The Sleepover Club

Three fantastic Sleepover Club
stories in one!

Have you been invited to all these sleepovers?

1 The Sleepover Club at Frankie's
2 The Sleepover Club at Lyndsey's
3 The Sleepover Club at Felicity's
4 The Sleepover Club at Rosie's
5 The Sleepover Club at Laura's
6 Starring the Sleepover Club
7 Sleepover Girls go Pop!
8 The 24-Hour Sleepover Club
9 The Sleepover Club Sleeps Out
10 Happy Birthday Sleepover Club
11 Sleepover Girls on Horseback
12 Sleepover in Spain
13 Sleepover on Friday 13th
14 Sleepover Girls go Camping
15 Sleepover Girls go Detective
16 Sleepover Girls go Designer
17 The Sleepover Club Surfs the Net
18 Sleepover Girls on Screen
19 Sleepover Girls and Friends
20 Sleepover Girls on the Catwalk
21 The Sleepover Club Goes for Goal!
22 Sleepover Girls go Babysitting
23 Sleepover Girls go Snowboarding
24 Happy New Year, Sleepover Club!
25 Sleepover Girls go Green
26 We Love You Sleepover Club
27 Vive le Sleepover Club!
28 Sleepover Club Eggstravaganza
29 Emergency Sleepover
30 Sleepover Girls on the Range
31 The Sleepover Club Bridesmaids
32 Sleepover Girls See Stars
33 Sleepover Club Blitz
34 Sleepover Girls in the Ring
35 Sari Sleepover
36 Merry Christmas Sleepover Club!
37 The Sleepover Club Down Under
38 Sleepover Girls go Splash!
39 Sleepover Girls go Karting
40 Sleepover Girls go Wild!
41 The Sleepover Club at the Carnival
42 The Sleepover Club on the Beach
43 Sleepover Club Vampires
44 sleepoverclub.com
45 Sleepover Girls go Dancing
46 The Sleepover Club on the Farm
47 Sleepover Girls go Gymtastic!
48 Sleepover Girls on the Ball
49 Sleepover Club Witches
50 Sleepover Club Ponies
51 Sleepover Girls on Safari
52 Sleepover Club Makeover

Mega
Sleepover Club ⑦

Sleepover Girls and Friends
Sleepover Club Bridesmaids
Sleepover Girls on the Ball

Angie Bates
Narinder Dhami

The Sleepover Club ® is a registered trademark of HarperCollins*Publishers* Ltd

Sleepover Girls and Friends first published in Great Britain by Collins 1999
The Sleepover Club Bridesmaids first published in Great Britain by Collins 2000
Sleepover Girls on the Ball first published in Great Britain by Collins 2002

First published in this three-in-one edition by Collins 2003

Collins is an imprint of HarperCollins*Publishers* Ltd
77-85 Fulham Palace Road, Hammersmith
London W6 8JB

The HarperCollins website address is www.**fire**and**water**.com

1 3 5 7 9 10 8 6 4 2

Sleepover Girls and Friends
Sleepover Girls on the Ball
Text copyright © Narinder Dhami 1999, 2002

The Sleepover Club Bridesmaids
Text copyright © Angie Bates 2000

Original series characters, plotlines and settings © Rose Impey 1997

ISBN 0 00 715258 2

Sleepover Kit List

1. Sleeping bag
2. Pillow
3. Pyjamas or a nightdress
4. Slippers
5. Toothbrush, toothpaste, soap etc
6. Towel
7. Teddy
8. A creepy story
9. Food for a midnight feast:
   chocolate, crisps, sweets, biscuits.
   In fact anything you like to eat.
10. Torch
11. Hairbrush
12. Hair things like a bobble or hairband,
    if you need them
13. Clean knickers and socks
14. Change of clothes for the next day
15. Sleepover diary and membership card

Sleepover Girls and Friends

by Narinder Dhami

Collins

An imprint of HarperCollins*Publishers*

CHAPTER ONE

SURPRISE! It's me, Kenny. It's my turn to tell you what's been happening to us recently, and boy, have I got a story to tell you! You just won't believe it!

You remember the Sleepover Club, don't you? As if you could forget! There's five of us – me (I'm the wild one), Frankie (the sensible one – well, sometimes), Lyndz (the Hiccup Queen), Fliss (who can be a bit of a fusspot) and Rosie (who's a lot happier since we decorated her bedroom for her – but that's another story). We've had our Sleepover Club going for ages now. It's Top Secret, but we don't mind our friends like *you* knowing all about what we get up to.

But when all this started, we weren't getting up to much anyway. In fact, we were all feeling pretty down...

"I'm fed up with all this rain!" I moaned as we trailed back into school when the lunch hour was over. "I wish it was summer."

"Yeah, so do I," said Fliss. "EEEK!"

Ryan Scott, who's in our class, had just gone past and flicked his wet scarf at her.

"He fancies you, Fliss!" Frankie remarked, winking at me.

Fliss turned pink. "Oh, don't be silly!" she said, but you know what Fliss is like. She's had a thing about Ryan Scott for ages.

"I don't think we're going on holiday this year," Frankie sighed. "Not with the baby and all that." (Frankie's mum's having a baby, remember?)

"Nor are we," Lyndz added gloomily, "but my gran and grandpa might be coming to stay with us."

"My dad *says* he's going to pay for us to go

on holiday," Rosie muttered, "but I'll believe that when I see it!" (Rosie's dad says a lot of stuff, but he doesn't always get round to doing it.)

"Did I tell you—" Fliss began eagerly.

"Yeah, about fifty million times!" I said, taking off my coat.

Fliss looked offended. "You don't even know what I'm going to say!"

"I'll take a guess." I grinned at her. "*We're going to Majorca and it's going to be great!*"

Fliss had nearly sent us all bananas going on and on about her holiday to Majorca. Secretly though, I was a bit jealous. My mum and dad love going to places like Scotland and Wales, and although I like being out of doors, I don't mind a bit of sun either.

"Well, it *is* going to be great!" Fliss said crossly. "I can't wait!"

"Remember when we went to Spain?" Frankie said as we trooped into the classroom. "That was brilliant!"

We all looked out of the classroom window at the rain coming down in sheets and felt even more miserable. That school trip to Spain was everyone's best holiday *ever*. The weather had been scorching, the beaches were fab and best of all we'd made friends with five Spanish girls called Pilar, Maria, Isabella, Elena and Anna. At first we'd hated each other – that was sort of my fault. OK, it *was* my fault. But then we'd got over it and had a brilliant time together. We'd told the girls all about our Sleepover Club and they'd started one for themselves. Since we'd got back from Spain we'd kept in touch by emailing them every week from our class computer.

"Come on everyone, sit down quickly." Mrs Weaver came in, glancing round the room and glaring at anyone whose bottom wasn't firmly on a seat. "Emma and Emily, didn't you hear what I said?"

"Sorry, Miss," Emma Hughes said in a sugary-sweet voice. "Emily and I thought the bookshelves were looking a bit messy, so we were just tidying them up."

"Oh, thank you, girls," said Mrs Weaver.

I just looked at the other Sleepovers and

pulled a face like I was about to be sick. The M&Ms *always* have that effect on me!

The M&Ms, in case you've been asleep for the last zillion years and don't remember, are our *biggest* enemies. They're also known as the Queen and the Goblin because Emma Hughes just thinks she's so cool, and Emily Berryman's small and has got this really gruff voice. We totally hate them, and they hate us. Oh hang on a sec, I didn't tell you what happened at Katie's party last week, did I? It was so coo-ell!

Katie Dawson, who's in our class, had a birthday party last week and she invited just about everyone, including us and the M&Ms. It was a really brill party with loud music and masses of food. Katie's mum had ordered loads of pizzas from the pizza place in the High Street, so we were all well pleased.

Then the M&Ms had to go and spoil it by putting a piece of squishy tomato on Fliss's chair. So when Fliss sat down on it, it stuck to the white jeans she was wearing and ruined them. Fliss went totally ballistic, so I decided

13

it was time for the Sleepover Club to get their revenge.

I strolled over to the M&Ms, as cool as anything.

"Looks like Fliss has had a bit of an accident!" Emily was chortling in that stupid deep voice of hers.

"Yeah, Fliss, you're supposed to eat tomato, not wear it!" Emma called, laughing her head off.

"Talking of wearing things, Emma," I said, grabbing the nearest pizza from the table, "is this your size?"

And I turned the plate over and dropped the pizza on to Emma's head. Toppings side down.

Oh, *what* a laugh that was! Emma just sat there open-mouthed for a second or two. Then all this cheese and tomato and onion started dripping down her face. The other Sleepovers were in hysterics.

'Course, we all got told off and sent home, but it was totally worth it just to see the look on Emma's face! Anyway, now the M&Ms hate us more than ever, and they're sure to try and get back at us somehow. We've got to watch our backs for a bit.

"Right, I've got some good news for you," Mrs Weaver said, after she'd taken the register. "It's particularly good news for those of you who went on the school trip to Spain a while back."

We all sat up, ears flapping.

"I've been in touch with the teachers of some of the Spanish students we met while we were over there," Mrs Weaver went on. "And we've arranged for eleven of the pupils to come over to visit Cuddington in July."

The Sleepover Club started nudging each other and whispering. What we all wanted to know was, were our friends going to be coming over on that trip or not? So I put my hand up.

"Yes, Laura?"

"Miss, are those girls we made friends with coming?" I asked.

Mrs Weaver asked their names, then checked the piece of paper in her hand. "Yes, they're all down on the list."

I turned to the others. "*Ex-cellent!*"

"It'll be great to see them all again!" Rosie gasped.

"I can feel a gi-normous sleepover coming on!" Frankie whispered.

"Quiet for a moment, please," Mrs Weaver said, glancing over at us. "The students and their teachers will be arriving on Friday July 12th and staying until the end of the summer term, Tuesday 23rd. I know it's only April now, but we have to find them places to stay. If anyone would like one of the Spanish pupils to board with them, please take one of these letters home tonight, and see me tomorrow morning *after* you've checked with your parents."

We were all getting pretty excited now. It would just be *so* cool having our Spanish friends staying with us! I really hoped that Maria would want to come and stay with me – we could talk about football all night!

"Right, get out your books for silent reading, please," Mrs Weaver told us.

Everyone started talking then, and we all

got our books out as slowly as possible so we had more time to natter about what Mrs W. had just told us.

"They're coming at the end of the summer term – that's *brill*!" Lyndz exclaimed. "There's always loads of stuff going on then!"

"Yeah, there's Sports Day and the Summer Fete," I pointed out.

"And we'll hopefully get a class trip to WonderLand, that fab new theme park!" Frankie added.

"Oh, and don't forget the fancy-dress competition on the last day of term!" Fliss squealed.

Rosie was looking a bit put out. "Yeah," she said pointedly, "and there's something else too!"

"What?" I asked, but Frankie nudged me in the ribs.

"It's Rosie's birthday, of course!" she hissed.

"Oh, right, July 15th!" I grinned. "What about an extra-special sleepover?"

Rosie was beaming all over her face by now. "That'd be excellent!"

It was then that I noticed the M&Ms standing by the bookshelves near our table, looking seriously grumpy.

"Oh, I forgot!" I said loudly. "*Some* people in this class weren't lucky enough to go on the school trip to Spain!"

The Queen had had chickenpox at the time and the Goblin didn't want to go without her, so now we could *really* rub their noses in it!

The M&Ms flounced off, looking annoyed, and left us all giggling.

"I can't *wait* for July!" I said. "It's going to be seriously brilliant!"

But I didn't know just how wrong I was…

CHAPTER TWO

"Quick, check the email box, Kenny!" Fliss poked me hard in the back. "See if Isabella and the others have replied to our last email!"

"OK, OK!" I said crossly, as the others crowded round me eagerly. "Stop hassling me!"

It was a few days after Mrs Weaver had told us about the Spanish pupils coming to visit. It was mine and Lyndz's turn to use the class computer, and, although we were supposed to be finishing off the story we were writing together, Mrs W. had agreed to let us check the email box and send a reply.

"We've got an answer!" Frankie announced triumphantly as a new message popped up on

19

the screen. "Quick, Kenny, see what they say!"

I hit the mouse, and opened the message.

```
Hi, Sleepover Club!
We look forward very much to see
you all in England in July. We
are all very excited. Can we have
a special sleepover when we are
staying with you?
   Love from Pilar, Maria,
Isabella, Elena and Anna
```

"Go on, Kenny!" This time it was Rosie who poked me in the back. "Tell them it's my birthday, and we're going to have a big sleepover on the day they arrive!"

Frankie tapped me on the shoulder. "Tell them we're going to sleep out in a tent in Rosie's garden if the weather's good!"

"And tell them they're going to be staying with us!" Lyndz added, jogging my elbow.

"Will you lot get off!" I moaned. "I'm going to be black and blue all over at this rate!" And I started typing in our reply.

Dear Spanish Sleepover Club,
We're really excited too, and we
can't wait for July! We've got
loads of exciting stuff happening
here. First, it's Rosie's
birthday a few days after you get
here, so we're going to have a
big birthday sleepover on the day
you arrive! We'll have a party in
Rosie's garden, and then we're
going to sleep out in a big tent.
We're going to play loads of
games, give each other makeovers,
have a fashion show and stuff our
faces with birthday food!

"No pizzas though!" Fliss said as I typed that,
and we all started laughing.

"I heard that!" snapped Emma Hughes, who
was sitting nearby. "And it wasn't funny!"

"Oh yes, it was!" I retorted wickedly. "Seeing
you with tomato sauce sliding down your face
would make anyone laugh!"

"You think you're so clever, Laura

McKenzie!" Emily Berryman chimed in.

"Well, at least I'm not stupid enough to wear a pizza on my head!" I pointed out, and the other Sleepovers fell about.

"Take no notice of them, Emma," said Emily.

"I won't," Emma said, and stuck her nose in the air.

"Wait till our Spanish friends get here!" Frankie said gleefully. "Then there'll be *ten* of us to get on your nerves!"

"These Spanish girls must be crazy," Emma sniffed. "Fancy wanting to be mates with a bunch of losers like you!"

I nudged Frankie. "Emma's looking just a little bit green, don't you think?"

"Oh, definitely," Frankie agreed. "She's starting to go green all over!"

"I am *not* jealous!" Emma snorted furiously. "I don't care if you've got a *million* Spanish friends!"

"So how many Spanish people do *you* know, Emma?" Fliss asked.

Emma picked up her work and stormed across the classroom to queue up at Mrs

Weaver's table. Emily followed, leaving us all in fits of giggles.

"This visit is really winding the M&Ms up!" Frankie said.

"Good!" I replied. "They deserve it!"

"Come on Kenny, get on with the email," Lyndz said. "Mrs Weaver keeps giving us dirty looks."

Quickly I began to type again:

Has your teacher told you you're going to be staying with us? Pilar's staying with Frankie, Isabella with Fliss, Elena with Lyndz, Anna with Rosie and Maria with me. So you and me can have lots of arguments about footy, Maria!
Got to go now, because our teacher's giving us dirty looks! REPLY SOON.
Kenny, Lyndz, Frankie, Rosie and Fliss

"It's funny how you and Maria both like football, Kenny," Frankie remarked as I sent the email on its way to sunny Spain. "And you're both a bit mad too."

"Well, what about you and Pilar?" I retorted. "You're both about six feet tall and bossy with it!"

We'd discovered that the Spanish girls were so much like us, it was spooky. Isabella and Fliss were scarily alike – they'd even had exactly the same swimsuits on holiday! Elena and Anna, who were twins, were a bit like Lyndz and Rosie too. Elena was pretty easygoing, like Lyndz, and she was always getting hiccups too! And Anna was kind-hearted, but she could be a bit prickly sometimes (sound like anyone you know?). Anyway, the reason why we got on so well with them was probably because we *were* so alike.

"How many days to wait before they get here?" I asked.

"Seventy-five," Frankie said immediately. "I worked it out last night."

"Seventy-five days!" I groaned. "That's ages!

We might be dead by then!"

Frankie gave me a shove. "Oh, look on the bright side, Kenny, why don't you!"

"Anyway, it gives us lots of time to plan what we're going to do," Lyndz added.

"Yeah, this has got to be special!" I said firmly. "We want to make sure Pilar and the others have a trip they'll never forget!"

* * *

"Are they here yet?" Fliss asked for about the millionth time, standing up to peer out of the classroom window.

"Not unless they're invisible, and so is their coach!" I said impatiently. "I'll tell you as soon as I see them."

It was Friday July 12th at *last*. It seemed a very long time since Mrs Weaver had first told us that the Spanish pupils were coming over, but at last the day had arrived. They were coming to our school from the airport by coach, and because I had the best view of the playground gates from my seat, I was watching out for them. We were all supposed to be doing silent reading, but Mrs Weaver wasn't bothering much about keeping us quiet. She was pretty cool about things now that we were almost at the end of term.

"I hope it doesn't rain tonight," Rosie said anxiously, glancing out of the window. "Not now we've decorated the garden and put the tent up."

The rest of us looked at each other and giggled. The sun was blazing into the classroom – there'd been a heatwave for the last two weeks and the weather was *scorching*. It was even hotter than it was when we'd gone to Spain.

"It's going to be brill sleeping outside tonight!" I said. We'd spent the last few days round at Rosie's after school, getting everything ready for the Grand Sleepover that evening. Although the Cartwrights' garden, like their house, was a bit of a mess, we'd hung streamers and balloons in the trees, and my dad had brought our big tent over and put it up on the grass.

"Yeah, but no horror stories, Kenny, all right?" Fliss insisted nervously.

"Nah, 'course not!" I said, crossing my fingers behind my back and winking at Frankie. I had a fab story to tell at the sleepover that night, all about a mummy, a werewolf and a haunted house. Fliss was going to wet herself!

"I wonder why Pilar and the others didn't reply to that email we sent them the other day?" Lyndz said.

Frankie shrugged. "Maybe their teacher wouldn't let them."

We hadn't heard anything from the Spanish girls for nearly two weeks now.

"Maybe they were too busy getting ready for the trip," I suggested. "Hey, here's the coach!"

Everyone in the classroom jumped out of their seats and rushed over to the windows, except the M&Ms. Typical. Meanwhile, Mrs Weaver had grabbed her clipboard and hurried outside.

"There's Maria!" I yelled, as the Spanish kids

began to file off the coach, looking a bit tired and crumpled. Maria was at the front, wearing her Real Madrid football shirt as usual. I banged on the glass and waved. "MARIA!"

Maria glanced over, but she didn't wave back.

"I guess she just didn't see me," I said, disappointed.

"There's Pilar!" Frankie began to bang on the glass too, but Pilar wasn't taking any notice either. Neither were Isabella, Elena and Anna, who got off behind her.

"Maybe they don't like you any more!" remarked Emma Hughes with a spiteful grin, but we ignored her.

We watched Mrs Weaver leading the Spanish kids and their two teachers into school, and then they came into our classroom.

"Hey, Maria!" I shouted, trying to attract her attention, but I had to shut up when Mrs W. gave me one of her mega-gruesome glares.

"Sit down, everyone, please!" she called. "*Quietly!*"

Although we couldn't say anything, we kept on grinning and giving Pilar, Maria and the others thumbs-up signs. But it was really strange because they weren't doing anything back. In fact, they were acting as if they didn't even know who we were. They were staring straight through us.

"What's going on?" I whispered to Frankie. "Why're they being so funny?"

Frankie shrugged. "Maybe they're just tired after the flight," she suggested.

"What, too tired to *smile* at us?" I said.

I stared hard at Maria until I caught her eye. You know what she did? She just stared right back at me. She didn't smile. She didn't wink. She didn't do anything. It was really strange.

There was *definitely* something very weird going on. And I was determined to find out exactly what it was...

CHAPTER THREE

"And this is where you'll be sleeping!" I threw open the door of my bedroom, and grinned at Maria. "My sister Molly the Monster's gone to camp with her school, so you'll be sharing with me. Cool, huh?"

Maria didn't say anything. Which wasn't surprising really because she'd hardly said a word to me at all. We hadn't had much time to chat at school because the home bell had rung about fifteen minutes after the coach had arrived, and then my mum turned up in the car to drive us home. I could see the other Sleepovers looking just as puzzled as I was, as they went off with their mum or dad and the Spanish girl who was staying with them. It was *weird*.

I'd been mega-nice to Maria in the car when my mum took us home, but she'd hardly said a word to me. I'd told her all about the special sleepover at Rosie's and even that hadn't made any difference. She was fine when my mum spoke to her though! And that had really got right up my nose. I was getting seriously annoyed.

"Come on," I said, still trying to be nice. "Let's go and kick a ball around in the garden or something."

"No, thanks." Maria shrugged. "I want to unpack my suitcase."

"OK," I said. "Do you want some help?"

"Not from you!" Maria retorted rudely, and I almost choked with fury.

"What's *that* supposed to mean?"

"It means I not want you to help me!" Maria glared at me, and that just about did it. I was *boiling*.

"You're really starting to get on my nerves!"

I hissed, clenching my fists. "What's going on?"

"Why you ask *me* what is going on?" Maria snapped. We were standing nose-to-nose now like a couple of heavyweight boxers. "*You* start it!"

"Start what?" I asked, bewildered. I totally didn't have a clue what she was going on about.

Maria looked like she was about to say something, but then she just stuck her tongue out at me. If Molly the Monster had done that to me I'd have grabbed my pillow and whacked her round the head with it, but somehow I managed to stop myself. Instead I stomped out of the room, leaving Maria unpacking her suitcase.

I just couldn't understand what was going on. Up until a week or two ago we'd all been great mates. So what had gone wrong?

When I got downstairs, I picked up the phone and called Frankie.

"Hey, Franks, how's it's going?"

"Gruesome!" Frankie groaned. "Pilar's being a right pain!"

"So's Maria," I agreed. "Did Pilar tell you why they're acting like total morons?"

"Nah, she won't even *talk* to me!" Frankie said in disgust. "I just phoned Lyndz and she said Elena's being just as weird!"

"Right, I'll phone Fliss and you phone Rosie," I decided. "Somehow we've got to find out what's going on, or the next few weeks are going to be a total disaster!"

"Isabella's driving me bananas!" Fliss complained when I got through to her. "She keeps on making nasty remarks about my teddy-bear collection – she says hers is much better!"

"Never mind that!" I said impatiently. "Has she told you why they're all being so weird?"

"No," Fliss replied. "I just phoned Rosie and she says that Anna won't tell her either."

"Well, maybe we'll find out at the sleepover tonight..."

I said goodbye to Fliss, and put the phone down. I was beginning to wonder if the Grand Sleepover we'd planned so carefully was going to be quite so grand after all...

* * *

"Er – shall we start the sleepover now?" Rosie asked, looking round at us.

We all nodded silently. Rosie opened the French windows that led out of the Cartwrights' living-room into the garden, and we all trudged gloomily after her. What a great evening this was going to be. Since we'd all arrived at Rosie's place, no-one had said a word to each other. We'd all just sat on the sofas, the Sleepover Club on one and the Spanish girls on another, and we'd glared across the room at each other. Rosie was already looking pretty hassled, and I didn't blame her. This was supposed to be her birthday sleepover, and by the look of it, it was going to be about as jolly as a three-hour maths test.

"Oh, hello girls." Rosie's mum was laying out loads of food on a table which had been set up near the tent. "I bet you're looking forward to this, aren't you?"

Nobody said anything. Mrs Cartwright took

one look at our faces, blinked and then decided not to say anything.

"Have a good time!" she called as she went back to the house.

Yeah, right. We were *really* going to enjoy ourselves when everyone was walking around with their faces down to their knees. Well, it looked like it was up to me to get this party going a bit!

"OK, what shall we do first?" I asked loudly, making everyone jump. "Shall we play International Gladiators?"

"Nah, let's eat!" said Lyndz.

"We could give Rosie her presents first," Frankie suggested.

"No, let's have makeovers first!" Fliss chimed in. "I've borrowed some make-up from my mum."

"Yes, I think makeover is a good idea!" Pilar said suddenly. She looked at the other Spanish girls, who nodded.

"Yeah, OK," I agreed. I'm definitely not into trying out hairstyles and make-up like Flissy is – I was just trying to be friendly.

"We give you makeovers first!" Isabella announced, grabbing the make-up bag Fliss had just taken out of her rucksack. "We make you look beautiful!"

Frankie had brought some make-up and nail varnish too, as well as brushes and combs, and Rosie ran into the house to get some mirrors. Then we started the makeovers. Maria was doing mine, and although I told her not to use too much make-up because I didn't like it, it felt like she was using *tons* of it.

"What are you doing, Maria?" I asked, trying to twist round a bit so that I could get a look at the others.

"Keep still!" Maria grabbed my arm and pulled me round to face her again. "I cannot make it right if you move!"

"Hey, that tickles!" I heard Frankie complaining. "What's that, Pilar?"

"I use lipliner and lipstick," Pilar said. "Now stay quiet!"

The other Spanish girls started giggling, and that made me a bit suspicious. Then we heard barking, and Adam came into the garden with three of his mates and his dog Jenny. Adam's got cerebral palsy and he's in a wheelchair. He can talk, sort of, but mostly he uses a computerised voicebox.

"Hey Adam," I called. "You all right?"

Adam stopped in his chair and stared at us. Then he and his mates all started to roar with laughter.

"Maria, what've you done?" I yelled, grabbing one of the mirrors.

I had *loads* of black eyeliner slapped on all round my eyes and a big red mouth. I looked like Bobo the clown! And the others weren't any better.

"Look at me!" Frankie gasped. Pilar had drawn a pair of glasses and a fake moustache on her face with eyeliner!

"My hair!" Fliss wailed, grabbing a mirror. "What've you done to my hair?" Isabella had backcombed it so that it was all frizzy and looked like a bird's nest.

"I look stupid!" Rosie spluttered. She had enough blusher on her cheeks to sink the

37

Titanic, and her hair had been gelled into spikes which stuck up all over her head. She looked gruesome.

"I look like I've got the measles!" Lyndz howled, glaring at Elena, who'd put little black spots of eyeliner pencil all over her face.

"Right, that's it!" I leapt to my feet, rubbing hard at the make-up with a tissue. "You lot are dead!"

Maria and the others were rolling on the grass, crying with laughter.

"It serve you right!" Isabella said triumphantly.

"You should not send us those emails!" Pilar added. "Now we pay you back!"

"What are you talking about?" I stared at them. "What emails?"

"You know what we talk about!" Maria said scornfully. She put her hand in her bag and pulled out some papers. "*These* emails!"

She shoved them into my hand and I read the one on top, which was dated a week or so ago.

```
Dear Spanish girls
Why don't you learn how to talk
English properly?
  Kenny, Frankie, Rosie, Lyndz
and Fliss
```

"You say other things too," Elena said. "Nasty things about our country!"

"Yes, we are proud to be Spanish!" Anna added fiercely.

"We didn't send these!" I said, showing them to the other Sleepovers. "No way!"

"We've never seen them before!" Frankie backed me up, and the others nodded.

Maria and the other girls obviously didn't believe us. "So who send them then?" Maria asked.

I looked at the others. "I bet I know who it was!" I hissed. "I bet it was—"

"Kenny!" Maria called, and I spun round.

"AARGH!"

A cream doughnut hit me right in the middle of my face!

CHAPTER FOUR

Well, that was IT! I wasn't in the mood to try and sort things out any more – this was WAR!

"You shouldn't have done that!" I spluttered as I wiped cream and sugar off my face while the Spanish girls roared with laughter. "You're really going to get it now!"

"Kenny, be careful!" said Fliss and Lyndz together, but I was too mad to listen. I grabbed a cheese and pickle roll off the table and threw it at Maria. She ducked, but it hit Pilar instead, and Branston pickle spilled out all over her jeans.

"Hey!" Pilar shouted, "you dirty my jeans!"

And she scooped some cream off the top of the trifle with a spoon, and flicked it at us. It hit Fliss right in the eye.

"Ow!" Fliss wailed, and she lobbed a ham roll in the Spanish girls' direction.

Next second it had turned into a free-for-all as we all started grabbing food missiles and hurling them at each other.

"Stop it!" Rosie yelled. "You're ruining my birthday sleepover!"

Then she got a sausage roll in the eye, and that made her so mad, she started to join in. It was like something out of a comedy film. Everyone was screaming and trying to dodge flying cakes and rolls, Jenny was barking madly and Adam and his friends were all watching us and laughing their heads off.

I hadn't managed to land a direct hit on Maria yet, so I spooned some strawberry jelly into a bowl, and flung it in her direction. I didn't get Maria. But I did manage to get Rosie's mum. Right in the middle of her face!

"Well!" Mrs Cartwright stared furiously at us, trying to wipe strawberry jelly out of her eyes. She must have come out to see what all the noise was about, and we'd been so busy fighting, we hadn't heard her. "What on *earth* is going on here?"

"Er – we were having a food fight, Mum," Rosie muttered sheepishly, while the rest of us shuffled our feet and tried to brush the crumbs out of our hair.

"I can see *that*," Mrs Cartwright replied in a freezing tone. "I think you'd better clear everything up straightaway. And then I'm going to ring your parents and you're all going home."

"What about the sleepover?" Rosie wailed, but her mum just gave her a look that shut her up.

"*You* started that!" I hissed at Maria when Mrs Cartwright had gone back into the house. "This is all your fault!"

Maria shrugged. "You start it with all your nasty emails!"

"We didn't send them!" I began, but I could see it was no use. They just didn't believe us.

Rosie was looking really upset. "This has

been my worst birthday ever!" she groaned. "And it isn't even my birthday till Monday!"

"Never mind, you've still got your prezzies to look forward to," said Lyndz.

"Mum's so mad with me, I probably won't get *anything*!" Rosie muttered.

"What're we going to do now?" Frankie asked as we began to pick up squashed cakes and rolls from the grass and put them into bin bags. The Spanish girls started clearing up too, but they kept well away from us, and they were whispering to each other and giving us filthy looks.

"We're just going to have to prove to them that it wasn't us who sent those emails!" I said.

"How?" asked Lyndz.

"We need to find out who sent them," I said. "And I've got a pretty good idea who it was too…"

* * *

"Right, hands up everyone who thinks it was the gruesome M&Ms who sent those emails!" I announced.

Everyone's hand immediately went up, and I grinned.

"Yeah, so do I!" I agreed. "So what're we going to do about it?"

It was the day after the not-so-Grand Sleepover, and Frankie, Lyndz, Fliss and Rosie were round at my place to discuss exactly what we were going to do. We'd all been well and truly roasted alive by our parents when we got home after the food fight, and Pilar and the others had been told off by their teacher, Miss Moreno. We'd also been told that we couldn't have a sleepover next weekend. For once, we didn't care that much though. It wouldn't have been any fun with Maria and the rest of her Gruesome Gang!

"I tried to talk to Elena last night," said Lyndz, "but she was still in a right mood."

"Yeah, Anna was too," Rosie agreed. "She even asked my mum if she could sleep in a different bedroom instead of sharing with me!"

"Well, Isabella wouldn't speak to me either," Fliss chimed in. "*And* she snores!"

"I got the big freeze from Pilar too," Frankie

said. "What about you, Kenny?"

"I tried talking to Maria when we went to bed," I said. "But she wouldn't listen. She put her headphones on so she couldn't hear me, and she had her Walkman on really loudly!"

"They're really mad with us," said Rosie. "Those emails must have been pretty bad."

"I could murder the M&Ms!" I muttered. "They're not gonna get away with this!"

"We'll have to have another go at talking to Pilar and the others," I said. "What time do they get back from Leicester?"

"They should be back pretty soon," Lyndz replied. Miss Moreno and Mr Cortez, the Spanish teachers, had come round in a minibus that morning and collected the pupils to take them to Leicester on a shopping trip. "Then they're going to the park for a picnic."

"Right, let's get over there then and tell them about the M&Ms!" I jumped to my feet. "We'll make them believe us even if we have to sit on their heads and bounce up and down on them!"

"Oh, right, like *that* can't fail!" Frankie said

sarcastically. "They'll *really* want to be friends with us after that!"

"Just keep cool, will you Kenny!" Fliss said nervously. "We don't want to start another fight!"

I gave her a shove. "That wasn't my fault, it was Maria's. You know me, I'm just not the fighting type!"

The park wasn't far away from my place, and we were allowed to go to it on our own, so we set off.

"We ought to start thinking about making our fancy-dress costumes soon," Lyndz remarked. "We've only got a week and a bit to get them ready."

We always have a fancy-dress competition at school on the last day of the summer term, which is really wicked. Even the teachers dress up, and there's prizes for the best home-made costumes.

"I was just going to wear my Leicester City football strip," I began, but everyone else started groaning loudly.

"Bor-ing, Kenny!" said Frankie. "That's what

you've worn for the last three years!"

"My mum says she'll hire a costume for me," said Fliss. "It'll be a lot easier than making it."

"Even *more* bor-ing!" the rest of us said together.

"You've got to make it yourself or you can't win a prize," Lyndz added.

"I think I might go as an alien," Frankie said. "Then I can wear my cool new silver nail varnish."

"I could go as a clown," I suggested. "Then I could get Maria to do my make-up!"

The others started to laugh.

"You'd probably frighten the kids in the Infants to death!" Fliss pointed out.

"I wonder if Maria and the others are going to dress up too?" Rosie said. "They're going to be there on the last day of term, after all."

"Maybe we could offer to help them with their costumes," Lyndz suggested.

"Yeah, that might be a good way of making friends with them again," Frankie agreed, as we arrived at the park.

"They're back from Leicester," said Lyndz.

"There's the minibus."

"All right," I said as we walked up to the park gates. "Now everyone just stay cool and calm. Nobody loses their temper, OK?"

"What're you telling us for, Kenny?" Fliss sniffed. "*You're* the one who's likely to thump them if they won't listen to us!"

"What a cheek!" I began indignantly, but then I stopped. I'd just caught sight of the Spanish pupils sitting around on the grass in groups, eating their picnic. Maria, Pilar, Elena, Anna and Isabella were sitting near the swings, surrounded by lots of carrier bags full of shopping. And they weren't on their own either. They were laughing and chatting and sharing their picnic... *with the gruesome M&Ms!*

48

CHAPTER FIVE

We all stood and stared at them. Honestly, we must have looked like a bunch of stunned goldfish, standing there with our mouths open! The Spanish girls and the M&Ms didn't notice us though because they were too busy having a laugh together. It was unbelievable!

"They're making friends with the M&Ms!" Rosie gasped. "They must be crazy!"

"What're the M&Ms doing here anyway?" Lyndz asked.

"Who cares!" I was burning with fury. "They're here, and they're trying to get in with our mates! I'm going over to tell them exactly what I think of them!"

"No, Kenny!" Frankie grabbed one of my arms and Lyndz clutched at the other. "You'll just make things worse!"

When I get mad though, there's no talking to me! I pushed Frankie and Lyndz off and stormed across the grass towards Maria and the others. They glanced up and saw me coming, and they started to laugh and nudge each other. Meanwhile the Queen and the Goblin looked so smug, I could have pushed them both into the boating lake.

"What do you want?" Maria snapped. "Go away, we try to eat our picnic."

"I want to talk to you!" I retorted. "About those emails!" I saw Emma Hughes flash a grin at Emily Berryman when I said that, and that wound me up even more. "If you want to know who sent them, just take a look over *there*!" And I pointed at the M&Ms.

"Oh, stop being a pain, Kenny, and go and play in the traffic!" said Emma Hughes with a pretend yawn. "Nobody wants to listen to you!"

Pilar and the other Spanish girls were all glaring at me. "Yes, go away, Kenny!" they chorused.

"We want to eat our picnic with our friends," said Maria pointedly.

Their friends! I almost choked. The M&Ms had done their best to split us up, and now they'd won and they were taking our mates away from us!

"You'd better tell them the truth, Emma Hughes!" I said threateningly, "or else!"

The Queen was beginning to look a bit worried by now, but just at that moment the other Sleepovers caught up with me and grabbed my arms again.

"Back off, Kenny!" Frankie hissed in my ear. "You're just making things worse!"

Even though I was mad, I could see what she meant. Pilar, Maria, Isabella, Elena and Anna just didn't believe what I was saying – not now that the M&Ms were being as nice as pie to them. I took a deep breath and tried to calm myself down.

"Look, we just want to talk to you," I said.

"Well, we not want to talk to *you*," said Elena, and the others nodded in agreement.

"'Bye, Kenny!" said Emily Berryman with an infuriating grin.

"Come on, Kenny," Frankie whispered. "We don't want to talk to them with the Gruesome Twosome here anyway!"

"Yes, come on, Kenny!" Fliss tugged at my arm and took a step backwards. She accidentally trod on one of the bags of shopping lying on the grass, and there was a loud CRACK.

"My bag!" Isabella squealed. She pulled the carrier bag open, and took out an object wrapped in tissue paper. Inside was a pretty blue bowl. Well, it would have been a pretty bowl if it hadn't been in two pieces.

"I buy that for my mother!" Isabella yelled, her face turning red with fury. "Now you break it!"

"I didn't mean to," Fliss stammered.

"She did it on purpose!" Emma Hughes had to stick her nose in and try to stir things up as usual. "I saw her!"

"No, I didn't!" Fliss snapped. "You can shut up, Emma Hughes!"

"Make me!" Emma sneered.

"OK, if Fliss won't, I will!" I lunged forward, but Frankie caught my sleeve and dragged me back. She and the others hustled me away across the grass, leaving the Spanish girls furious and the M&Ms laughing.

"That Emma Hughes is *history*!" I snapped as Frankie and the others pulled me over to the park gates. "This mess is all down to her!"

"And now she's made friends with Anna and the others, they won't believe us if we try to tell them what she and Emily are *really* like," Rosie pointed out.

"No, I bet the Queen and the Goblin are being really nice to them!" I said, clenching my fists. "You know how two-faced Emma Hughes is!"

"Well, there's not much we can do about it, is there?" Frankie muttered, and nobody could think of anything to say.

We all trailed back miserably to my place, and went out into the garden. The sky was blue, the sun was shining, it was warm, and in just over a week's time we'd be finishing school for the summer holidays. But we couldn't help feeling fed up. We'd been looking forward to Pilar and the rest of the gang coming over so much, and now the M&Ms had gone and ruined it all.

"Why don't we design our fancy-dress costumes?" Lyndz asked.

No-one was that keen, but it was better than sitting around doing nothing. So I went inside and nicked some paper and pens from my dad's study, and then we lay around on the grass, sketching. I can't draw though, so I just doodled.

"I think I might go as the Tin Man," said Lyndz.

"What?" I glanced over at her.

"The Tin Man from *The Wizard of Oz*," Lyndz explained.

"That sounds like a hard costume to make," said Fliss.

"No, I'll just use loads of cardboard boxes and paint them silver," Lyndz said. "And I can make myself an oil-can to carry. It'll be great!"

"Well, I want to dress up in something glamorous!" said Fliss. "I don't want to be a rusty old Tin Man!"

"You could go as Barbie," I suggested, winking at Frankie. Fliss has got long fair hair, she's dead skinny and she's got about as many clothes as Barbie has! I meant it as a joke, but Fliss immediately looked interested.

"That's a good idea – then I wouldn't have to make a costume! I could just wear one of my dresses."

"I think I might go as the Witch from *The Lion, The Witch and The Wardrobe*," said Frankie. "Then I can still wear my silver nail varnish! What about you, Rosie?"

"I don't know," Rosie said gloomily, "I can't think of anything!"

"We'll help you," Lyndz told her.

"Hey, I've just had a great idea for my costume!" I said triumphantly. "And it's not my Leicester City strip either!"

I jumped to my feet and ran into the house. It took me a while to find what I was looking for, but when I did, I took it outside.

"Remember *this*?" I said with a grin, holding it up.

"The mummy mask!" squealed Lyndz and Fliss together.

"I didn't know you'd still got that!" said Frankie.

Remember when went on that school trip to the museum and slept over, and we frightened the M&Ms to death with the mummy mask I'd made? That was just so cool!

"I'll go as a mummy!" I announced, putting the mask over my face. "All I've got to do is nick some bandages from my dad's surgery, and I'm sorted!"

"Maybe you can scare the M&Ms into telling the truth about those emails!" Lyndz suggested.

"Yeah, what are we going to do about that?" Rosie asked.

Everyone looked gloomy again.

"I wish I hadn't broken that bowl of Isabella's," Fliss sighed.

"If only there was some way we could prove

that the M&Ms sent those emails," Frankie said. "Then everything would be OK."

"And maybe I could buy Isabella another bowl," Fliss added.

"Well, we could find out what time the emails were sent by checking them," Lyndz pointed out. "But that doesn't help us very much because we can't prove who was using the computer at the time—"

"Lyndz!" I gasped, "you're a genius!"

Lyndz looked at me blankly. "I am?"

"Yeah, you are!" I said triumphantly. "We *can* prove who was using the class computer when those emails were sent!"

The others stared at me. They *still* didn't get it.

"Look," I gabbled impatiently, "how do we *always* know whose turn it is to use the computer?"

"Because Mrs Weaver puts a list up on the classroom noticeboard," Fliss replied.

"Exactly!" I grinned round at the others. "So all we've got to do is check out the list to see who got to use the computer and when last week, and compare it with the dates and times on the emails! Simple!"

"Kenny, you're brilliant!" gasped Frankie. "I'd like to see the M&Ms talk their way out of this one!"

"They won't be able to!" I said confidently. "We're going to prove to Maria and the others that the M&Ms are the bad guys – not us! I can't *wait* to see Emma Hughes' face on Monday morning!"

CHAPTER SIX

"Happy birthday to you,
Happy birthday to you,
You look like a monkey
And you smell like one too!"

"Thanks, Kenny!" Rosie gave me a shove as I finished singing and took a bow. "Now where's my prezzie?"

I dived into my schoolbag and pulled out a square-shaped parcel wrapped in Bacofoil. "Sorry, I forgot to get any wrapping-paper!" I grinned as I gave it to Rosie, and the others started giggling.

"Typical!" Rosie snorted, rolling her eyes.

It was Monday morning, and we'd all got to school early so we could give Rosie her presents. Everyone was pretending to be really jolly and up-for-it, but that was just because we didn't want Rosie's actual birthday to end up being more of a downer than it already was. The weekend had been pretty grim. Our sleepover had been ruined, we were in deepest doom with the Oldies because of the food fight and I was having to put up with sharing my bedroom with Maria, which was nearly as gruesome as sharing with Molly the Monster! Luckily the Spanish kids had been taken out again on Sunday by their teachers – they'd gone to visit some local museums, so at least we hadn't had to spend the day with them. We'd started making our fancy-dress costumes instead.

"Oh, that's great, Kenny!" Rosie said as she unwrapped the scented bath stuff I'd bought her. She'd already got a box of choccies from Frankie, a set of different nail varnishes from Fliss and a groovy pink fluffy purse, shaped like a heart, from Lyndz.

"Now you won't smell like a monkey even if you look like one!" I pointed out, and Rosie thumped me.

"Hey, take a look over there," Frankie said suddenly in a low voice.

We all glanced across the playground. Pilar, Isabella and the others were standing in the corner chatting away to – you've guessed it, the Gruesome Twosome themselves, the M&Ms.

"They're getting pretty matey, aren't they?" Lyndz said.

"Not for long!" I said confidently. "You wait till we get into class and I show them Mrs Weaver's computer list!"

We all started grinning and giving each other high fives. Pilar and the others were going to find out exactly what the M&Ms were really like!

"I guess we can't blame the Spanish girls for being mad about those emails," Lyndz said as we charged into school the minute the bell rang. "I mean, they must have thought we were being really nasty."

"Yeah, well, they should have known we'd never do anything like that!" I retorted. "And they could have asked us about them first instead of getting their knickers all in a twist!"

"What, you mean, like you'd have done if someone had sent you nasty emails?" Lyndz said with a grin.

"Oh, yeah, right!" Fliss chimed in sarcastically. "As if Kenny wouldn't have flattened them first and asked questions later!"

"All right, all right!" I groaned. "Let's just get this sorted, OK?" I slung my tracky top on to my coat peg and headed for the classroom, the others right behind me. We'd rushed into school so fast that we were first through the door. We had to get our hands on that computer list before the M&Ms arrived and realised what we were up to!

The classroom noticeboard was behind Mrs Weaver's table, next to the board. It was usually full of notices about the football and netball teams, the various school clubs and lots of other stuff, including the computer rota. *Usually…*

"Girls! One at a time, please!" Mrs Weaver snapped as we all tried to elbow our way through the door at the same time. She was standing by her table, sorting through a pile of folders. "I know it's getting towards the end of term, but there's no need to behave like a bunch of football hooligans!"

"Yes Miss, sorry Miss," we all said together.

Then I stopped dead and nudged Frankie hard in the ribs. She nudged Fliss and Fliss nudged Lyndz and Lyndz did the same to Rosie. We all stared at the noticeboard on the wall. The *empty* noticeboard.

There wasn't a single piece of paper pinned up on it at all. Everything had vanished – including the computer list!

"Miss, what happened to the stuff that was on the noticeboard?" I gabbled.

It was then that I noticed the two large, bulging black bags lying next to Mrs Weaver's table.

"Oh, I've thrown all that away now," Mrs Weaver replied, ripping up a couple of sheets of paper and shoving them into one of the bin bags. "The whole classroom's got to be cleared by the end of term, so I'll be needing some help this week." She raised her eyebrows at us. "Any volunteers?"

We were too busy staring at each other in horror to reply. The computer list was now in one of those two bulging black bags! How were we going to get it back?

"Um – the thing is, Miss," I said, "there was something on the noticeboard I really needed. Can I go through the bags and look for it?"

Mrs Weaver stared at me as if I'd gone mad. "Don't be ridiculous, Laura! You'll never find it – in fact, it's probably been ripped into pieces!"

I just couldn't believe it. That list had been our one chance of proving to Maria and the others that we hadn't sent those emails. Now we didn't have a hope!

"But, Miss—" I began.

"Leave it, Kenny." Frankie grabbed my arm and pulled me away as the rest of the class began to come in. "There's nothing we can do about it!"

"Rats!" I muttered under my breath as Mrs Weaver picked up the bags and went out to throw them into the huge steel bins behind the canteen. "What about if I climb into the bins at lunch time and try to find it then?"

"Urgh, don't be so disgusting!" Fliss wrinkled up her nose. "Anyway, Mrs Poole said anyone who climbs into those bins is going to be in big trouble."

"Yeah, that was just because Ryan Scott did it last year for a dare and got stuck!" I retorted. "But that wouldn't happen to me."

"Forget it, Kenny!" Frankie said firmly. "You wouldn't know which bin it was – you wouldn't even know which *bag* it was. It'd take forever!"

"We can't just give up!" I muttered as Isabella, Maria, Pilar, Elena and Anna came in, talking and laughing with the M&Ms. What was worse, they even went over to sit on their table with them!

"Hurry up and settle down," Mrs Weaver called, as the rest of the Spanish kids came in with Miss Moreno and Mr Cortez. "We've got a visitor arriving in a moment or two – a photographer from the local newspaper!"

We all looked at each other in surprise.

"The paper has heard about our visitors from Spain, and it wants to do a piece about them," Mrs Weaver went on. "So we're all going to have our photo taken, and hopefully it will be in the newspaper tonight!"

Everyone started talking at once, while Mrs Weaver went over to speak to the two Spanish teachers.

"We're going to be in the paper!" Fliss squealed. "Quick, where's my comb?"

"Cool!" said Rosie. "Let's make sure we get to the front!"

"Yeah, we will!" I said in a determined voice, "Even if we have to trample all over the M&Ms to do it!"

"Look!" Frankie whispered, elbowing me in the ribs. "Maria's coming over!"

Pretty shocked, we all stopped talking. But Maria was actually *smiling*. Well, sort of.

"Hi." Maria stopped in front of us, looking a bit shy. "I come to say – we are sorry about the makeover."

That was a *big* shock! Our mouths dropped open and none of us could say a word for a second or two.

"That's OK," Frankie said at last.

"And I'm sorry about breaking Isabella's present for her mum," Fliss chimed in quickly.

Maria shrugged. "It was accident, no? So, we are friends again?"

The Sleepover Club all looked at each other.

"What about the M&Ms?" I asked.

"Who?" Maria looked blank.

"Emma and Emily," Rosie explained.

"Oh, we can *all* be friends, can't we?" Maria asked.

"Not on your flippin' life!" I began until both Frankie and Lyndz trod heavily on my toes under the table. "Ow!"

"Great!" Maria put her hand in her pocket, and popped a sweet into her mouth. "Sorry, you want one?" She pulled out a bag of liquorice and held it out to us.

"We're not supposed to eat in class," Fliss began virtuously, but Frankie gave her a look.

67

"Come on, Fliss, it's the end of term! Take a risk!"

We all took a sweet from Maria and quickly popped them in our mouths before Mrs Weaver saw us. It looked like we'd managed to sort things out with the Spanish girls after all! Although there was no way we were going to be friends with the M&Ms...

"We see you at playtime, yes?" Maria winked at us and went back to the others, just as a man with a camera hanging round his neck popped his head round the door.

"Mrs Weaver? I'm James Robinson from the *Evening Echo*."

"Oh, good, come in." Mrs Weaver ushered him in, while Fliss grabbed her comb and started preening herself. "Now, what would you like us to do?"

"Well, if we could gather everyone at the front of the room, with the Spanish children in the middle, that would make it easier for me to get everyone into the picture," the photographer said.

We spent the next few minutes pushing

tables and chairs around, and being posed by the photographer.

"There's no way I'm being best buddies with the M&Ms!" I muttered to Frankie as we carried a table between us. "Not even to make friends with Maria and the others again!"

"Let's just wait and see what happens, OK?" Frankie replied in a low voice, still chewing on her sweet.

Finally, everything was ready. We hadn't quite managed to get to the front of the photo because the photographer wanted the Spanish kids there, but we were right behind them, kneeling on a couple of tables, with the rest of our class around us.

"Right, now let's have some nice big smiles please!" called Mr Robinson.

We all began to smile – and then we all nearly jumped out of our skins as Mrs Weaver gave a loud scream.

"Laura! Francesca! Lyndsey! Felicity! Rosie! What on *earth* has happened to your teeth? They're all *black!*"

CHAPTER SEVEN

"What?" I said, puzzled. I didn't have a clue what Mrs Weaver was going on about – until I glanced at Frankie. It looked like she had no teeth at all because they were totally black! And the rest of the Sleepover Club were just the same!

"You've obviously been eating something you shouldn't have!" Mrs Weaver said grimly. "I suggest you go and wash your mouths out!"

"But, Mrs Weaver, we'll miss the photo!" Fliss gasped.

"That's OK, girls," said the photographer with a grin. "You'll only frighten the readers looking like that, anyway!"

Everyone started laughing, especially the Spanish girls and the M&Ms, who were just about killing themselves. Angrily the five of us stomped out of the classroom, and went into the girls' toilets.

"We've missed our chance to be in the newspaper because of that trick Maria played on us!" Fliss said crossly as she rinsed her mouth out. "Those were joke sweets!"

"I thought they tasted a bit funny!" Lyndz said as she used her finger as a toothbrush.

"I guess that was to pay us back for breaking Isabella's bowl," I muttered. "They must have thought we did it on purpose."

"And I bet the M&Ms have been egging them on as well!" Frankie added. "You know what those two are like!"

"Yeah, well, we're not going to let them get away with it, are we?" I asked. "This means WAR!"

The others looked at each other and nodded, although they all looked a bit glum. It *was* a bit of a downer after we'd looked forward to the Spanish girls visiting for so long, but we couldn't let the M&Ms walk all over us, could we?

By the time we got back to the classroom, the photographer had gone and the rest of the class were moving all the chairs and tables back into place.

"Oh, there you are," said Mrs Weaver sternly as she stared at us. "I suppose that was meant to be funny! Well, if you girls have any more jokes like that lined up, you won't be taking part in any of the end-of-term activities. Do I make myself clear?"

"Yes, Miss," we mumbled together, trying not to look at the Spanish girls and the M&Ms, who were all grinning.

While we were putting our table and chairs back in place, the M&Ms came over to have a quick gloat.

"I don't think Mrs Weaver's too pleased with you!" Emma Hughes said gleefully. "And *what* a shame you aren't going to get your picture in the paper!"

"Our friends the Spanish girls are really fed

up with you!" Emily Berryman chimed in smugly. "They wish they were staying with us instead of with you lot!"

"Oh, take a jump off a very high cliff, you two!" I snapped.

The M&Ms went off, giggling. They went back over to Pilar and the others, and they all put their heads together and started whispering and sniggering.

"You know what?" I said to the others as we all sat down. "I'm going to think up a really gruesome trick to play on that lot on the last day of term!"

"No way, Kenny!" Fliss said firmly. "You know what Mrs Poole said about playing tricks at the end of term – she banned them!"

"Yeah, that was after some of the leavers flour-bombed her in the corridor!" Frankie giggled.

"Hey, I wish I'd seen that!" Rosie said.

"It was before you started here," Lyndz said. "*And* they threw eggs at the teachers' cars – it was really funny!"

"Quiet, please." Mrs Weaver was looking

round the room waiting for everyone to settle down. "Right, we have a couple of things to sort out. As you know, it's Sports Day tomorrow and then it's the school Summer Fair the day after."

That cheered us up a bit. Sports Day was a great laugh. We'd held the heats a few days before Pilar and the rest of her gang had arrived, and all of us had made it into at least one of the races which would be taking place tomorrow, even Fliss.

"Right, don't forget that those of you who are taking part in the races tomorrow must have your sports kit with you," Mrs Weaver went on, "or you won't be allowed to compete. Do ask your mums and dads to come along if they can. And, by the way, I'm sure you'll be pleased to know that our visitors will be taking part in the races too!"

We all sat up when we heard *that*! Well, I was going to make sure that if Maria or the others were in any of the races *I* was in, I was going to beat the pants off them!

"And now for the Summer Fair on

Wednesday afternoon," Mrs Weaver went on. "As you know, it's organised by some of the parents…"

We all started nudging Lyndz, because her mum, Mrs Collins, was in charge of the Parents' Association.

"… and this year it's our class's turn to help out." Mrs Weaver glanced round the room. "Everyone, including our visitors, will be given a job to do, and please try to do it *sensibly*. You'll have plenty of time to have a look at the stalls and enjoy yourselves, but the parents who are organising the fair are relying on your help as well."

"I hope we get to do something good!" I whispered to Frankie.

Mrs Weaver glanced at the list she was holding. Then she frowned and glanced at us. "Francesca, Laura, Felicity, Lyndsey and Rosie – Mrs Collins has suggested that you be in charge of the tombola."

"Excellent!" I muttered to Frankie.

"I just hope I can trust you to behave yourselves," Mrs Weaver said sternly, fixing us with her beadiest stare. "You know that the Mayoress is coming to open the fair, and we don't want anything going wrong."

"No, Miss," we said virtuously. The tombola was one of the best stalls to be on, so we were all pretty excited. We were even more pleased when the M&Ms got the boring job of selling programmes, and Pilar and the others were put down to help Lyndz's mum with the cake stall! That was one in the eye for them!

"And don't forget that we have our class trip to the theme park next Monday." Mrs Weaver had to raise her voice because the bell had gone for break time and everyone was talking again. "Plus the fancy-dress competition on the last day of term. I hope you're all busy making your costumes!"

"Oh, yes, Miss!" said Emma Hughes in a treacly voice. "I'm working really hard on mine!"

"So am I, Miss!" said Emily Berryman.

"We can't let those creeps win *again*!" I said, as we went outside. "They've walked off with the prizes the last three times!"

"Still, we got the best job at the Summer

Fair!" said Lyndz. "I had to nag my mum for ages to give us the tombola!"

"Nice one!" I said, as we all crowded round Lyndz and slapped her on the back. "Hey, maybe we can fix it so we win all the prizes!"

"What about Sports Day tomorrow?" Rosie asked. She hadn't been to Sports Day at our school before. "Do you get a prize if you win?"

"Yeah, book tokens usually," said Frankie.

"Let's see how many the Sleepover Club can win!" I said.

"I tell you – none at all!" Maria said scornfully. We hadn't heard the Spanish girls come up behind us, and now they were giggling and sticking their tongues out at us.

"We'll win every race we're in!" I snapped. "Just wait and see!"

Fliss looked a bit nervous at that. She'd made it into the skipping race, but only because Ryan Scott had tripped over his rope and knocked over three other kids, including Frankie, in their heat.

"*We* win more than you!" Pilar retorted. "We are better at sport!"

"No way!" Frankie cut in.

"Then we have competition, yes?" said Maria. "We see who wins the most prizes. If you win – we give you all our prizes. If *we* get more, you give us *your* prizes!"

"OK – but this is just between us, not the M&Ms as well!" I said firmly. Maria nodded, and I stuck out my hand, and we shook. She tried to crush my fingers but I was ready for her, and I crushed hers instead! "You're on!"

CHAPTER EIGHT

"I wish we weren't having this stupid contest!" Fliss moaned for about the millionth time as we changed into our sports kit the following afternoon. Sports Day was due to start in the next half hour, and we were all up for it! At least, I thought we were...

"Stop saying that, will you!" I poked her in the back. "We've got to win, so I hope you've been practising your skipping!"

Fliss didn't look too happy. "Well, sort of..." she muttered. "But Pilar's in the skipping race too, and Isabella says Pilar's really good at skipping so—"

"Hang on a minute!" I grabbed Fliss's arm. "*What* did you say?"

Fliss turned bright red. "Nothing."

"You said *Isabella* told you!" I stared hard at Fliss. "Have you been talking to her?"

"No. Well. Yes. A bit." Fliss looked even more flustered.

"I don't believe you, you traitor!" I snapped. "What're you talking to our enemies for?"

"Well, she's sharing my bedroom, and we just got talking last night," Fliss defended herself. "I think she wants to be friends with us again!"

"I bet it's some sort of con!" I said crossly. "And you fell for it, Fliss! You're such a wally!"

"I am not!" Fliss snapped.

"Yeah? Well, you're the *only* one of us who wants to make friends with them after what they did!" And I looked round at the others.

Lyndz had gone a bit pink, and was clearing her throat and shuffling her feet.

"Um – me and Elena sort of got talking last night too," she confessed.

"What!" I glared at her. "What did she say?"

"She said she wished we were all friends again," Lyndz muttered, "But that Maria and some of the others were still mad at us."

"There you are then!" I said triumphantly, as Mrs Weaver began to round everyone up to take us over to the sports field. "They don't like us and we don't like them!"

Lyndz and Fliss looked doubtful, and so did Frankie and Rosie! I was really beginning to lose my cool now.

"Well, if Isabella and Elena want to be friends," Frankie said slowly, "maybe we should all give it a go—"

"No way!" I cut in firmly. "Look what they did to us – they can't get away with that!" Secretly I was a bit annoyed that Maria hadn't said she wanted to make friends with *me* again. We'd got on really well in Spain… But if she was going to be mean, then so was I – and I could be a lot meaner than she could! "Anyway," I went on, "we don't want to be mates with them while they're hanging round with the M&Ms, do we?"

The others shook their heads, although

Lyndz and Fliss still looked a bit uncertain.

"Come on, line up in twos, please," Mrs Weaver called. "When we get to the field, I want you sitting in rows ready for your races, just like we practised last week."

We all lined up by the classroom door. Rosie went over to get something from her locker – and I couldn't believe my eyes when I saw Anna go over to talk to her! They were smiling at each other too! So when Rosie came back to line up, I pounced on her straightaway.

"What did Anna say to you?"

"Er – she just wished me good luck," Rosie muttered, looking embarrassed.

"Oh, don't tell me – you and Anna are big buddies again!" I said sarcastically. I was pleased to see that it looked like Maria was telling Anna off for speaking to Rosie too! At this rate, there wouldn't be any contest if everyone started being mates again… Deep down I wasn't sure if I was glad or sorry. But if Maria wasn't giving in, then neither was I!

The rest of the school was already out on the field by the time our class got there. There were lots of parents there too, sitting on chairs next to the track so that they got a good view. There was a refreshments stall, and a little platform where Mrs Poole stood to present the prizes at the end.

"There's my mum!" Fliss started waving madly at Mrs Sidebotham, who was sitting next to Mrs Thomas, Frankie's mum. Mrs Thomas was a few months pregnant, and a bump was beginning to show.

"Save your energy for the skipping race, Fliss!" I told her.

The first race for our year was the girls' sprint. I was in that, and so was Frankie. So were Maria and Pilar! I nudged Frankie as they lined up next to us.

"Go for it, Franks!" I whispered. Frankie was faster than me, and I reckoned she could easily beat Pilar and Maria too! But if I could get second place, I'd win a prize too. That would put us ahead in the contest right from the start!

"You have no chance!" Maria said as we waited for Mrs Weaver to blow her whistle.

"We beat the trousers off you!"

"You mean beat the pants off us!" I corrected her. "And you won't, so dream on!"

"On your marks!" Mrs Weaver shouted. "Get set!" And then she blew the whistle. Frankie shot off like a bullet from a gun, and she was halfway down the track before I'd even moved. I ran as fast as I could, but Pilar overtook me easily, although she couldn't catch Frankie. I could hear Fliss, Rosie and Lyndz cheering me on, and I tried even harder, but I couldn't overtake Pilar. Then I heard footsteps behind me – Maria was catching me up!

I had to really push it to stay ahead of her. Frankie got to the tape first, followed by Pilar and I was third – with Maria about a millimetre behind me! Panting hard, I slapped Frankie on the back.

"Nice one! We got two prizes – that means we're in the lead!"

"You were lucky!" Maria snapped. "We beat you in the next race!" And she stormed off.

"Well done, Frankie," Pilar said quickly,

before she ran off after Maria.

Frankie looked surprised. "That was nice of her," she said.

"Don't *you* go all soft on me!" I said crossly, giving her a shove.

There were some other races next, involving some of the other kids, so we sat and watched. Then it was time for our year again. It was the sack race, and Rosie and Isabella were taking part in it.

"Watch out for Ryan Scott, Rosie-Posie!" I told her as Rosie lined up inside her sack. It was a mixed race so there were boys and girls in it together. "He's pretty fast."

"Yeah, he can jump like a frog!" Frankie added with a grin.

"He looks like one too!" I said under my breath, and we all giggled.

"Hey, I heard that!" Ryan shouted, poking me in the back.

"On your marks!" Mrs Weaver called.

"I wonder if Isabella's any good at sack racing?" Lyndz said as we waited for the whistle to blow.

"She's got no chance against Rosie!" I said confidently.

The race began. We were all yelling and cheering loudly for Rosie, but although she was jumping along so fast she was purple in the face, we could see that she wasn't going to win. Ryan Scott was leaping along in front of everyone else, and he was miles ahead. Emma Hughes was second, and Danny McCloud was third, close behind her!

I groaned. "We haven't got a chance of winning a prize!"

"Well, neither has Isabella!" Frankie pointed out. Isabella was ahead of Rosie, but she was only in fourth place.

Then, all of a sudden, Ryan Scott tried to jump too far. He fell forward and landed flat on his face! Emma Hughes began grinning, thinking that she was going to win, when next second Danny McCloud stumbled, fell over and knocked the Queen over too! We all started cheering – but then I stopped. Isabella was in the lead now and she was jumping neatly towards the finishing-line!

"Come on, Rosie!" I yelled, but it was too late. Isabella had won! And Rosie was last – that meant we were equal with two prizes each...

Maria tapped me on the shoulder. "We catch you up – and now we beat you!" she said with a big grin.

"We'll see!" I retorted, as Rosie trailed over to us, looking a bit sheepish.

"Sorry," she muttered.

"Oh, it doesn't matter," Lyndz told her.

"What d'you mean? Of *course* it matters!" I yelled. "We've got to beat Maria and that lot out of sight! And that means you've all got to try harder!"

The others didn't look that keen, and that made me mad. Just because *they* were all being wimps and wanting to be friends with the Spanish girls again – well, *I* wasn't! Although I might have given in if Maria had been a bit nicer... But she was too busy shouting at the other girls in Spanish – probably telling *them* they had to try harder too!

Anyway, we had some ups and some downs during the next few races. Lyndz and Frankie won the three-legged race which put us ahead, but then Anna evened things up by winning the obstacle race. Maria and Elena came second and third in the Potato Grab, but then Frankie won the egg and spoon and I was second in the hurdles. So by the time we got to the last race, the skipping race, we were on a dead heat with five prizes each.

"You'd better win this, Fliss!" I said in a determined voice.

Fliss looked a bit pale. "I'm not very good at skipping," she muttered.

"You're going to win this race if it kills you!" I told her.

"I feel sick!" Fliss moaned. "I don't want to do it!"

"Hey, that's an idea!" I bounced to my feet. "Fliss, go and tell Mrs W. you feel ill, and you don't want to be in the race. Then Frankie can take your place – she's the best skipper out of all of us! And she would have been in the race anyway if Ryan Scott hadn't knocked her over in the heats."

"Do I have to?" Frankie grumbled, looking less than keen.

"Yeah, you do!" I said firmly. What was going on here? Looked like I was trying to run this feud single-handed, because the others just didn't seem interested...

Looking relieved, Fliss went off to speak to Mrs Weaver. Meanwhile I glanced over at Maria and the others. Maria was having a real go at Pilar in Spanish, waving her arms about and talking really loudly. I guessed that Maria was saying that Pilar had to win the race – but Pilar looked about as keen as Frankie did.

"OK, it's all sorted." Fliss came back. "Frankie's in."

"Oh, great," Frankie muttered.

They all lined up for the skipping race. Maria looked well sick when she saw that Frankie had taken Fliss's place, and she came storming over to me.

"Where is Fliss? She should be in this race!"

"Fliss isn't very well," I said coolly, "so Frankie's doing it instead."

"You make that up!" Maria snapped. "You know Fliss will not beat Pilar!"

"Prove it!" I retorted, glaring at her until Elena and Anna came over and dragged her away.

"On your marks!" called Mrs Weaver. "Get set!"

The whistle blew.

"Go for it, Frankie!" I yelled.

Pilar and Frankie sped off neck and neck. They both had long legs so they could take big strides, and they'd soon left the others behind. But they were still so close together, it was hard to tell which one of them was in the lead. First it looked like it was Frankie, then Pilar.

"COME ON, FRANKIE!" I shouted.

And then it happened. Pilar's skipping rope suddenly hooked itself on to one of the gold earrings she was wearing. She skidded to a halt and gave a yell, trying desperately to untangle it.

"Go, Frankie!" I leapt to my feet gleefully. We had the race in the bag now!

Then I just couldn't believe my eyes. Frankie stopped skipping and dashed over to Pilar! She started trying to help her untangle the rope, but it was well and truly stuck. A few seconds later, everyone else in the race skipped past them!

"Frankie!" I screamed, dancing up and down in frustration. "Go on! Don't stop!"

But it was too late. Everyone else had already crossed the finishing-line!

CHAPTER NINE

"All right, Kenny, stop going on about it, will you!" Frankie snapped as she threw a handful of raffle tickets into the tombola drum. "It was no big deal!"

"No big deal!" I retorted. "You stopped to help Pilar, which meant we didn't win the race! We could have walked it – *and* we'd have got their book tokens too!"

"Frankie was just trying to help Pilar," Lyndz chimed in.

"Yeah, her ear was all red and sore afterwards, didn't you see?" Rosie added.

"I think it was really nice of Frankie to stop

and help," Fliss said.

It was the day after Sports Day, and it was almost time for the Summer Fair to start. All the stalls had been set up on the sports field that morning, and there was a long queue of people at the gates, waiting to come in. We'd all really been looking forward to the fair, but after yesterday we weren't getting on too well. We didn't argue very often, but now the others were really bugging me. I knew they all wanted to get matey with the Spanish girls again, but there was *no way* I was up for that! Not while Maria was still keeping the war between us going.

Maria and the others were over on the cake stall with Lyndz's mum, and they were all looking pretty sulky. I reckoned Maria was having exactly the same problem as me...

"If you and Maria would just sort things out, we could all be mates again!" Frankie said, throwing some more tickets into the drum.

"Well, she started it!" I retorted.

"You two are as bad as each other!" Frankie said. "You both need a kick up the behind!"

"Maria's a pain!" I said crossly. "I wish Molly the Monster was back home instead of her!"

"Well, you'd better behave yourself today," Fliss warned me, as Mrs Weaver walked round inspecting the stalls. "Mrs Weaver's got her beady eye on you!"

"We've got some good prizes, haven't we?" Lyndz looked at our stall. We had a mixture of cuddly toys, bath stuff, sweets and bottles of soft drink. "I *love* this Dalmatian!"

The stuffed Dalmatian was our best prize, and Frankie had sat him right at the front of the stall where everyone could see him. He was really big and made of soft white fur. I wasn't into cuddly toys much, but even I wouldn't have minded winning him! All the winning tickets ended in 0 or 5, and the Dalmatian was number 500.

"That should get a lot of people coming to our stall!" Frankie said.

"Hey, I've just had an idea!" I announced. "Why don't we challenge Maria and that lot to see which of us makes more money on our stall?"

The others groaned. "No, Kenny!" they said together.

"Oh, well, if you want to be a bunch of wimps..." I muttered.

"Look, the caretaker's opening the gates," Lyndz said quickly. "And here comes Mrs Poole with the Mayoress!"

All the people queuing outside started to file in. They crowded round the little platform, which had been left there yesterday after Sports Day. Mrs Pontefract, the Mayoress, was chatting to Mrs Poole as she went up on to the platform to make a speech. Mrs Weaver had warned us that we weren't allowed to sell a single ticket until she'd declared the fair open.

"Well, firstly let me say how very happy I am to be here," declared Mrs Pontefract, looking at all the people clustered round the platform. She was wearing her robes and gold chain, but because she was very short and round, she looked like a Teletubby! Mrs Pontefract had been to our school a few times before, and whenever she made a speech she always went on and on, so none of us bothered listening.

"I wonder who'll win the Dalmatian," said Fliss, giving it a pat.

"I bet it's still left over at the end," I said. "The best prizes always are!"

"... and now I am happy to declare this Summer Fair open!" said the Mayoress, and everyone clapped. Then they all started rushing over to the stalls. Mrs Poole and Mrs Pontefract left the platform, and they started looking round the fair too.

"Hello, I want to buy some tickets," said a familiar voice. We all looked round, and there was Isabella with her purse in her hand.

"That was quick!" said Fliss with a shy smile. "You're our first customer, Isabella!"

"Hold on – you're supposed to be helping Lyndz's mum on the cake stall, aren't you?" I asked, glaring at Isabella.

"Mrs Collins say I can come and buy some tickets." Isabella pointed at the Dalmatian. "I want to win this!"

"Yeah, he's gorgeous, isn't he?" Frankie said enthusiastically.

Isabella held out a pound coin. "Please can

I have five tickets?"

"I suppose so," I muttered, taking the money.

"Isabella!" Maria slipped out from behind the cake stall and rushed over to her. She gave me an evil stare, and then began jabbering away in Spanish to Isabella. Even though we couldn't understand what they were saying, it was obvious they were having an argument. I guessed that Maria didn't want Isabella to buy any tickets from us!

Isabella wouldn't take any notice though. She put her hand into the drum, and pulled out some folded tickets. She took three herself and gave two of them to Maria to open.

"Anything ending in 0 or 5 wins a prize!" Lyndz said helpfully, and I glanced at her, annoyed. I didn't want Isabella to win *anything*!

Isabella said something in Spanish and threw her tickets in the bin by the side of the stall, looking disappointed. Meanwhile, Maria was looking at one of the two tickets she had in her hand with a big smile on her face.

"I win a prize!" She grinned smugly at me. "I

have a number with 0 at the end!"

"Trust her!" I muttered to Frankie.

"I have number 500!" Maria announced, waving the ticket over her head.

"Yes! We win the dog!" Isabella shouted, beaming all over her face.

"No, you can't have!" I gasped, and the other Sleepovers looked gobsmacked too. Our best prize *couldn't* have been won by the first customer who bought a ticket! And there was no way I was letting Maria and Isabella have it!

"Yes! We win!" Maria and Isabella were celebrating, doing high fives, but I had an idea. Quickly I whipped the 500 ticket off the front of the Dalmatian and swopped it with the one on a can of Coca Cola, which had 225 on it. The other Sleepovers could hardly believe their eyes!

"Kenny, you can't do that!" Fliss began, but I elbowed her in the ribs. "Ow!"

"Here's your prize, Isabella," I said casually. "A can of Coke!"

Maria and Isabella stared at me. "No, I win the dog!" Isabella said with a frown.

"No, I don't think so!" I shook my head. "The Dalmatian's number 225!"

Isabella and Maria both blinked as if they were seeing things. "No, it was 500!" Isabella said furiously. "You change it so we do not win!"

"I did not!" I said.

"You should let us have a free go!" Maria said, trying to grab some more tickets out of the tombola drum.

"No way!" I legged it round to the front of the stall, and tried to push her away, but Maria picked the drum up off the stall and held it tightly.

"Give it back!" I yelled, and we started to have a tug-of-war!

By now quite a lot of people were looking round at us to see what was going on. I was so mad I didn't care, not even when I saw that Mrs Poole and the Mayoress were heading in our direction. Pilar and the other Spanish girls also dashed over from the cake stall to find out what was happening, and they started calling to Maria in Spanish.

"Kenny, stop it!" Frankie was saying, and so were the others, but I just pulled my end of the tombola drum even harder.

Unfortunately, the drum was a bit rickety and it couldn't take the strain. It split in two, and Maria and I both fell backwards...

"What on earth's going on here?" Mrs Poole began with a frown, but next second she and the Mayoress were both showered in *hundreds* of raffle tickets!

CHAPTER TEN

"Well?"

Mrs Poole sat at her desk the following morning and stared hard at the ten of us lined up in a row – me and the rest of the Sleepover Club as well as Maria and the Spanish girls. Usually Mrs P. was a bit of a pushover, and talked more about how sorry she was that we'd let her down, rather than just going ballistic. But this time she looked like she was going to tear us to bits.

"I was very ashamed of your behaviour in front of all our visitors, *and* the Mayoress too," Mrs Poole went on sternly. "Poor Mrs Pontefract was picking raffle tickets out of her

101

hat for at least ten minutes afterwards."

I bit my lip, hoping I looked upset, but really I was trying not to laugh! We'd spent the rest of the Summer Fair on our hands and knees sweeping up the tombola tickets, and we'd had tellings-off from Mrs Weaver, the Mayoress and from Lyndz's mum. Now it was Mrs Poole's turn.

"There'd better be a good reason for such appalling behaviour," Mrs Poole went on, looking hard at us, one by one, "or I'm afraid to say that none of you will be going on the class trip to the theme park next Monday."

That wiped the smile off my face! I'd been looking forward to going to WonderLand for months, and now it was all Maria's fault that I might not be going. Well, I suppose it was my fault a bit as well... Anyway, I knew I'd have to speak up and tell the truth, because I couldn't let the others take the blame when they'd had nothing to do with it. So I cleared my throat.

"Er – Mrs Poole, I—"

"Mrs Poole, I tell you what happened," Isabella interrupted me, and I glared at her. I reckoned Isabella was now going to drop me right in it by telling Mrs Poole all about how she'd won the Dalmatian and I'd switched the tickets round!

"I buy some tickets," Isabella said in a loud voice. "I ask Maria to help me pull them out and she have her hand stuck in the tombola."

Mrs Poole frowned. "So why were she and Kenny fighting over it?"

What's going on? I wondered with a frown. Why wasn't Isabella dropping me in it? I just couldn't understand it.

"They weren't fighting, Mrs Poole," Frankie said quickly. "Kenny was just trying to pull Maria's hand free."

"Yes, and the tombola break," Pilar added.

"And that's when all the tickets flew out," Lyndz finished off.

"We're really sorry, Mrs Poole," said Rosie.

Mrs Poole looked slightly less furious. "Is that what happened, Maria? Kenny?"

I glanced sideways at Maria. She looked pretty sulky, but Pilar was nudging her in the ribs.

"Yes, Mrs Poole," she muttered.

"Yes, Mrs Poole," I said, heaving a silent sigh of relief. It looked like I wasn't going to be banned from the trip after all, but I just couldn't understand why. Maria had had the perfect opportunity to get me into trouble big-time and she hadn't taken it. Why not? Now that Isabella had helped me out too, I felt really bad that she'd hadn't got the Dalmatian in the end. Maria had dropped the winning ticket in all the fuss after the tombola had broken.

"Well, if it was an accident, I think I can overlook it just this once," said Mrs Poole. "But I want you all to spend this morning writing letters of apology to Mrs Pontefract. And I want them given to me by the end of the morning. Is that clear?"

We all nodded. We'd got off pretty lightly, considering we'd annoyed the Mayoress *and* the headteacher! And at least we were all still going on the class trip. We all filed out of Mrs Poole's office trying not to grin at each other with relief.

"Whew, that was close!" I said to Frankie as

soon as we were outside in the corridor. "I thought I was going to miss out on WonderLand!"

"Well, you were lucky Isabella thought fast and came up with a good excuse!" Frankie told me. "You owe her one!"

"Yeah, OK…" I muttered. Then I noticed the other Sleepovers staring hard at me. "What?"

"Isabella got you out of trouble," said Fliss pointedly. "You *could* say thank you!"

I pulled a face. "Oh, all right then…"

"And maybe you and Maria can make friends now," Lyndz added eagerly.

I didn't say anything. I was beginning to feel a bit ashamed of myself for messing about with the tickets the day before. Maybe if I asked Mrs Poole nicely she'd let Isabella have the Dalmatian after all…

The Spanish girls were crowded round Maria, who still looked sulky, and they were having a go at her in Spanish. I reckoned they were telling her to make up with me. If she wanted to, well, so would I.

"Er – Isabella, thanks for coming up with

that story for Mrs Poole," I muttered. "It was really nice of you."

Isabella grinned at me. "It is OK!"

"And I'm really sorry about changing the ticket on the Dalmatian," I went on. "I'll tell Mrs Poole you won it fair and square, and maybe she'll let you have it."

For some reason Isabella stopped smiling and looked over at Maria. "Do you tell her or do I?" she asked sternly.

"Tell me what?" I asked, puzzled.

Maria was staring down at her feet. "I did not have the winning ticket," she muttered sheepishly.

"*What?*" My mouth fell open. "But you had number 500!"

"No, it was not 500," Maria said. "I just *say* I had it to make you angry! I knew you do not want to give Isabella your best prize!"

"What a stupid trick to pull!" I was so furious I could hardly speak. "I nearly lost out on the class trip because of you!"

"Well, you should not change the tickets!" Maria snapped.

"I wouldn't have had to if you hadn't told that fib in the first place!" I retorted.

"Oh, you're both as bad as each other!" Frankie cut in. "Why don't you just give it up and make friends?"

"Yes, and then we forget all about this!" Pilar added.

"I'll be friends with Pilar, Elena, Anna and Isabella," I said pointedly, "but I'm not going to be friends with *her*!"

"And I am friends with Frankie, Fliss, Rosie and Lyndz," Maria said, "but I am not friends with *her*!"

"Fine!" I snapped.

"Fine!" agreed Maria.

And we turned on our heels and stalked off in opposite directions, leaving the others behind us.

CHAPTER ELEVEN

"WonderLand, here we come!" I said as I climbed on to the coach behind Fliss. "This is going to be cool!"

We'd just had another weekend without a sleepover because of the Oldies still making a fuss about the food fight, so this trip to WonderLand would make up for that.

"We only just made it, though!" Frankie pointed out.

"Yeah, so don't do anything crazy today, Kenny!" Fliss warned me.

"Me! Why should *I* be the one to do anything crazy?" I asked innocently, poking Fliss hard in the back. She squealed and nearly whacked Emma Hughes on the head with her rucksack as she went past her seat.

"Watch where you're going, you idiot!" Emma snorted.

"Yeah," chimed in Emily Berryman, who was sitting next to her. "You could have taken Emma's head off!"

"That would have been an improvement!" I said sweetly, and the Terrible Twins both glared at me.

Maria and Pilar were sitting behind the M&Ms, with Elena and Anna behind them, and Isabella was across the aisle on her own. Anyway, when I made that crack about Emma, I *thought* I saw Maria *almost* smile. But maybe I didn't really. Maybe I imagined it... After all, we still weren't speaking to each other, and the others had given up trying to make us. They couldn't really be friends properly unless me and Maria were too, so the Spanish girls were still going round with the M&Ms.

We all went further on down the coach, and sat down – me next to Lyndz, Fliss next to

Rosie and Frankie on her own.

"What have you got in your packed lunch?" Lyndz asked as soon as we sat down.

"Two packets of cheese and onion crisps, two ham and tomato rolls, a Snickers, a Twix, a packet of chocolate Hob-Nobs and a strawberry milkshake," I said.

"I'll swop you a packet of salt and vinegar for a cheese and onion," Lyndz offered.

"And I'll swop a sausage roll for half your Hob-Nobs," Fliss said.

Anyway, swopping and changing our lunchboxes around took up lots of time, and by the time we arrived at WonderLand, we all had totally different lunches from the ones we'd set out with! Then we all stopped thinking about food for once, and started getting pretty excited instead. Fliss had been to WonderLand before, but none of the rest of us had. It looked pretty spectacular. The front was built like a huge castle, and you had to walk on a drawbridge over a moat to get in.

"Wow! This is coo-ell!" I gasped as the coach pulled up in the car park next to all the others.

"What's the best ride, Flissy?"

"I liked the riverboat ride," Fliss said.

"Oh, great big fat hairy deal!" I snorted. "I mean, what's the *scariest* ride?"

"The Mega-Loop!" Fliss gave a shudder. "You're upside-down most of the time. I went on it with my mum and my brother, and my mum was sick when we got off!"

"Right, we're definitely going on that one then!" I jumped to my feet. "Come on, what're we waiting for?"

"Sit down, Kenny!" Lyndz grabbed my arm. "Mrs Weaver's waiting to speak to us!"

"Right, I want you all to listen carefully," said Mrs Weaver, who was standing at the front of the coach. "We've talked about this already, but this is a reminder for those of you who don't always act sensibly."

And she stared grimly down the coach at the Sleepover Club. What a cheek!

"You are allowed to go round the theme park on your own, but stay with your friends at all times. Myself and the other teachers will be patrolling around, keeping an eye on things, and if you have any problems, you can always speak to the park stewards."

We were all fidgeting away in our seats with ants in our pants, waiting for Mrs Weaver to stop rabbiting on. As soon as she did, we all jumped up and pushed our way off the coach. Then Mrs W. led us over to one of the ticket offices, and we all got given a luminous pink wristband to wear that would let us go on all the rides.

"Quick, let's get away from the boring old teachers!" I hissed in Frankie's ear as soon as we had gone over the drawbridge and we were inside. Everyone agreed, and we sneaked off while Mrs Weaver was still reminding everyone where we were meeting for lunch, and that we had to be on our best behaviour at all times.

"Come on, let's go on the Secret Garden ride." That was Emma Hughes, wittering on behind us and being a bossy-boots as usual. "It doesn't sound too scary!"

"*That* ride look good." Maria was pointing at a deadly-looking rollercoaster-type ride which towered high above our heads and twisted and turned like a corkscrew.

"That's the Mega-Loop!" Fliss whispered in my ear.

The Queen turned green (hey, I'm a poet!). "No, I don't want to," she said firmly. "Come on!"

I saw Maria pull a face at the others as they trailed off after the M&Ms.

"Poor them!" said Lyndz. "They're going to have a really gruesome time with the M&Ms!"

"Serves Maria right!" I muttered, but secretly I couldn't help feeling a bit sorry for her too. The M&Ms wouldn't want to go on any of the cool rides!

We took it in turns to choose what we wanted to go on. Rosie went first, and she chose the log flume. We all got sore throats because we screamed so much, and we all got soaked, especially me and Frankie 'cos we'd bravely volunteered to sit at the front. But it was a roasting hot day, so we soon dried off!

"Right, my turn now!" Lyndz said when we climbed off. "I want to go on the Jolly Roger!"

That was a huge model of a pirate ship that swung up and down and side to side. It looked fab!

"Look, the queue's pretty small." Frankie nudged me. "Come on!"

We all charged over to join the end of the line. Just as we got there, three older boys we didn't know jumped in and pushed their way in front of us.

"Hey, get out of the way!" I yelled indignantly. "We were here first!"

"No, you weren't!" sniggered one of the boys, who had floppy dark hair and sticking-out ears. "Look, we're in front of you!"

"That's because you pushed in!" Frankie pointed out.

"So make us move then!" said one of the others, a tall skinny boy with ginger hair.

"OK, I will!" I yelled. I charged forward, but I wasn't moving because Fliss and Rosie had both grabbed hold of my arms.

"Kenny, no!" Frankie hissed. "Mrs Weaver"ll go mad if you get into trouble again!"

"Yeah, Kenny! Mrs Weaver'll go mad!"

mocked the third boy, who was short and stocky with a skinhead hair-cut.

If looks could kill, those boys would have dropped down dead! But that was all I could do – look. I didn't want to get into trouble again, and spoil the end of term.

"All right," I muttered, trying to cool myself down. The boys started sniggering and doing high fives because they'd got one over on us, and that *really* made me mad! But I just about managed to stop myself from kicking their butts!

After the Jolly Roger ride, which was really good, it was my turn. I wanted to go on the Mega-Loop, of course! So we made our way over to it.

It looked even bigger and scarier when you were standing right underneath it! The queue was a bit longer than for some of the other rides, but it wasn't too bad. We went over to join the end of it – and you'll never guess what happened! Those creeps appeared again right behind us and pushed in again! We were so shocked, none of us could do anything about it, even me! We just stood and stared at them while they killed themselves laughing.

"Right, that's it!" I clenched my fists. "You're going to move this time or else!"

"Who's going to make us?" jeered Sticking-Out Ears.

"We are!" Frankie told him.

"Get off!" scoffed Ginger. "We're not afraid of five wimpy little girls!"

"What about *ten* girls?" said a familiar voice right behind us.

CHAPTER TWELVE

Surprised, we all looked round. Maria and the others were standing behind us in the queue, staring hard at the three boys.

"These are our friends," said Pilar. "So now we are *ten* girls!"

I stared at Maria. Then I moved next to her so that we were standing shoulder to shoulder. "Yeah, so you'd better move out of the way!" I said with a grin.

"We're not scared of ten girls!" said Ginger, although his two mates didn't look quite so sure. "We're not scared of a *hundred* girls!"

"Hey, I've got an idea!" Frankie announced.

"Why don't we grab them and *kiss* them to death!"

This time the three boys went quite pale.

"Yeah, good one, Frankie!" Lyndz agreed. "Then their mates will really take the mickey out of them!"

"Now wait a minute—" Ginger began, starting to back away.

"Let's get them!" I yelled. "Come on – kissy kissy!"

And we all rushed forward. The three boys panicked and ran for their lives, nearly tripping over in their eagerness to get away. We all had to hold each other up, we were laughing so much.

"Did you see the look on their faces?" Rosie gasped.

"They look like... like we going to beat them up!" Isabella giggled.

"I don't think we'll be seeing *them* again in a hurry!" said Frankie.

"Good – I would not like to kiss them!" Pilar laughed. "They are very ugly!"

After we'd stopped laughing, Maria and I

started shuffling our feet and looking a bit awkward. Everyone else was standing round waiting for us two to say something.

"Thanks for helping us out," I muttered at last.

"Is OK." Maria shrugged. "We want to go on Mega-Loop, and when we get here, we see you have problem."

"I thought the M&Ms didn't want to go on the Mega-Loop," Frankie said.

"We say goodbye to M&Ms," Maria muttered, looking even more embarrassed. "We – how you say – dump them!"

"They annoy us very much!" said Pilar with a grin. "They not want to go on *any* good rides!"

"Typical M&Ms!" I said. "They're right wimps!"

"Yes, you are right about them!" Maria said. "And we think maybe they *did* send those nasty emails!"

"They not like you at all!" Isabella added.

"Well, we don't like them either!" I said firmly.

"We forget everything now and have a good time, yes?" Maria looked at me.

"You bet!" I said, and I meant it!

Now that there was ten of us going on all the rides, everything was even better. The Mega-Loop was *wicked*! You got spun round upside-down so fast it made your teeth rattle inside your head! Fliss and Isabella both looked pretty green when we got off, and I felt just a little bit funny myself. After that we went into the Haunted House, and then to the Hall of Mirrors. That had those weird mirrors that give you really funny reflections, and we nearly died laughing when we looked at ourselves.

Then it was time to go to the picnic area and meet the others for lunch. Boy, I wish you could've seen the M&Ms' faces when the ten of us turned us laughing and chatting and being best mates. The Queen and the Goblin looked as if they were going to burst with rage!

We all stuffed ourselves silly, and then Mrs Weaver and the other teachers rounded

120

everybody up and we went to watch some of the afternoon shows. There was a show with animals doing tricks, and one with acrobats, and afterwards we were allowed to go shopping. I got a cool blue baseball cap with *WonderLand is Wonderful!* written on it.

"I wish we didn't have to go home," Rosie said with a big yawn as we climbed on to the coach. "We didn't get to go on all the rides."

"But at least Maria and Kenny made friends at last!" Fliss added as we all filed down the coach. I sat next to Maria, Frankie sat next to Pilar, Rosie and Anna sat together and so did Lyndz and Elena and Fliss and Isabella.

"Hey, look at the M&Ms!" I nudged Maria. "They look like they've swallowed a wasp!"

The M&Ms had just got on the coach, and they were glaring at us. They found seats as far away from us as possible, and then turned their backs on us.

"I am glad we not have to be friends with them any more!" said Maria. "They are – how you say – a pain in the neck!"

"Definitely!" I agreed.

Although we were all pretty tired, the trip home was great. We showed each other what we'd bought, shared what was left of our packed lunches and played games.

"That was my best day ever!" Rosie sighed as the coach pulled into the school playground. We were a bit late getting back and all the other kids had already gone home.

"And tomorrow's the last day of term – even better!" Frankie added. "Then it's the summer holidays!"

"It's a real shame we can't play any tricks tomorrow though," I grumbled as we collected up our empty crisp packets and picked up our bags. "Mrs Poole's a real meanie!"

I was a bit surprised by what happened next. Maria stared at me with her mouth open as if I'd just told her the sky was about to fall on her head! She immediately jumped to her feet and began gabbling away in Spanish to Pilar, who was sitting behind her. Then the others started joining in.

"Hey, what's going on?" I asked.

"I set a trick for your teacher!" Maria said

breathlessly, looking worried. "In her table. When she opens the drawer, flour will fall out over her!"

We all stared at her. "You set a trap for Mrs Weaver?" Frankie said, eyes wide. "Why?"

"It was Emma's idea," Maria muttered, looking ashamed. "She say it will be good fun."

"Well, it's too late to do anything about it now," I said. "Anyway, Mrs W. won't know who's done it, so you'll be OK."

"No, you not understand!" Pilar looked worried too. "Emma say we have to blame *you*!"

"What do you mean?" I asked.

"She put two more bags of flour in your – how you say – locker, Kenny," Pilar explained. "Then Mrs Weaver think it is all your fault!"

"The nasty little ratbag!" I hissed furiously, bouncing right out of my seat. "Right, Emma Hughes is for it!"

"Never mind that now, Kenny!" Frankie said. "It's more important that we go into school and get rid of that booby-trap. Or you're dead tomorrow when Mrs Weaver gets flour all over her!"

"Yeah, she'll go ballistic and so will Mrs Poole!" Lyndz agreed.

"We get rid of it," said Maria. "I go into school now and do it."

"I come with you," Pilar told her.

"Come on, girls." Mrs Weaver was waiting impatiently at the front of the coach, glancing at her watch. "Off you go."

We looked up and realised that everyone else had got off and we were last. So we scrambled our stuff together, and hurried over to the door.

"Right, we're a bit late getting back, so hurry straight home or your parents might start getting worried." And Mrs Weaver started ushering us over to the playground gate.

"Miss, I have to go into school for something," Maria began, but Mrs Weaver shook her head.

"Sorry, Maria. Whatever it is it will have to wait until tomorrow."

"But, Miss, I have to go into school!" Maria insisted.

"And it's still open, Mrs Weaver," Frankie

pointed out. "The caretaker hasn't locked up yet."

"Yes, that's because the cleaners are here, and we don't want you getting in their way." Mrs Weaver stood by the gate and watched as we all reluctantly filed out. "Now make sure you go straight home."

We didn't have any choice. We walked down the road, staring gloomily at each other.

"So what are we going to do NOW?" Frankie asked.

CHAPTER THIRTEEN

"We've got to get into school somehow," I said grimly, "or tomorrow I'm going to be in the biggest trouble ever!"

"You might even get expelled!" Fliss wailed.

"Oh, thanks a lot!" I snapped.

"Shut up and let's think about this!" Frankie said, taking charge as usual. "Look, we've got to go home first, or our parents are going to start climbing the walls."

"I have to come back later," Maria decided. "In one hour, when the teachers go home."

"Is good idea," Pilar agreed. "I come with you."

"I'm coming too," I butted in, "'cos _I'm_ the one who's going to be in deepest doom if Mrs W. gets covered in flour!"

"I'd better come as well then," Frankie said. "Someone's got to be there to control Kenny!"

"Cheek!" I said indignantly.

"I'm coming too then!" chorused Lyndz, Elena, Rosie and Anna together. Fliss and Isabella looked at each other, then they both nodded too.

"We can't _all_ go!" I spluttered. "With ten of us creeping round the school, we're bound to get caught!"

"No, hang on, I've got an idea!" Frankie said thoughtfully. "We'll split up!"

"What difference will that make?" I asked impatiently.

"We'll split up and go into the school through different doors," Frankie explained. "Then, if anyone gets caught, at least someone else has got a chance of making it to our classroom!"

We all thought about that. It made sense.

"OK, so we'll meet back here in about an

hour," I said, checking my watch. "Then it's Operation Flourbag!"

"D'you think the school'll still be open?" Lyndz asked.

"I dunno," I said doubtfully. "How long does cleaning a school take?"

We all looked at each other. No-one had any idea.

"We'll just have to risk it," said Lyndz.

"Yeah," I muttered. "I just hope this plan works…" Because if it didn't, the last day of term was going to be ruined, I was going to be history, and the Queen and the Goblin would have the biggest laugh ever at our expense…

"Where are Pilar and Frankie?" I hissed, looking at my watch for the millionth time.

Everyone else had met up outside the school gates right on time, except for those two, and now we were all getting edgy. We'd all told our parents that we had to go back to school to collect something we'd forgotten – none of them had minded, 'cos we were allowed to stay out longer anyway now that it was light in the evenings.

"Let's go without them," Fliss suggested, her teeth chattering with nerves.

"No, give them a few more minutes," Lyndz said. "Look, the school's still open." We could see that some of the windows were still ajar, so it was obvious the caretaker hadn't locked up yet.

"The cleaners must still be in there." I glanced impatiently up the road again, and there were Pilar and Frankie racing towards us. "At last!"

"Sorry!" Frankie gasped. "My mum went shopping for baby clothes today and she wanted to show them all to us!"

"Is the school still open?" Pilar panted.

I nodded. "But we've got to be quick. The caretaker might start locking up any minute."

"What if Mr Coleman starts locking up while we're inside?" Fliss asked nervously.

"We will be shut in?" Isabella squeaked, looking scared.

"'Course we won't!" I said confidently. "We can easily climb out of one of the windows!

Now, let's get a move on!"

Quickly we divided ourselves up into three groups. Fliss and Maria and I were going in through the main entrance doors; Elena, Rosie and Anna were going round the back; and Frankie, Pilar, Isabella and Lyndz were taking the short route through one of the cloakrooms.

Silently we crept in through the playground gates. It was still daylight so we had to run for cover behind a wall, and wait there for a few seconds to make sure that the caretaker hadn't spotted us.

"OK, let's go for it!" I whispered. "Good luck – and I hope we all make it!"

"Just a sec!" Frankie grabbed my arm as I was about to shoot off with Fliss and Maria. "Look over there!"

Frankie was pointing at the teachers' car park. To our horror, it was still full of cars – *and Mrs Weaver's red Metro was there too*.

"The teachers are still here!" Fliss wailed. "I thought they'd have gone home by now!"

"What're they doing here?" I groaned.

"Ssh! Listen!" Elena held up her hand. We all listened hard – and in the distance we could just about hear a Spice Girls song playing very faintly. The windows of the staffroom were wide open, and the noise seemed to be coming from there.

"They must be having an end-of-term party!" Lyndz said.

"Oh, great!" I said. "And the staffroom's really close to our classroom!"

"We can't give up now," Rosie pointed out. "Anyway, they'll probably be too busy having a good time to hear us!"

"Rosie's right," said Frankie. "We've got to go for it!"

We all took a deep breath and started slapping each other on the backs and doing high fives, trying to make ourselves feel braver. Then we split up and set off.

"I'm scared!" Fliss moaned in my ear as the three of us hurried over to the main entrance. "What if we get caught?"

"We just say we forgot something and we came to get it," I replied. "Don't say anything about the flour!"

Fliss, Maria and I had the longest journey through the school to get to our classroom, but at first it wasn't too bad. We went through the Infants, and cut through the hall, and then we were in the corridor that led up to Mrs Weaver's room. The staffroom was at the end of the corridor, and although the door was shut, we could hear the sound of music and people laughing and talking.

"Quick!" I grabbed Fliss and Maria, and dragged them along with me towards the classroom. The door was slightly ajar, and we rushed in. To our relief, the others were already there.

"We all made it!" I exclaimed.

"Yeah, but let's get a move on!" Frankie whispered. "Maria's got to get rid of that flour!"

Maria was already standing by Mrs Weaver's table, pulling a big black bin bag out of her pocket.

"Stand back!" she said. She pulled the top drawer open a very little way, and slipped the black bag over it. Then she pulled it out further, and we saw a small puff of flour as it all disappeared neatly into the black bag – instead of over Mrs Weaver tomorrow!

"Hey, that was cool!" I said admiringly. "How did you set that up?"

"Not now, Kenny!" Fliss hissed. She and Isabella were the look-outs over by the door. "Come on, let's get out of here!"

"Don't forget the flour in Kenny's locker!" Lyndz reminded us. Lucky she remembered! Quickly I went across the room, and looked in my locker. It was empty except for a really old and smelly pair of trainers, an empty crisps bag – and two big packets of flour.

"Creeps!" I muttered angrily as I took the flour out. It weighed a ton. "What am I supposed to do with this now?" Then I grinned as I had a really fab idea. "Hey, guys, what do you think of this?"

But I didn't get a chance to tell them what I was planning to do because Fliss and Isabella suddenly jumped away from the door, and gasped in fright.

"What is it?" asked Elena.

"M-M-M-Mrs Weaver!" Fliss stuttered, looking absolutely terrified. "She's just come out of the staffroom, and she's coming this way!"

CHAPTER FOURTEEN

Everyone had a major panic. If Mrs Weaver came into the classroom, we'd had it because there was nowhere we could hide.

"Close the door, Fliss!" Frankie hissed. "*Quietly!*"

Fliss's hands were shaking so much she could hardly manage it, but she did it. Meanwhile the rest of us crawled under the tables and tried to make ourselves as small as possible. If Mrs Weaver went past the classroom we were OK. If she just glanced through the glass at the top of the door as she went by, we would *probably* be OK. But if she opened the door and came in… we were dead meat.

I kept my eyes on the door. I saw Mrs Weaver's head appear in the glass at the top – and then she went by. I heaved an enormous sigh of relief.

"She's gone!"

"Let's get out of here then!" Fliss wailed.

"No, wait!" Frankie cut in. "It might be better to stay here till she's gone back to the staffroom. Otherwise there's a chance we might bump into her while we're trying to escape!"

We couldn't argue with that, although none of us were very keen on staying in the classroom a minute longer than we had to. But I had something to do before we left anyway.

"Kenny, what're you up to?" Frankie asked as I picked up the two bags of flour.

"Oh, just paying back the M&Ms for getting us into this mess!" I said cheerfully. "Maria, give me a hand, will you?"

* * *

Maria and I had just finished setting up our surprise for the M&Ms when Elena and Rosie, who were being look-outs, started waving madly at us.

"Mrs Weaver's coming back!" Rosie mouthed silently at us. We all dived under the tables, and waited. Mrs Weaver went past again, and then we heard the staffroom door open. A blast of noise came out.

"What's that!" Frankie gasped, covering her hands with her ears. "It's horrible!"

"It sounds like a dog howling!" Fliss added.

"No, it isn't." I started laughing. "It's Mr Coppins singing! The teachers are doing karaoke!"

We all started giggling and we had to stuff our hands in our mouths to muffle the sound. Rosie opened the door a bit wider so that we could hear it better. After Mr Coppins had finished murdering a Boyzone song, Mrs Weaver did a Madonna impression! We all nearly died laughing.

"Come on, let's get out of here!" Frankie said at last. "We've wasted enough time already!"

Still giggling, we tiptoed across the room, and peered out of the door. Luckily the staffroom door was closed, but the teachers were making so much noise, I don't think they'd have noticed if we'd dropped a bomb on them!

"Right, shall we split up again?" I whispered.

"Nah, no point," Frankie whispered back. "Let's just get out of here as fast as we can!"

We all ran down the corridor. We were nearly back at the main entrance, when suddenly Elena, who was at the front, stopped dead in her tracks, and the rest of us all bumped into each other as we skidded to a halt.

"I can hear noise!" Elena gasped. "Someone is outside!"

We all listened. She was right. There were definitely footsteps approaching!

"Quick, hide!" Frankie hissed, diving into a nearby classroom.

We all scattered. Isabella, Fliss and Rosie followed Frankie, while Lyndz, Anna and Pilar dashed into the hall. Maria, Elena and I raced into the Infants' cloakroom, and flattened ourselves against the wall.

The footsteps got louder. Someone was coming in through the door.

"Hello?" said a familiar voice, and I nearly dropped dead with fright! It was Mrs Poole, our headmistress! "Who's there?"

She'd heard us! I glanced at Maria and Elena, who both looked as scared as I was.

"I said, who's there?" Mrs Poole repeated. "You'd better come out, whoever you are!"

None of us moved.

"Right, I'll have to come and find you then!"

We heard the sound of heels tapping across the entrance hall – and they were coming in our direction! Mrs Poole was coming over to the cloakroom!

"What we do now?" Maria whispered urgently in my ear.

For once I didn't have a single bright idea. Mrs Poole was going to catch us red-handed, and there was nothing we could do about it. I just hoped the others kept quiet and managed to get out safely after we'd been captured…

"Betty! We've been waiting for you!"

That was Mrs Weaver's voice! I groaned silently. How many more teachers were we going to have to get past before we could escape?

"Oh, hello, Jane," Mrs Poole replied. "I was just wondering if some of the staff were lying in wait for me – you know, to play an end-of-term trick on me!"

"Not this time!" Mrs Weaver said with a laugh.

"Yes, I still remember last term when you turned all the furniture in my office upside-down!" Mrs Poole started to laugh too. "How's the party going?"

"Fine, but we're waiting for you to come and give us a song!"

"Right. Funny though, I could have sworn I heard someone moving around..." Mrs Poole was coming closer to the cloakroom. "Maybe we ought to check the classrooms."

I held my breath.

"Oh, come on, you're missing all the fun!" Mrs Weaver said firmly. "We'll ask the caretaker to look around if you're worried."

Mrs Weaver and Mrs Poole walked off down the corridor together. We waited till the sound of their voices had died away, and then we sneaked out of our various hiding-places.

"Did you hear *that*?" I asked indignantly. "The teachers are allowed to play tricks at the end of term, but we're not!"

"I didn't know the teachers behaved like this at the end of term!" Frankie grinned as we tiptoed out of the door. "I thought they spent all their time tidying the classrooms and moaning at us!"

"They'd die if they knew we'd heard them doing karaoke!" Rosie giggled.

It was still light when we got out into the playground, and we had to be careful making our way over to the gates. When the last one of us had finally dashed out, we all heaved a big sigh of relief.

"We made it!" I said triumphantly.

"Just about!" Frankie grinned. "Mrs Weaver nearly caught us a few times!"

"I've got to get home right now," Rosie said,

glancing at her watch. "I've got to finish off my fancy-dress costume for tomorrow."

"Me too," said Lyndz and Frankie together.

"Let's get out of here." I walked off up the road, and the others followed. "I've had enough of school to last me a lifetime!"

"This was all my fault," said Maria. "I am very sorry."

"Yes, if we did not listen to M&Ms, this would not happen," Pilar chimed in.

"No, it wasn't your fault," Frankie said, slapping her on the back. "This was all down to the M&Ms! They were the ones who started everything off by sending those emails!"

"Yeah, and tomorrow they're going to get exactly what they deserve!" I said with a big grin. "And I'm *really* looking forward to it!"

CHAPTER FIFTEEN

"Hey, Kenny!" The others were already waiting in the playground the following morning when my mum drove me and Maria to school. When they saw me, they all started laughing like drains.

"D'you want some help, Kenny?" called Frankie as I tried to climb out of the car. "You look like you're having problems!"

It was a bit hard getting out of a car with my mummy case on. I had my mask on top which was really big, and then the cardboard boxes Frankie and I had stuck together covered me from my neck almost down to my feet. Frankie and Lyndz had helped me to paint the boxes all over with hieroglyphics. Underneath I'd wrapped some bandages round myself too, so that I could burst out of the boxes just like a mummy in a horror film! I looked cool, even if I did say so myself!

"'Bye, girls!" My mum waited patiently until I'd managed to heave myself out of the car. Maria, who was dressed in her Real Madrid football strip, gave me a hand. "Have a good day."

"'Bye, *Mummy*!" I said and the others giggled.

"You look gruesome, Kenny!" said Fliss, who was just wearing a pink dress and a pink headband to match. It must have taken her all of thirty seconds to come up with *that* Barbie costume!

I stuck my arm out of one of the armholes in the side of the box. "Like my bandages?"

The others fell about.

"Hey, Maria, Kenny – guess what?" Rosie, who was dressed as a black and white cat and had a really fab mask with long whiskers, was nearly bursting with excitement. "I nagged my mum all evening yesterday, and she gave in and said we could have another sleepover at mine tonight!"

"Excellent!" I gasped. "An end-of-term sleepover!"

"And a goodbye sleepover because we go home tomorrow," Maria added.

"Let's have a really good one," Frankie said. "But no makeovers!"

I grinned and had a good look at everyone else's costume. Lyndz's Tin Man was brilliant! The silver paint she'd used was really shiny, and made the cardboard boxes look just like tin, and she'd made a wicked oil can as well.

"Can you guess who Elena is?" Lyndz asked.

I looked at Elena. She was wearing a blue dress with a white apron, and carrying a little basket with a stuffed dog sitting inside it. I didn't have a clue who she was meant to be – until I looked down and saw the red shoes she was wearing.

"Hey, you're Dorothy from *The Wizard of Oz* too!" I said.

145

Elena grinned and nodded.

"So what do you reckon, Kenny?" Frankie did a twirl so that I could see her *The Lion, The Witch and The Wardrobe* costume. It looked pretty good. It was a long dress all in white and silver, and she had a wand with a big glittery star at the end, silver make-up and silver nail varnish.

"Good one!" I nodded. Then I glanced at Anna who was all in green with a funny hat on her head. "What're you, Anna? A pixie?"

"What is pixie? No, I am Robin Hood!" Anna said, looking a bit put out. "I made a – how you say – a bow and arrow, but Maria sit on it and break it!"

"Sorry!" Maria said with a grin.

Isabella and Pilar looked pretty good too. Isabella was a butterfly, with big chiffon wings in bright colours, and Pilar was Mickey Mouse! She had the trousers and the white gloves, and she'd made herself some mouse ears out of some cardboard and a pair of black tights!

"I reckon one of us is bound to win a prize!" I said. "That'll be one in the eye for the M&Ms!"

"I'm not so sure about that!" Frankie nudged my mummy case. "Look over there…"

We all looked across the playground. The Queen and the Goblin were just getting out of Mrs Hughes' car. They were both dressed up like Victorian ladies, and they were wearing long dresses with big skirts and bonnets and high-heeled lace-up boots. Emma was carrying a lacy parasol and so was Emily. We all stood and stared at them, our mouths open. They *were* the Gruesome Twosome – but we had to admit they looked good.

"They didn't make those costumes themselves – no way!" I said angrily. "You're supposed to make the costume yourself to win a prize!"

"It looks like their parents have been slaving over those cozzies for weeks!" Frankie complained. "They're bound to win!"

"I do not think so!" said Maria, winking at me. "We have surprise for them, remember?"

That started us all giggling.

"Come along, girls, didn't you hear the bell?" Mrs Weaver came hurrying across the

147

playground from the car park, looking a bit the worse for wear. She was dressed up as a clown in a baggy white suit and she had a big red nose stuck on too!

"You look good, Miss!" Frankie said, winking at the rest of us.

"Oh, thank you, Frankie." Mrs W. gave a huge yawn. "So do all of you!"

We all filed into class, having a good laugh when we saw what other people were wearing. I had to go in sideways so I could get my mummy case through the door! Ryan Scott was an alien, Danny McCloud was Dracula and other kids in our class were dressed up as a werewolf, a Teletubby, Superman and lots of other things.

"Mrs Weaver looked a bit sick, didn't she?" Frankie said with a grin. "Where is she anyway?"

"Probably gone up to the staffroom to take some aspirin!" I replied. "That was some wild party last night!"

At that moment the M&Ms swept into the room, holding up their dresses and looking snooty. We all started nudging each other and giggling.

"Hey, Emma, what're you and Emily meant to be then?" called Ryan Scott, looking puzzled.

"We're Victorian ladies, you wally!" Emma snorted.

"Bor-ing!" Ryan stuck his tongue out at her. "Why didn't you come as something decent?"

Emily glared at him. "You wait – Emily and I are going to win the prizes for best costume!" she snapped, as she rustled over to her locker. Emily followed her, and we all glanced at each other. Obviously we knew what was going to happen next, but we didn't want to give it away!

Emma reached out to open her locker.

"EEEK!" she roared as the booby-trapped bag of flour tipped over and showered her dress and face with white powder. Emily saw what had happened and tried to jump back out of the way, but it was too late. She'd already started opening her locker, and the same thing happened to her! They were both covered from head to toe!

"W-w-who— w-what—!" Emma spluttered, coughing as she got some flour in her mouth.

"Hey, Emma, you're not Victorian ladies now – you're ghosts!" yelled Ryan Scott, and the whole class collapsed into giggles.

"What on earth is all this noise about?" Mrs Weaver came into the room, yawning her head off – and nearly dropped down dead with shock when she saw the M&Ms covered in flour! "What's going on?"

"Someone put flour in our locker, Miss!" Emma coughed furiously, "and I bet I know who it was too!" She spun round and glared at us, and we all started laughing again. We couldn't help it – her face was completely white!

"Ryan, go and get Mr Coleman and ask him to clear up this mess," Mrs Weaver said briskly. Then she turned to stare at us with narrowed eyes. "Does anyone know anything about this? Francesca? Laura?"

"They must have set it up last night, Miss!" Emily Berryman roared, "after we got back from the theme park!"

"But we went straight home, Miss!" Frankie chimed in quickly. "You saw us!"

"Yes, that's true…" Mrs Weaver frowned. I reckon she *thought* it might be us, but she couldn't see how we'd done it.

"You must have done it this morning then, Kenny!" Emma snapped, still wiping flour off her face.

"What! Like this?" I looked down at my mummy case. "I can hardly move without someone helping me!"

"Well, one of the others must have done it then!" Emma yelled.

"We only got here a few minutes before the bell so we wouldn't have had time!" Rosie said.

"Well, it's certainly a mystery." Mrs Weaver stared hard at us, and we all looked innocently back at her. If she asked us right out if we'd set the trap, Maria and I would have to say yes. But unless she did, we were keeping quiet! "What a shame your costumes are ruined, Emma and Emily. They look very nice too. What I can see of them."

"I know you did this, Laura McKenzie!" the Queen hissed as the caretaker arrived to sweep up the flour. "And you're not going to get away with it!"

"Serves you right for sending those emails!" I hissed back, and Emma turned purple with rage. "Anyway, we got away with it before, didn't we!" And I waggled my mummy mask at her. "Remember this?"

Emma stalked off, trailing a cloud of flour, and she and Emily went off to the girls' loos to try and sponge their dresses clean.

"That was close!" Fliss muttered nervously. "Mrs Weaver looked dead suspicious!"

"I think she's too tired after the party to care very much!" Frankie grinned. "The M&Ms are crushed to bits – what a great way to end the summer term!"

"It's not quite finished yet," I reminded her. "We've still got the sleepover tonight!"

CHAPTER SIXTEEN

"I told you my mummy costume was cool!" I said triumphantly as we lay inside our sleeping-bags in the tent in Rosie's garden that evening. "Mrs Weaver thought it was ace!"

Lyndz and Pilar had won the prizes for best costumes in our class, and they'd got book tokens. But Mrs Weaver had said that mine was so unusual, she was giving me a Mars bar as a special prize! I was dead thrilled. I'd never won a prize for anything I'd made in my life before!

"Yeah, well done, Kenny!" said Frankie. "Now stop going on about it, will you!"

"I'm going to keep this Mars bar for ever and ever!" I announced, holding it up so that everyone could see it. "I'm never going to eat it, even if I'm starving! Is there any more chocolate left?"

Fliss sat up and searched through the empty packets lying around. "No, we've scoffed it all!"

"Oh, well!" I pulled the paper off the Mars bar and bit off a chunk. I passed it round, and in a few seconds it had disappeared.

"Did you see the M&Ms' faces when we won the prizes?" Frankie giggled. "They were so furious they had steam coming out of their ears!"

"What?" asked Pilar, looking puzzled.

"Not really!" Frankie told her.

"They are your big enemies now," Elena said seriously. "You must be careful."

"Oh, we can handle the M&Ms!" I said, screwing the Mars wrapper up and flicking it at Fliss. "They don't scare *us!*"

It had been a brilliant sleepover so far. Lyndz had brought her little brothers' paddling-pool with her, and we'd blown it up and filled it with water, and then we'd spent ages jumping in and out of it, splashing each other. It was too small for us, but that was part of the fun! Then we all tried getting in it together – it was a real laugh! After that we'd played International Gladiators, and then Rosie's mum had come out and told us it was time for bed, so we'd all crawled into the tent. Maria had pulled the tent flap back so that we could see outside, and now we were lying in rows, looking up at the stars as it got dark.

"This has been the best end of term ever," Fliss said sleepily.

"And the bestest sleepover ever," Rosie added.

"And this has been my best holiday ever in my life," Elena said solemnly.

"I think so too," Anna agreed. "And you are our best friends."

"And you're our best friends!" Lyndz told her.

"And Leicester City are the best football team in the world!" I said.

"No, they're not – Real Madrid are the best!" And Maria kicked me through the sleeping-bag.

"Oh, shut up, you two!" Frankie groaned. "Don't start a football argument!"

"Shall we sing our Sleepover song?" Lyndz asked.

"Wait till I get back." I climbed out of my sleeping-bag and winked at Maria. We had something else in mind – one last trick before the Spanish girls went home tomorrow! "I've just got to nip to the loo."

"Me too." Maria got up and followed me out of the tent. Then we hid behind a tree and waited, trying not to laugh.

We could hear Lyndz humming our Sleepover song – "Down by the river there's a hanky-panky…" And then we heard her say "Poo! What's that smell!"

Maria and I nudged each other and doubled up with silent laughter.

"Urrgh! It's horrible!" That was Fliss.

"It smell very bad!" squealed Isabella.

"It's Kenny and Maria!" Frankie yelled.

"They've let off a stinkbomb!"

Next second all eight of them were fighting to get out of the tent, and flapping their hands in front of their noses. Maria and I just couldn't keep quiet any longer – we hung on to each other and laughed out heads off!

"Right – let's get them!" Frankie roared, and the others grabbed their pillows and chased us right round the garden.

So we ended up having a fight on the last day of the visit just like we'd had on the first day – but this time it wasn't for real! It was just a good laugh.

It was really sad saying goodbye to our mates the next day, but at least we've got the summer holidays to look forward to. We're going to have lots of sleepovers, but from now on I'm going to keep out of trouble! No, don't laugh – I mean it!

Oh-oh, got to go. Molly the Monster's just got back from camp, and I've got an ace trick to play on her. I'm going to let my pet rat Merlin curl up and go to sleep on her bed – that'll freak her out! See you later!

The Sleepover Club Bridesmaids

by Angie Bates

An imprint of HarperCollinsPublishers

CHAPTER ONE

Yikes! You really made me jump then. I thought it was one of the others coming upstairs.

I left them all watching a video. Actually, I started out watching it too, but Kenny said she couldn't concentrate with me sitting next to her. She said she could FEEL me fizzing, like a Disprin in water.

Well, can you blame me for being a bit fidgety, after the incredible day I just had? (Actually, better make that incredible *week*!!)

Anyway, I didn't want to spoil the film for everyone. Also to be honest, I really needed some peace and quiet. So I came up here to write in my diary. Don't laugh, but in the run up to Mum and Andy's Big Day, I've been keeping two diaries – my official Sleepover Club diary *and* a mega-secret Wedding Diary.

I'm not joking – I've been under stress like you wouldn't believe. There were times when letting off steam in my Wedding Diary was the only thing which kept me sane. Unfortunately, it was practically impossible to find the privacy to actually *write* in it – that's how mad it's been at our house lately.

Have a peek inside, and you'll see what I mean.

Oops, ignore all that gory stuff I scribbled on the front cover. That curse doesn't apply to our trustworthy Sleepover fans. What? No, of *course* you won't die a horrible agonising death if you read it! I mean, I formally *invited* you to peek, didn't I? OK, if it makes you feel better, I'll cross my heart!! Anyway, here's yesterday's entry:

In just a few hours, it'll be my mum's wedding day. Forget butterflies – I think I've got giant rhinos rampaging in my tummy. I'm really tired but there's no way I'm going to get a WINK of sleep! Until recently I thought weddings were like, mega-happy family events. But if you ask me, they just bring out the worst in everyone. Practically everything that could go wrong with this one has. And the worst thing was – it was ALL my fault! I should never have—

Oh-oh, Amber's whingeing at me to turn out the light, so she can get her beauty sleep. 'Bye for now!

Heh heh heh! I bet that got you going. Now you're going crazy, wondering who on earth the mysterious Amber is, aren't you? Which is excellent news, because I'm DYING to tell you. In fact, if I don't tell someone the whole amazing story pretty soon, I'll probably EXPLODE!

I wasn't exaggerating in my Wedding Diary, by the way. A few days back, my whole life went totally haywire. And I don't want to worry you or anything, but at one point, things got so bad that the fate of the entire Sleepover Club *trembled* in the balance...

Are you shocked? Then just imagine how *we* felt!

So hang on for your life, lovely reader, because we're going on a bumpy rollercoaster ride back in time, to the day when my mum's wonderful wedding began to go HORRIBLY pear-shaped...

CHAPTER TWO

Wouldn't it be great if life was like films? Just imagine if you woke up each morning to your very own movie soundtrack! Then, the minute you heard those creepy *durn durn DURN* chords, you'd instantly know to avoid the very bad thing which was lying in wait for you around the corner.

As it was, one of the worst days of my life came without warning.

Actually, it started out great. The sun shone. Mum and Andy giggled over breakfast like two love-birds. I didn't think it was possible for my wildly happy mum and soon-to-be-official step-dad to get any happier, but they were practically GLOWING! And my little brother was in such a sweet mood that he presented me with a truly bizarre drawing.

"Ooh, that's erm, *lovely*, Callum," I said cautiously. I had no idea why Callum had given me a drawing of five orange space aliens, but like Mum says, it's the thought that counts.

"That's you and that's Kenny," he said proudly. "There's Frankie and that's Rosie and Lyndz. You're all wearing your bridesmaids' frocks, look!"

"And what's that?" I asked, pointing at a green figure lurking in the corner of the page.

"Oh, that's a dinosaur out to kill you all," Callum said airily.

Well, he IS seven! But when I bluetacked his drawing to our fridge alongside his other masterpieces, Callum looked really hurt.

"Don't you want to show my brilliant drawing to your friends, Fliss?"

"Oh, silly ole me, what was I thinking of," I said, and I stuffed it into my school bag instead.

I showed it to the others before we went into school, and not surprisingly they fell about.

"Which one's me again?" asked Kenny.

"Isn't it obvious? The one with three eyes," giggled Lyndz.

"Duh," said Rosie. "Anyone can see that's not an eye, it's a nose."

Kenny looked uneasy. "We're not really going to wear dayglo orange dresses, Fliss, are we?"

Honestly, that girl is *so* impossible! She can describe just about every goal scored by Leicester City football team ever since there's BEEN a Leicester City football team, but when it comes to style, she hasn't got a *clue*!

"No, we are NOT wearing dayglo orange," I said patiently. "I've told you about a billion times. We're wearing this really pretty shade of *peach*, OK? Orange was just the closest colour Callum could find in his crayon box."

Kenny pulled a face. "I can't believe you're putting us through this, Fliss," she moaned.

"We're going to look totally stoo-pid. Like a bunch of icky *meringues,* or something."

But Kenny didn't fool anybody. She'd never admit it, but Miss Cool 'n' Sporty was every bit as keyed-up about Mum's wedding as the rest of us.

Frankie had gone misty-eyed. "Just think," she breathed. "One day Izzy will be doing cute little drawings for *me!*"

Frankie's baby sister must be about six months old now, but Frankie's still totally mushy about her.

Rosie gave me a nudge. "Fliss, quick! Check out the M&Ms!"

Now there's two girls who should *definitely* come with a warning soundtrack. In case you've forgotten, Emma Hughes and Emily Berryman are the Sleepover Club's deadliest enemies. They're also completely two-faced, which is why grown-ups never believe us when we tell them how mean the M&Ms are. In fact, like Kenny says, most grown-ups think the sun shines out of the M&Ms' you-know-whats!!

I sneaked a look over my shoulder, in time

to catch Emma and Emily madly pretending they weren't eavesdropping on our conversation. You should have seen their faces. They looked exactly like they'd been sucking lemons! The M&Ms can't *stand* anyone else being the centre of attention.

"Heh heh heh," chortled Lyndz. "They must have heard about your mum's wedding. One-nil to you, Flissy."

I've got to admit, it gave me a definite boost, seeing my ten minutes of bridesmaid fame get under our enemies' skins like that. You know, sometimes I think us Sleepover Club girls must be telepathic, because we didn't have to say a single word! We just stalked past the M&Ms, as if we were wearing our long floaty dresses and flowery crowns already!

For the rest of that day, whenever the M&Ms were in earshot, we kept up a non-stop gush of bridesmaid talk. And that's where everything started to go wrong. I'm so sure of this, that if I was making a film of my life, that is *definitely* the part where I'd put in some doomy *durn durn DURN* chords.

You see, the M&Ms are our sworn enemies for one very good reason.

They are NOT nice people, OK?

By the end of the day, we'd managed to get so far up their noses that those girls were practically spitting with envy. If we'd had any sense, we'd have let it go at that. Instead, we decided to carry on flaunting our bridesmaid superstar status to the max.

For obvious reasons, we usually avoid walking home the same way as the M&Ms. But today we trailed them so closely, we were practically walking in their shoes!! We all knew we were playing with fire really, but we were having such a great laugh, we didn't care.

We skipped along arm in arm, swanking loudly about how we were going back to my house for a dress fitting, and how our dresses were totally lush and how Mum and Andy's wedding was going to be at this mega-posh country house.

Then all of a sudden, the M&Ms darted across to the other side of the street, giggling like idiots. And at the same moment Frankie flashed me a worried look. The kind that says "uh-oh."

And there it was, blocking our path. An absolutely MASSIVE ladder.

I don't think the bloke was much of a decorator, because there were paint drips everywhere. I could hear the ladder creaking and swaying like a ship in a storm, as the painter sloshed white gloss on the gutterings and anything else within splattering distance.

The others have probably told you that I'm really superstitious. *Everyone* knows this. So you won't be surprised to hear that walking under ladders is not normally my idea of a fun time. And so this was definitely a *durn durn DURN* moment.

I stopped dead a few metres from the ladder and swallowed hard. I could hear the Gruesome Twosome whispering on the other side of the street, and I just KNEW they were cooking something up.

Suddenly Emily squawked:

"I dare you to walk under that ladder, Felicity Sidebotham!"

"Yeah, right," jeered Emma. "And pigs might fly!"

And from the way the M&Ms smirked, you could tell they thought they'd totally trapped me.

I can't explain what got into me then. It's not like I've ever been the daredevil type. It's true that I was on a serious wedding high, but it was more than that. Maybe I was just fed up with people calling me a wimp all the time.

I gave the M&Ms my iciest stare. "OK," I snapped. "Then you'd better start looking up and checking for flying pig poo!"

The others gasped and Frankie actually made a grab for me, but they were all much too late.

I sailed under that ladder, as smooth as butterscotch. I didn't even cross my fingers inside my pockets. In fact I moved so fast, the others had to put on a real spurt to catch up.

No-one spoke after that. We just kind of marched along in deadly silence. The others looked a bit stunned. The M&Ms had totally vanished. I suppose they'd slithered off to their coffins, or whatever the undead normally do after school.

Finally Frankie said, "Personally, Fliss, I wouldn't have done that. Not *this* week."

"Me neither," said Rosie in an awed voice.

Kenny shook her head. "What got into you, Fliss?"

Lyndz had turned deadly pale. "If that was me, I'd have been wetting myself in case I jinxed the entire wedding."

"Yeah," agreed Frankie. "Walking under ladders pretty much *guarantees* seven days' bad luck. Everyone knows that."

"Rubbish," I said uneasily.

Lyndz practically wrung her hands. "But it's true," she said.

Rosie had been counting on her fingers. "Seven days," she squeaked. "But that takes you right up to the eve of the actual wedding! I mean, Fliss, *anything* could happen. Your house could be struck by a meteorite or something!"

Rosie's words went through me like a knife. And suddenly I totally went to pieces.

"Why didn't you guys stop me?" I wailed. "I don't want Mum and Andy to have bad luck. I want everything to go BRILLIANTLY for them!" I covered my face. "I can't *believe* it. I just hexed my mother's future happiness!!"

Usually when I start one of my major doom monologues, the others say sensible things like, "Don't be stoo-pid, Fliss. Have a Cheesy Wotsit and look on the bright side."

But this time, I couldn't help noticing that no-one exactly rushed to contradict me. In fact, no-one said a WORD.

I looked up in a panic, and saw four worried faces staring back at me. This was terrible. All my friends thought I'd ruined Mum's wedding too!!

That DID it. I had the howling heebie jeebies right there in the middle of the street. "I'm such a bad person! I ruin *everything*. I should never have been born!"

The others didn't know what to do. They made sympathetic noises and someone patted me once or twice, but I was in such a state it didn't register. At least, not until Kenny suddenly whacked me really hard.

"Will you shut up!" she yelled. "I'm going to tell you how to cancel the bad luck, OK?" And she fished a clean tissue out of her pocket and handed it over.

I stopped yelling immediately. "Really?" I quavered. I gave my nose a big comforting blow. Then I gazed at Kenny like a hopeful puppy, while she told me what I had to do.

I have no idea where that girl picked up her wedding know-how, but I bet it wasn't at Leicester City football club! I was impressed. I mean, *I'm* the girly superstitious one, right?

Apparently, all I had to do was find four mysterious "somethings" by the actual wedding day and give them to Mum, and the jinx would be like, cancelled!

"Find four what?" frowned Rosie. "Speak English, Kenny."

Kenny sighed and gabbled a quaint little rhyme that went: "Something old, something new, something borrowed, something blue."

"Oh, *those* somethings," the rest of us said immediately.

I wiped my eyes. "I didn't know that was like a good *luck* thing," I sniffled.

Lyndz wasn't too impressed. "Fliss's mum seems like the mega-organised type to me," she objected. "She probably had her somethings sorted ages ago."

I gave my nose another big blow. "Uh-uh," I said. "She's been too busy organising all the dresses and the reception and everything to even *think* about good luck stuff."

"Well, there you go," said Kenny smugly. "Now you can take care of them *for* her. That way you get to be a good daughter AND cancel the wicked M&Ms' ladder spell all in one go."

"Yippee!" grinned Rosie. "Now let's go and try on our meringues – I mean, dresses!"

"You'd better not call them that in front of my mum," I warned, cheering up a bit more.

Mum was making our bridesmaid dresses herself. I helped pick out the colour, actually. It was also my idea to have like, cute little ballet shoes dyed to match. Mum had gone to loads of trouble, sitting up night after night, stitching away, and now the dresses were almost ready. The fitting was just for Mum to check the hems before she finished them on her machine.

Actually, I think Mum was as excited about the dresses as we were, because she whipped open the door before I could even get my key out.

"Do you girls fancy a little snack," she said, "before we do the fitting?"

Frankie giggled. "Maybe we should have the fitting and *then* have our little snack," she said. (I don't know if the others have told you, but my mum's snacks are sometimes a wee bit over the top and take *forever* to prepare!)

"Good point," agreed Kenny.

"Oh, well, if you're sure." Mum flew upstairs to fetch the dresses. She called down to us from the landing: "Shut your eyes, girls!"

"Mu-um!" I moaned. "We're not five years old."

We shut our eyes all the same. There was loads of mysterious rustling as Mum came back downstairs. Suddenly I got this wildly excited feeling, like you do just before you open your eyes on Christmas morning.

"You can look now," said Mum, sounding breathless.

She had draped the dresses over the sofa, so we could see them properly. We gasped.

"Oh, they are so-o *gorgeous*," breathed Rosie.

The last time I'd seen the fabric, Mum was struggling to cut out gazillions of fiddly little pattern pieces on our living-room floor. So I was every bit as dazzled as the others.

"We're going to look like fairy-tale princesses," whispered Lyndz.

"Some of us, maybe," muttered Kenny. "The rest of us will look like total—"

"You first, Kenny dear," said Mum brightly.

Good ole Kenny! We could tell she was absolutely freaking out inside, but she stood there like a docile little lamb and let Mum slip her rustly satin dress over her head. Though it was just as well Mum was concentrating on Kenny's hemline, because Kenny's *face* was a total picture.

The minute Mum disappeared to hunt for a tape measure, Kenny clenched her fists. "Don't any of you say a WORD," she hissed.

"I KNEW I'd look like a meringue."

Frankie frowned. "Actually," she said, "you look really pretty."

"*Pretty!*" Kenny snarled. "Huh! Don't make me laugh!"

Honestly, I wish you could have seen that girl, pulling hideous troll faces at us in her frothy peachy bridesmaid's dress. We all cracked up.

Naturally, Kenny thought we were laughing because she looked awful in the dress. She clawed at it furiously, trying to get it off, but Mum had pinned the material at the back, so she was basically trapped.

Luckily, just then Mum walked back in and said a totally perfect thing.

"Oh, Kenny," she said softly. "You make that dress look so special."

We could see Kenny struggling to figure out if "special" was some kind of polite adult code for "weird". Then she gave my mum a shy little grin.

"Hey, thanks Mrs Sidebotham," she said. "Erm – about that snack?"

CHAPTER THREE

Did I tell you we'd planned to hold our next sleepover the following Saturday? In other words, immediately AFTER the wedding?

Don't laugh, but for some reason I felt completely unhinged every time I heard myself say those three little words.

After the wedding. After the wedding. After the...

It was like I couldn't imagine it. As if the wedding was making HUGE quantities of fog, and I couldn't see anything beyond it.

I'd known about Mum and Andy getting married since New Year, yet I still couldn't quite believe it was going to happen. I think Mum felt that way too. She'd been really stressed out the last few days. In fact, on Friday night she went to bed practically the same time I did!

When I woke up on Saturday morning I snuggled under my duvet, picturing how thrilled Mum would be with me for tracking down her lucky somethings all by myself. Obviously I didn't plan to spoil my good deed by mentioning the evil ladder spell. Besides, if Kenny was right, that stupid ladder didn't have a chance against my four magical gifts.

I chanted the rhyme softly under my quilt. "Something old, something new, something borrowed, something blue."

Suddenly I sat up, totally freaked out. *Yikes!* I had exactly one week left to get my act together!! Not to mention that I still hadn't figured out what my brother and I were giving Mum and Andy for a wedding present...

"Oh well," I sighed. "I've got all today to crack that one."

But as it turned out, I was totally wrong about this.

When I went downstairs, Mum and Andy were rushing round like maniacs, cleaning the house.

"What's up, you two? Is the Queen Mum dropping by?" I joked.

My mother gave me a funny look, scurried off with the vacuum cleaner and started blasting the hall with Shake 'n Vac.

Andy looked surprised. "Didn't Nikky tell you my mother's coming to stay?" he said.

"Uh-uh," I said.

"She probably forgot," said Andy. He lowered his voice. "It's not surprising. Your mum's got a lot on her mind."

"Tell me about it," I sighed. I filled a bowl with my favourite strawberry cereal and joined Callum in front of *Live & Kicking*.

"Hey, shorty!" I hissed. "What can I get Mum that's like, *old*? Oh, I also need something blue?"

My brother frowned. "Andy's got some stinky old cheese in the fridge," he suggested. "That's quite blue." He suddenly remembered something. "You probably shouldn't give it to Mum though. I heard her tell Andy to put it in the bin. She said it made her want to throw up, *big* time."

I sighed. Looks like you're on your own with this one Fliss, I told myself.

Andy popped his head round the door. "I'm just going to fetch my mum from the station. Anyone want to come?"

"ME ME ME!" yelled Callum, jumping up and down.

"How about you, Fliss?" Andy asked.

I pointed to my pink baby doll pyjamas. "I don't *think* so, Andy," I giggled.

Mum came scurrying back with the vacuum cleaner. She stared at me. "Why aren't you dressed?"

"Duh! It's Saturday," I said. Then I saw what she was doing. "Mum, are you nuts? You vacuumed in here three minutes ago."

Mum seemed amazed. "Are you sure?"

"Totally."

Mum giggled. "Oops," she said. "Look, Fliss, get a move on, there's a love. Patsy will be here in half an hour." She looked as if the very idea of meeting her future mother-in-law made her want to faint.

"I'm going, I'm going," I grumbled. "You're not the only person with stuff to do, you know," I added mysteriously.

Personally I thought Patsy was an incredibly sad name for an adult, but apart from that, I was looking forward to meeting Andy's mum. Maybe she could help me out with my four somethings. Plus, she'd probably bring us cool presents. After all, she was *kind* of our grandma.

Andy never talked much about his family. But it was obvious he totally worshipped his mum. Andy's dad died when Andy was really little, so his mum brought him up by herself.

After my shower, I tried on practically everything in my wardrobe. In the end I decided to put on this new summer dress Mum got me in Leicester. I expect you can guess what colour it was!

Actually this particular dress is a really *delicious* pink, that delicate sugar-mouse colour which looks really perfect with blonde hair. Then I brushed my hair and fastened it back with some sweet little slides.

"Why haven't we met Patsy before?" I asked, as Mum and I waited for everyone to arrive. "I mean, you and Andy have been together for AGES."

But at that moment Mum vanished rather suddenly into the downstairs loo, so I never heard the answer to my question.

By the time she came out again, Andy's car was pulling up outside. Then his mum got out (*Durn durn DURN!*) and I figured it out for myself in ten seconds flat.

I'd have probably figured it out sooner, but I was distracted by Patsy's clothes at first. They were *gorgeous* – well, you know, for an old person. But then I got a good look at Patsy herself, and my heart sank.

You know how some people have naturally friendly faces? Well, Patsy Proudlove has a naturally UNfriendly face.

Mum rushed out and gave her a big hug. Patsy forced a smile, but you could see hugging wasn't her favourite activity.

"And this is Fliss," said Mum brightly.

"So I see," said Patsy, as if she'd been

spying on me by satellite and wasn't too impressed.

"We've all been dying to meet you, Patsy," said Mum.

Then we all stood around like a game of statues, and it was glaringly obvious that no-one could think of ANYTHING to say!

Andy rubbed his hands together, something I never *ever* saw him do before. "Well, isn't this, er – great!" he beamed. "Shall we go into the living room, and catch up with everyone's news?"

"I'd rather see my room first, if you don't mind, dear," said Patsy in a brisk voice. "And perhaps someone would show me where I can wash my hands. You wouldn't believe the state of those trains." And she said it as if the state of Britain's trains was *our* fault!

Andy carried Patsy's stuff up to the spare room. Patsy followed stiffly in her gorgeous clothes.

What's *her* problem, I thought.

Without looking at me, Mum crossed the hall and moved a harmless little vase for absolutely no reason. "Erm, did you put out those guest towels like I asked you?" she said. She sounded really uptight.

I was getting that churning feeling. The one I get when Mum's stressing about something and I don't know what to do about it.

"Mum," I whispered. "Is Patsy going to be staying here all *week*? You know, until the wedding?"

Mum looked shocked. "Where else would she stay? She *is* Andy's mother. It's really good of her to offer to lend us a hand."

"Mmn," I said in a neutral kind of voice. But what I was thinking was EEK! I'd rather win a night out with Darth Maul!!

Anyway, I won't go into too many lurid details about our first day with Andy's mum. All you need to know is that it was deeply depressing.

Patsy was the kind of person who has strong views on everything. Pop music, TV soaps, dog poo, you name it. And once she got started she just kept on and on, battering away at Mum like a bulldozer. And Mum just sat there, smiling bravely, and totally letting herself be bulldozed!

I kept expecting Andy to tell his mum where to get off, but it was like he didn't even *notice*! And all at once these scary new thoughts came slithering into my mind like poisonous snakes. Like, what if Andy didn't really love us after all?

I felt like I was seeing a totally different side of my almost-step-dad. I got the definite feeling that if you asked Andy to choose between us and his sour-puss mother, he'd root for her every time.

After lunch, I escaped into the kitchen to make tea for everyone. And can you believe Patsy had the *nerve* to follow me!

"No, no dear," she said impatiently. "You've put enough water in that kettle to sink the Titanic. Do you think your stepfather's made of money?"

That was the last straw. And the minute Patsy left the kitchen, I made a sneaky phone call to Rosie.

"Can I come over?" I hissed. "It's an emergency."

"Sure," she said. "I'll tell the others."

I popped my head round the living-room door. "Erm, I've just remembered I was meant to meet up with my friends today," I fibbed. "I won't be long. See you later everyone." Then I grabbed my jacket and slammed out of the house.

I stormed along, getting to Rosie's house in record time.

Luckily Rosie let me in and we went straight up to her room, so I didn't even have to be polite to her mum or anything.

I paced up and down Rosie's bedroom until the others turned up, and then I just splurted out the whole story.

"Since I walked under that ladder, everything's fallen apart," I ranted. "Mum's gone totally wobbly. Andy's mother is this like, nightmare person! And Andy's not even *trying* to stop her."

Kenny rolled her eyes. "I already told you how to cancel the ladder spell. You were meant to get cracking on those somethings today."

"How could I? I haven't had a minute to

myself," I fumed. "How was I supposed to know Patsy Proudlove was coming? No-one ever tells me *anything*!"

Lyndz grinned. "You make Andy's Mum sound like one of those huge thingummies!"

We stared at her.

"You know," she said. "The things that flatten towns and stir up tidal waves."

"What, like a hurricane?" asked Kenny.

Lyndz nodded, her eyes glinting wickedly. The others cracked up.

"Yikes! Hurricane Patsy's coming. Everyone down into the cellar!" cackled Frankie.

But I couldn't even raise a smile. "It's so unfair," I moaned. "She's spoiling everything. And Mum's just letting her." I slumped to the floor. "And I STILL don't know what to get them for a wedding present."

"Well, we can't do much about Hurricane Patsy, but we could give you some prezzie ideas," suggested Rosie. "That might take some of the pressure off."

"Thanks, Rosie Posie," I croaked. "That would be great."

Rosie tore some pages out of a notebook and handed them round, along with various-sized bits of pencil.

"The thing is, it's got to be really unusual," I explained. "But it can't cost too much. And it can't be something they've got already."

Honestly, my friends are so sweet! They came up with masses of things, from parrots to peg bags. Actually, I was really into the parrot idea until Kenny pointed out that they cost thousands of pounds.

"Plus they poo everywhere from a great height," giggled Lyndz. "I don't think Fliss's mum would be too happy about that."

"It was just an *idea*," said Frankie huffily. "Fliss *said* she wanted something unusual."

"Parrot poo is unusual all right," spluttered Lyndz.

And you can guess what happened then, can't you? Yep, Lyndz had one of her famous hiccup attacks.

By the time she'd recovered, I wasn't just confused. I also felt guilty. My friends were knocking themselves out trying to cheer me up. So why was I still so depressed?

Finally we all went downstairs and Rosie made us drinks. She wanted us to try her new craze – something called a smoothy. Basically, you put fruit and natural yoghurt in the blender and whizz it till it's (surprise surprise) SMOOTH!

This time, Rosie whizzed raspberries, bananas and mango with yoghurt, and it was totally velvety and delicious.

"Know what I wish?" I said suddenly. "I wish this whole stupid wedding business was over. Then everything could just go back to how it was."

Frankie sighed. "Dream on, Flissy," she said. "Because that's never going to happen. I mean, when it's over Andy's going to be your *official* step-dad. That's *big!*"

The others nodded. Kenny looked serious. "Everything's going to change, Fliss," she said. "Everything."

After I switched off my lamp that night, Kenny's words came back to me. *Everything's going to change. Everything.*

"What if it's a bad change?" I whispered to myself. "What if this whole wedding idea is a big mistake, and none of us is ever happy again?" And I had a scared little sniffle into my pillow.

Just as I was finally dozing off, the phone rang downstairs. Who on earth could it be? It was practically midnight!

Andy took the call, then yelled for Mum. Then next minute Mum totally screamed her head off. My heart started to race. Something terrible must have happened. I jumped out of bed and ran downstairs.

"Mum! Mum! What's wrong?"

Mum waved at me to keep quiet. "You're actually here at Heathrow!" she shrieked into the phone, beaming all over her face. "So how come you kept me in the dark all this time? Oh, it's a surprise all right! Oh, Jilly, you've completely made my day. Wait till I tell Fliss!"

I sat on the stairs with a bump. Jilly lived in the United States. She was Mum's oldest and most unpredictable friend. Mum had been really disappointed when Jilly wrote to say she couldn't make it to the wedding. And now she'd turned up in the UK, just like that!

"Wait till you tell Fliss what?" I asked as Mum put down the phone.

Mum grabbed me and twirled me round. "Jilly's daughter came over with her. Isn't that great? You two are almost exactly the same age. Oh, Flissy, you two are going to have such fun, just like Jilly and I used to. And you're going to meet her tomorrow!"

I went back to bed in a happy daze. Jilly doesn't just live in the USA. She actually lives in *Los Angeles*, where the film stars hang out. That practically made Jilly and her daughter film stars too.

I stretched out under my quilt, and grinned to myself in the dark. I was going to be best friends with a film star! I could hardly believe my luck!

It's going to be all right, I thought. Everything is going to be ALL RIGHT.

Suddenly I was so happy that even though Andy's mum was in the next room, rattling the wardrobe with her juicy snores, I didn't give a hoot!

CHAPTER FOUR

Next morning, I rushed downstairs, dying to tell the others my news. But the instant I picked up the phone, Mum flew out of the kitchen, hissing like an angry swan. "SSSH! You'll wake Patsy. She'll be wanting a nice Sunday lie-in!"

"Fat chance in this house," grinned Andy.

But as it turned out, all this tiptoeing around was a total waste of time. About half an hour later, Andy took his mum up a cup of tea and found her sitting on the edge of her bed in her Sunday best, waiting for us to tell her it was OK to come down!

Patsy didn't actually say, but it was obvious this was a major black mark against Mum for not making her feel more welcome.

"I'm sure I don't want to get in anyone's way," she sniffed, as she poured herself a bowl of branflakes.

I sidled up to Andy. "Now can I use the phone?" I whispered.

Patsy overheard. "Use the PHONE!" she said, horrified. "She's just a child! She might ring Australia by mistake!"

"Oh, Fliss wouldn't do anything like that," said Mum quickly. "She's far too sensible."

I thought Mum still looked horribly pale. This wedding business is wearing her out, I thought.

"Thanks, Mum, you're a star," I whispered in her ear as I went past. And I grabbed the phone and escaped upstairs to my room.

"ANOTHER emergency?" said Rosie disbelievingly. "That's TWO, in twenty-four hours!"

"Yeah, but this one is a *cool* emergency," I said.

"OK!" she sighed. "See ya."

An hour later, we all piled into Frankie's pad. Frankie's mum had given everyone home-made slush puppies, plus a stash of kitchen towel to mop up the drips. Everyone made themselves comfy on Frankie's silver floor cushions. That girl goes for silver in a BIG way!

"Go on, Fliss, give!" beamed Rosie.

"Yeah, we want all the goss about Jilly's daughter," said Lyndz.

I felt myself go bright red. I don't know why I blush so easily, but I really wish I didn't! "What do you want to know?" I said.

"Everything," said Frankie at once.

"Well, she's about our age and her name is Amber Glass," I began.

"That's such a cool name!" cried Lyndz.

"And apparently, she's amazingly pretty."

"Like that actually matters," growled Kenny.

"Did I say it mattered?" I snapped. "I'm just describing Amber, OK!"

"Ignore her, Fliss," said Frankie. "So what's she like?"

"She's meant to be incredibly talented," I

said. "She's on TV, like all the time. She's got an agent and everything."

Lyndz's eyes almost popped out of her head. "She's ten years old and she's a film star already!"

"Well, *practically*," I said. "She's done loads of commercials anyway."

"Wow," said Rosie. "A wedding and a Hollywood celebrity in the same week!"

"I want Amber to have a really good time while she's here," I said. "It'd be great if you guys could help out."

"Count me in," said Rosie at once.

Lyndz hugged herself. "Can't wait!" she said gleefully.

"I wish it was the holidays already," sighed Frankie. "We could take her to Alton Towers."

"Get real," objected Kenny. "You're talking about a girl who can pop into Disney World any time she likes."

Even Frankie agreed there wasn't much point trying to impress a girl who had her own mobile phone.

"Let's face it, Cuddington's not exactly

LA," I sighed.

Frankie did a cheesey double take. "Yikes! So *that's* why there's never any high-speed car chases round here!"

Kenny threw a pillow at her. "We're trying to think, Frankie!"

"We could go to Bradgate Park after school," suggested Lyndz. "We could have a picnic and check out the cute little baby deer."

"Excellent! We can show her Lady Jane Grey's house," gushed Frankie. "My dad says Americans *lurve* history!"

Bradgate Park is meant to be this major local beauty spot. I probably liked it when I was little, but now I think it's got WAY too much fresh air. I always come back with earache.

"Why would Amber want to see a load of old ruins?" I said. "I mean, it's not like Lady Jane's going to invite us in for strawberries and cream."

"But it's so romantic," Frankie gushed. "I mean Lady Jane was like a child *queen*. And all those—"

"Romantic! You're joking. The poor kid got her head chopped off!" Kenny's eyes gleamed. "And did you know, they hardly *ever* did it with one swing! Sometimes they had to hack away at their—"

"*Kenny*," pleaded Lyndz. "I'm eating a raspberry slush puppy here."

"Yeah, Kenny," glared Frankie. "Plus I hadn't actually finished what I was saying, which was, erm – that all those deer in Bradgate Park today are descended from the deer which Lady Jane Grey herself may actually have—"

"—eaten," Kenny grinned.

Frankie scowled. "You have to make fun of everything."

"Why don't we just do exactly what we always do?" said Rosie. "That way it will be a change for Amber. Plus we'll have a good time."

Everyone thought this was excellent advice. There was a short pause. Then Lyndz coughed. "Let me just get this straight. We're talking typical fun-type activities to share with Amber, is that right?"

"Right," said everyone.

"The usual wacky stuff we do?"

"Totally," we agreed,

There was another, longer pause.

"Any ideas?" I asked finally.

Kenny tapped the side of her head. "Nope. Total blank."

"Blankety blank," Lyndz agreed.

"Ditto," said Rosie.

Frankie tugged her hair. "This is so *stoo-pid*," she complained. "I mean, the five of us have SO much fun, like *constantly*."

"Constantly," Rosie echoed.

"Oh, absolutely," agreed Kenny, totally straight-faced. "In fact, I'm not sure I can take any more excitement."

Frankie's lips twitched. "You are such a pig, Kenny," she giggled. And suddenly we all cracked up laughing.

"Let's wait till Amber gets here," said Lyndz sensibly. "She's the guest. We'll ask her what she wants to do."

So after that, we just hung around at Frankie's house, enjoyably messing about, till it was time for everybody's dinner.

But as I turned into our street, I remembered something. I'd promised myself to come up with my Something Blue today. Also, I still hadn't a CLUE what to get Mum and Andy for a wedding present. Then my tummy gave a big rumble. Oh, well, I'll think about it after dinner, I thought greedily.

Sunday dinner is like, this major production in our house. Six days a week, Mum is incredibly diet-conscious. But on Sundays she totally goes to town. Just thinking about Mum's roast chicken, with all the yummy trimmings, made my mouth water. Mmmn, I couldn't wait!

I let myself in through our front door, getting ready to breathe in that special Sunday dinner aroma. Then…

What in the WORLD is that gruesome pong? I thought.

It smelled *exactly* like bad drains!! I flew into the kitchen, to warn my parents they had a major plumbing problem on their hands. But for some reason, our kitchen was completely deserted. Normally at this stage on a Sunday, Mum is whizzing about like a celebrity chef on *Ready Steady Cook*, draining veggies and crisping up the roast spuds.

Then I noticed a Bad Sign. (*Durn durn durn!!*)

Instead of three or four pans cheerfully steaming away on the hob, there was one MASSIVE pan, glooping and glopping like a witch's cauldron. I had accidentally located the source of the bad-drain smell.

The saucepan was getting alarmingly hyperactive, as its contents tried to escape from under the lid. Suddenly, green slime began to dribble over the sides.

Andy's mum bustled in. "So you're back, finally," she snapped. "Just as well. Dinner's practically ready."

"Erm, so where is it?" I said. I wasn't trying to be funny. It truly never occurred to me that my Sunday dinner could resemble the experiment of an evil scientist.

"I took over the cooking. Your mother needs a rest. She's worn out," Patsy sighed. She made it sound like my fault – as if I was some selfish vampire child, draining my mother's blood supply.

"But we *always* have a roast on Sundays," I wailed.

Patsy snorted. "The traditional Sunday roast is a waste of time and energy. Takes all morning, wrecks the entire kitchen, and in five minutes it's forgotten. My soup takes twenty minutes and requires one pan. Far more sensible, don't you think?" She gave a grim smile.

I stared queasily at the overflowing pan. "That's *soup*?"

"I knew your mother was diet-conscious, what with the wedding coming up. Cabbage soup is *perfect* for slimmers. Maybe you've heard of the Cabbage Soup diet?"

"Er no," I said, truthfully.

Patsy lifted the saucepan lid and sniffed rapturously. "I'll just add the finishing touches," she said.

Yeah, like stir in some scrummy cat-sick, I thought. And I rushed off to plead with my parents.

Andy seemed more interested in the

motor-racing than listening to me. He didn't even take his eyes off the screen. "Patsy's just being helpful," he mumbled.

"It won't hurt just this once, Fliss," said Mum. She dropped her voice. "Just have a couple of spoonfuls to be polite. There's chocolate fudge brownies for dessert. I thought we'd all have a little pre-wedding treat!"

A high-pitched whine came from the kitchen as Andy's mum operated our liquidiser at high speed.

I swallowed bravely. "I suppose," I said.

In a few minutes we were all sitting round the table. Patsy brought the pan to the table, still sputtering furiously. (The pan, not Patsy, you nutcase!)

Unfortunately, its trip through the liquidiser hadn't exactly improved Patsy's soup. Now it looked like those bubbling mud springs you see on documentaries.

My brother looked panic-stricken. "I can't eat that," he whispered. "It's still alive."

I wanted to giggle, but the soup smelled so terrible I was scared to breathe.

"Try some, Callum. It'll put hairs on your chest," said Andy in a jokey voice I'd never heard him use before today.

Callum blew on a spoonful of sludge, shut his eyes and downed it in one. "Ouf!" he shuddered.

"Well?" said Patsy stiffly. "What do you think?"

"Ooh, that's really yummy, isn't it, Callum?" Mum hinted.

My little brother stared wildly around the table. I could practically see his thought bubbles. Help! What do I do? Fibbing is bad. Being rude is also very bad.

Then his face suddenly cleared, as he came up with the perfect reply. "I'll tell you one thing," he said cheerfully. "It's not *nearly* as bad as it looks!"

"*Callum!*" said Mum.

"Well, REALLY!" huffed Patsy.

But I thought my little brother was a total star. I was pretty heroic myself. I actually forced down one whole spoonful. But once my throat knew what was coming, it went on strike, refusing to let any more khaki gloop near my stomach. So I just kept my spoon busy, to give the impression I was slurping away like Oliver Twist.

Even nightmares have to end, I told myself. Soon I'd be tucking into one of Mum's highly calorific chocolate brownies. I'd never been too crazy about brownies in the past, but now that Amber was coming, all things American seemed incredibly groovy! Not to mention the fact that I was STARVING!!

All through dinner, Patsy was getting more and more tight-lipped. Suddenly she started collecting up the soup bowls, rattling the crockery like you would not *believe*.

"Well!" she sniffed. "We all know what happens to boys and girls who don't eat their dinner, don't we?"

Everyone stared at her. Even Mum and Andy looked startled.

Patsy drew herself up to her full height. "NO PUDDING!" she thundered. And she flounced out to the kitchen.

Callum's face fell a million miles.

"She can't do that!" I said in horror. "Tell her, Andy! Tell her, Mum!"

But Mum and Andy didn't say a word.

"You're not going to let her get away with it?" I pleaded.

Andy cleared his throat. "Don't make a big deal out of this, OK."

"Big deal?!" I yelled. "Do you know what I've had to eat today? A piece of toast and a raspberry slush puppy, that's what!"

"Fliss, please," murmured Mum. "You'll hurt Patsy's feelings."

That was the last straw.

"*Patsy*'s feelings?" I screamed. "What about *MINE*?"

I stormed upstairs to my room and slammed the door.

I wasn't just angry. I was scared. What was going on? Overnight my parents had somehow turned into these weird strangers. I felt as if I'd walked into one of those sc-fi films, where no-one is what they seem, and the evil bodysnatchers are in town. If my parents were going to carry on like this, they didn't DESERVE a wedding present!!

I picked up my giant pink teddy bear and gave him a major cuddle.

Before I knew it, I'd drifted off into a deeply satisfying daydream, where Mum's friend Jilly and her daughter liked me so much that they insisted on taking me back with them to Hollywood, where they fed me all the chocolate fudge brownies I could eat...

CHAPTER FIVE

The minute I got into the school playground, I dashed up to the others and started pouring out my tragic story.

I was just describing my cabbage soup ordeal in heartrending detail, when Kenny started biting her lip. Then I noticed Frankie was madly stuffing her fingers in her mouth. And suddenly Lyndz gave this humungous piggy snort.

I couldn't believe it. My friends were LAUGHING!

"I'm glad YOU think it's funny," I said huffily.

"I'm sorry," Rosie gasped. "It sounds awful, Fliss. You must have been so upset."

Of course, that did it. Everyone totally cracked up!

All of a sudden I completely saw the funny side. (Which is most unlike me!) For some reason, all the things which seemed so terrible yesterday struck me as absolutely hysterical today!

By the time I'd got to the part about Mum and Andy being taken over by alien bodysnatchers, we were staggering around the playground, shrieking with laughter.

Honestly, talk about Giggle Therapy! I felt HEAPS better. Plus, my mates helped me put everything into perspective.

"It's not like Hurricane Patsy is going to be staying at your place for ever," Rosie pointed out, as we lined up to go into class.

"And don't worry about your mum and dad," said Frankie sympathetically. "Grown-ups often act weird around their parents."

"Amber's coming, that's the main thing," said Lyndz. "I can't wait! I never met a real film star before."

"Yeah," said Rosie. "It's SO great you don't mind sharing her with us, Fliss!"

"Mum thought we'd all go into Leicester after school tomorrow," I told them. "Want to come?"

And my friends were so obviously thrilled to be invited that I started to feel like a bit of a celebrity myself.

When I got home, I was surprised to find Andy home from work already. He looked so smart I hardly recognised him.

"Oooh!" I teased. "Is this in Jilly's honour? Should Mum be jealous?"

"Er, yeah," Andy said. "That's exactly it, Fliss. I like to keep your Mum on her toes."

I noticed that my laidback step-dad had this really tense expression for some reason. Plus both he and Mum seemed unusually quiet. But I decided they just had butterflies, like me.

I went rushing upstairs to make myself look especially nice for Amber. After I'd had a long hot shower, I put on my new ice-blue jeans, and a sweet little T-shirt with the word ANGEL on it, in really tasteful lettering. I've got this real thing about angels lately, I don't know why. Plus, apparently they're HUGE in America.

I brushed my hair till it was all soft and silky, then I put in my flowery clips.

I checked my reflection nervously in the mirror on my dressing table. And you know what? I'm not being vain or anything, but I thought I looked quite pretty. And for, like fifty seconds, everything felt so perfect that I honestly wouldn't have swapped places with anyone else in the world.

Actually my life was getting more and more like TV! Fifty seconds of pure happiness, then that music goes *durn durn DURN*, and you know everything is going to go drastically downhill...

Well, that's how it was with me.

Last Christmas, Andy gave me this cute hand-mirror. Don't tell the others, but secretly I thought it looked like the kind of thing a mermaid might own. It lived on my dressing table, next to this bottle of really expensive bath stuff which my real dad, Steve, got me.

Anyway, I suddenly thought I'd like to see how my hair clips looked close up, so I went to pick up the mirror.

CRASH!!!

It slipped from my hands, bounced off my dressing table, and smashed into pieces.

I stared at it in total shock. I have no idea how it even happened. The mirror wasn't heavy. And my hands weren't sweaty or anything.

I was still staring at the mess, when Andy's mum rushed in, like a bad fairy in a pantomime. "How could you be so thoughtless, Felicity!" she cried. "That's seven years' bad luck!"

"I didn't break it on purpose!" I wailed. But inside I was turning numb with horror. And I'd thought seven DAYS' bad luck was terrible news!

I realised Patsy had beetled off to tell my parents what I'd done. So I dashed downstairs to tell them my side of the story. But I was too late.

Andy's face was like thunder. "Is this true, Fliss?" he said.

"I don't even know how it happened!" I wailed. "We won't *really* get seven years' bad luck, will we?"

I should explain that normally Andy is the most easy-going guy on this planet. But as you know, these days my family was totally NOT normal.

"How COULD you be so careless?" he yelled. "A great big girl like you!"

Don't you hate it when people call you a "great big girl"? It makes you feel like some hideous troll child. All yesterday's bad feelings came whooshing back. Why was Andy being so mean? Couldn't he see I was miserable about breaking his special present to me?

When I'd found that little gift-wrapped mirror under our Christmas tree last year, I'd felt all warm and fuzzy inside, and I just knew my step-dad really and truly loved me. But right now, I wasn't sure Andy even *liked* me any more. And all at once I burst into floods of tears.

I hate how I look when I cry. I look exactly like those rabbits which those naff conjurors used to pull out of hats. The creepy white kind with pink eyes. (Pink-eyed rabbits, you wally, not pink-eyed conjurors!)

So it was bad luck that Mum's best friend, Jilly, picked that precise moment to lean on our bell, sending the door-chimes into a frenzy of ding-dongs.

"Omigod! It's them!" shrieked Mum. She rushed to the door.

And there on our step were Mum's friend and her famous film-star daughter. I stared at them, totally stunned.

As you probably guessed, it wasn't Jilly who took my breath away. She looked quite sweet and everything, but she was just average mum-material. It was Amber. She was the prettiest girl I've ever seen. Everything about her was gorgeous. Her eyes, her teeth, her hair. Her hair wasn't blonde. It was literally *golden*. As for her clothes, they were out of this world.

I do my best to keep up with the styles (which isn't easy when you live in a dump like Cuddington). But so far as I could see, Amber was in a completely unique style

216

category of her own. She was totally, devastatingly perfect.

Finally Mum and Jilly stopped hugging each other and Mum registered that I was still standing there, lost for words. "Well, say hello to Amber, darling," she said.

Adults can be so tactless. Personally, I'd have thought it was bad enough having perfect Amber see me with my pink-rimmed rabbity eyes, without Mum carrying on like I was some sulky little kid. But there you go.

I scowled. "Give me a chance," I hissed. Nice one, Fliss, I thought immediately. That made you look extremely mature.

Then Amber did something which really showed me up. She stuck out her perfectly manicured hand and gave me a dazzling smile. "Hi," she said. "You must be Fliss. I'm Amber."

"Hi," I mumbled, feeling a real wally.

As you can see, Amber and I hadn't exactly got off to a flying start. But I reassured myself we'd make up for it, as soon we were on our own.

I hung about politely, while Mum and Andy

showed our guests over the house and demonstrated the power shower – you know the kind of thing. And at last Mum said, "Fliss, we won't be eating till quite late. Maybe you could take Amber on a grand tour of Cuddington? You could introduce her to your friends."

I knew this was blatant mother-type code for "We're dying to have a juicy gossip so let's get you girls out of earshot!" But the words were music to my ears.

"Would that be OK with you, Amber?" I asked shyly.

"Sure," said Amber, without enthusiasm. "That would be great."

The minute we got outside, Amber produced a pair of designer sunglasses and perched them on her divine little nose, which only made her look more depressingly perfect than ever.

A wave of panic washed over me. Amber and I were alone together, like I'd wanted. But I still couldn't think of a thing to say.

I mean, plenty of stuff wafted into my mind, but when I imagined actually saying any of it out loud to Amber, it seemed so *babyish* somehow. So there was this squirmingly long silence, and I completely didn't know what to do. Silences don't crop up that often when I'm with my sleepover mates. I mean, Frankie even talks in her sleep!

At last, to break the ice, I blurted, "We're going to Frankie's house. I told the others to meet us there."

Amber made a neutral American "Uhuh" noise and kept on walking.

I was going hot and cold by this time. I had to say *something*!

"I thought Frankie's was the safest bet," I explained. "I'm honestly not being horrible. But you never know *what* state Lyndz's house is going to be in. Her dad's always doing these major renovations. One time they couldn't find the telly for like, days!"

"Really," drawled Amber, making it rhyme with "silly".

"It's just the same at Rosie's," I gushed. "But for a completely different reason. Her mum and dad bought this whacking great house that needed masses doing to it. But then her dad walked out on them. They've done loads of improvements since then, but Rosie still worries that people will think she lives in a real tip."

You really despise me now, don't you? You're thinking, was Fliss out of her fluffy pink mind? Slanging off her best friends to some girl she'd only just met? And I totally don't blame you. All I can say is I TRULY didn't mean to.

I just wanted Amber to know how incredibly, well – *interesting* all my mates were. Only for some reason it came out sounding like they all came from problem families or something!

"We could have gone to Kenny's house, I suppose," I wittered desperately. "But then we'd have had to put up with her sister, Molly, poking her nose in all the time. Also Kenny has this rat."

Amber crinkled her nose. "Ugh," she said faintly. "Shouldn't they put down poison or something?"

I burst into fits of girly giggles. "Oh, I didn't

mean they have, like – RATS. It's a pet. Kenny keeps it in the garage."

"But still," said Amber. "A *rodent*!"

To my relief, I saw that we were nearly at Frankie's house.

"You're going to love Frankie," I gushed. "She's SO much fun. Being with her is just one long party."

You probably won't believe this, but it turned out that my horrendous walk with Amber was actually the *good* part!

As Amber and I went upstairs to Frankie's room, I could hear all my mates merrily slanging off the M&Ms like normal.

"They SO think they're the centre of the universe," Lyndz was saying. And Kenny chortled. "Not!"

Then we opened the door, and everyone looked up, and there was this like, ELECTRIC moment. I could practically see their thought bubbles. "Eeek! What do we say to this perfect person!"

This time Amber showed us *all* up. She stuck out her hand, and said, "Oh, hi!" with that killing American politeness.

I hastily introduced everyone. And Amber looked Rosie right in the eye, and said (eek! it gives me goosebumps just thinking of it!), "So you're Rosie. Gee, that's too bad about your dad."

Rose gave me this murderous look. Luckily, before she could give me a piece of her mind, good ole Frankie went into her Famous Actress routine.

"So Amber," she gushed. "What's it actually *like* living in LA?"

Amber's eyes lit up. "You guys can NOT imagine. It's SO fabulous."

It was like Frankie had turned some magic key. Amber totally sprang to life, telling us about her huge house, the stars she'd met, the parties she went to, the soap she'd just auditioned for – oh yes, and her FABULOUS boyfriend Darryl.

Now and then one of the others opened their mouths to say something, but now Amber had started, she just went on and on. The rest of us just gradually glazed over. Afterwards Kenny said that if Amber had said "fabulous" one more time, she'd have been forced to bang her head on the floor. Her *own* head, Kenny meant. Personally I'd have settled for putting a large paper bag over Amber's.

It's quite funny really. On the way home, things were completely reversed. Amber was still in "fabulous" chat-show mode, and I hardly said a dicky bird!

When we got in, I immediately went in search of Mum. I was in serious need of a girly talk, I can tell you.

I started up the stairs. Andy must have heard me, because he popped his head out of the kitchen. "I wouldn't disturb your mum just yet, Fliss," he said. He had that weird, tense expression I'd noticed earlier, when I was winding him up about coming home especially to see Jilly.

"I can go to the loo, can't I?" I moaned. "Amber's in the other one."

Well it wasn't an actual lie. I did go to the bathroom *first*.

Then I stopped outside Mum's bedroom door and hung about for a couple of seconds. I could hear them talking in whispers. Then I heard these muffled choking sounds.

Someone was *crying*. I think I'm a bit psychic, because right away I just knew that the person doing the crying wasn't Jilly. It was my mum.

I went into a complete panic. I tapped on the door, and without waiting for an answer, I went in. "Mum?" I said anxiously. "Is everything OK?"

Mum had obviously been crying on Jilly's shoulder. She looked up with angry pink-rimmed eyes. "Will you please go away, Fliss," she snivelled. "I really can't cope with any extra hassle today."

I was so hurt, I gave this little gasp.

Then I shut the door and went straight to my bedroom. And even though it was still light, I put on my night things, drew my bedroom curtains and climbed into bed, because you know what?

I couldn't cope with any extra hassle either.

CHAPTER SIX

The first thing I saw when I opened my eyes next morning was a beautiful golden-haired girl, fast asleep in my spare bed.

Yuk! I thought. I've been sharing my oxygen with Awful Amber!

It's amazing what a difference twenty-four hours can make. Yesterday I'd been so sure Amber would turn out to be my dream best friend. I'd even wished it was the holidays, so we could spend more time together. Now it was like I couldn't get away from her fast enough.

I scowled down at her, like a grouchy bear

who just found Goldilocks. Can you believe Amber looks perfect in her sleep? She doesn't even dribble!

I got washed and dressed and went downstairs. I was SO dreading facing Mum. I could only think of one thing which would make someone sob her heart out, five days before her wedding day.

Either Mum or Andy must have decided that getting married was a big mistake. But for some strange reason, they hadn't got around to informing me.

Suddenly I pictured those pretty peachy dresses hanging up in Mum's bedroom. Promise you won't laugh, but in my mind's eye they were *drooping*. I got this huge lump in my throat. My parents' marriage was over before it had even begun.

But when I went into the kitchen, I felt totally confused.

Mum and Andy were in there having a SERIOUS cuddle!! As soon as they saw me, they sprang apart, and I saw Mum had been crying again.

She quickly wiped her eyes. "Fliss, love,"

she said. "Whatever happened last night? Andy came up to ask if you wanted to go with him to get a takeaway, and you were fast asleep."

"Oh, yeah," I said in a casual kind of voice. "I had this headache."

But I was having major pangs of jealousy. Our family only has takeaways like, once a year. But we always get them from the same place – a restaurant called Bamboo, and it's THE best Chinese food, this side of heaven.

Andy sighed. "I'd better go to work." He gave Mum a soul-searching look. "Are you sure you don't want me to stay home, Nikky?"

"No, I'll be fine, love," she said. And another long look passed between them, like they were talking in a code only they understood.

My heart gave a little flutter. They've kissed and made up, I told myself. They had a tiff, that's all. Now everything's cool and groovy again.

And for like five seconds, the five peachy little dresses perked up.

But deep down, my days as an ostrich were strictly numbered. Because if everything was so hunky-dory, why did both my parents still look worried to death?

As Andy went out, Callum came in, yawning. "I stayed up REALLY late," he boasted. "*And* I had Chinese food. YOU didn't, ha ha!" Boys just love to put the boot in, don't they?

"Great," I said drearily.

Callum rubbed his tummy. "Amber let me have her last spring roll," he added. And he swaggered off with his cereal to watch breakfast TV.

Mum grinned. "Callum thinks Amber's great. He actually fell asleep against her shoulder last night."

"Oh, really," I said, in what I hoped was a non-committal voice.

But inside Grouchy Bear was yelling, "Keep your hands off my brother, Goldilocks! He's mine!"

Mum poured me some juice. She kept darting anxious looks at me. "Don't worry. I'll keep Amber entertained while you're at school," she said brightly. "I thought I'd take her and Jilly to Bradgate Park."

"Mmnn," I mumbled.

Mum darted another look from under her lashes. "Erm, Fliss," she said. "About yesterday, when you came in?"

I didn't know what to say, so I had a tiny sip of juice.

Mum laughed. "I think everything just suddenly got on top of me." She was smiling, but her voice had a definite wobble in it.

"Mum, is everything OK?" I blurted out. "I mean you still love Andy, right?"

Mum gasped. "What EVER made you say that, you funny girl?" she asked.

I replayed that moment over and over, all the way to school. What EVER made you say that? What EVER made you say that? Each time, I got the same result.

Captured on my mental video tape, Mum looked and sounded genuinely shocked at my question.

As I saw it, there were three possibilities. Either:

1) I REALLY had nothing to worry about.
2) My mum should definitely be put up for Actress of the Year.

Or:

3) My mum was shocked because I'd finally twigged something was wrong.

In other words, the whole situation was still about as clear as mud.

I decided not to tell my friends about my latest worry. It seemed like I was always crying on their shoulders these days. Plus, the Mum and Andy worry was kind of private.

"Hi!" I said brightly, as we all met up at the school gate. "Mum says are you all still on for after school?"

They looked at me as if I was speaking Martian.

"We're going to Leicester, remember? Shopping, then a serious pig-out at Pizza Hut!"

For some reason my friends seemed uncomfortable.

"I'd love to," said Lyndz. "But I've got this stupid thing I have to do."

"Me too," said Frankie. "Not the same thing," she added hastily. "A different stupid thing, that I totally forgot about."

Rose had gone red. "I can't come, either."

Honestly, I felt embarrassed for them. I glared at Kenny. "What about you? Have you got a stupid thing you just remembered you forgot?"

Kenny shook her head. "Uh-uh. The fact is, I don't think I'd enjoy Amber's kind of shopping. Plus, I *totally* wouldn't enjoy her company!"

I stared at them. "But you said you'd love to come!"

"We hadn't met Miss Fabulous then," Kenny pointed out.

"But then it'll just be me and Amber," I said. The thought made me break into a cold sweat.

My friends looked sheepish.

"It's just a shopping trip," I pleaded. "You don't have to marry her. You don't even have to talk to her if you don't want."

"No," said Lyndz unhappily. "But we'd have to listen to her."

231

Frankie put her arm around me. "It's not personal."

"Yeah, right," I said gloomily.

"Just tell your mum you won't go," said Kenny. "That's what I'd do."

I shook my head. "I can't."

"Why not?" everyone said at once.

"Then she'd guess me and Amber don't hit it off."

"So what?" said Kenny. "There's no LAW which says you've got to be buddies with your mum's friend's daughter!"

"It would hurt Mum's feelings," I said.

Kenny rolled her eyes. "Fliss, you are such a lightweight."

I clamped my lips together and counted to ten. You don't know you're born, Laura McKenzie, I thought darkly. You have NO idea what I'm going through.

I think Rosie did, though. She said softly, "Probably Fliss thinks her mum has got enough stress with the wedding and everything."

"Yeah," I said. "I do actually."

"So how's it going with those four

somethings?" Lyndz asked, to change the subject. Then the whistle went and it was time to go into school.

As the day went on, I got more and more depressed. Then on the way home, I had another one of my psychic flashes. This trip was bad news, I just KNEW it.

The instant I stepped inside the house, I heard Amber in full flow. "Nikky, I had the *best* time today. That olde worlde house had such an *awesome* atmosphere! Gosh, I just came out in goosebumps all over!"

I was in the living room by this time, but no-one noticed me for ages. Mum and Jilly were too busy listening to Amber gushing on about Lady Jane's awesome house, until I thought I'd totally throw up!!

I went to give Mum a hug. "Mum," I hissed in her ear. "I'm really tired. Mrs Weaver made us work incredibly hard today. Maybe you should go to Leicester without me."

Mum laughed. "You'll feel better once you get out of those school clothes! I'll give you ten minutes to get changed, then we'll go."

She beamed at Amber. "Once that girl hits the shops, she just shops till she drops."

Amber went into fits of laughter. "Gosh that is SO spooky! Are you sure Felicity and I aren't long-lost twins?"

I looked up in surprise. But it was my mum that Amber was merrily bonding with, not me.

Poor old Callum was looking glum. Patsy had offered to babysit, and I think he was terrified she'd be cooking his tea!

"I'll bring you back a treat," I told him.

"Fizz Bombs," he said at once. "'They blast your buds'. Two packets. No, THREE!"

"Get out fast, before he demands a plane to Cuba," Jilly giggled.

But my brother flung his arms round me, giving me one of his desperate cling-on hugs. Mum had to peel him off me like Velcro. We closed the door on frantic yells of "It's not fair! It's not fair!"

"I'm sorry I didn't meet your friends, Fliss," said Jilly, as we drove out of the village. "Amber's been telling me all about them."

I bet she has, I thought.

Amber was staring out of the window, so I took the opportunity to pull a horrible face. It sounds babyish, but it made me feel a very tiny bit better!

Mum and Jill were nattering about all these people they used to know, back in the days before I was born. People with nicknames like Buzz and Miggsy, so you couldn't tell if they were male or female.

"You're very quiet in the back, girls," Mum said suddenly.

"Uhuh," we both mumbled.

"Not feeling sick are you, Fliss? My daughter suffers from dreadful travel sickness," Mum announced to the world.

Amber rolled her eyes. "Great," she muttered.

"I'm fine," I said stonily. "Don't you worry your head about me."

There was another long silence.

"I don't know what you girls want to do," Mum said at last. "But I've got to find *the* perfect going-away dress, for after the wedding."

"I'll help," said Amber at once. "I know just the style which will suit you. You are so lucky, Nikky. You've got bone structure most supermodels would *die* for."

I watched Mum turning pink in her driving mirror.

"Honestly, all this fuss!" I burst out. "I suppose next you'll have to get a coming-*back* dress? I mean, get real, Mum, you can't close your wardrobe as it is. What do you need *another* dress for?"

You're shocked, aren't you? So was I! I had no IDEA all this spiteful stuff was going to come splurting out of my mouth.

Suddenly Mum went all efficient. "It's probably best if I park in the shopping centre," she said. She gave a hurt little laugh. "If I don't miss the signs, that is."

"Perhaps you'd like me to look out for signs for you, Nikky?" Amber said at once, in her fake helpful voice. "I do that for Mom all the time, back home."

"Would you, Amber? That would be really useful," said Mum warmly.

Goldilocks was the perfect name for that

girl. In the space of one school day, this golden-haired girl wonder had totally taken my place.

Can you see what Amber was doing? She was being ME, only better! The Hollywood version of Felicity Sidebotham – the sweet, helpful, style-conscious daughter of my mother's dreams.

I trailed after them out of the car park, watching them all being giggly girls together. So what was I meant to do now? Disappear in a puff of smoke?

Suddenly this cold rage came over me. Huh, you *wish*, Goldilocks, I growled. So they wanted me to be Amber's long-lost twin, did they? Then that's what I'd be. The scary wicked twin who gets her revenge!!

I really went for it. I sulked and sighed and rolled my eyes all around the shopping centre. I'm not exaggerating. I was so bad, I made Wednesday Addams look like the Milky Bar Kid! Well, OK, so I'm exaggerating slightly. But you get the picture.

The spooky thing was, once I started I totally couldn't stop.

When Mum came out of a cubicle looking drop-dead gorgeous in this sweet dress and asked me what I thought, did I tell her how great she looked? I did not. I just yawned, and said "Whatever," as if I couldn't care less. I hated myself for doing it, but it was like my wicked twin sister had totally taken me over.

And that meant that Amber got to say MY lines. "Andy is going to go crazy when he sees you in that colour," she cooed.

"He'll go even crazier when he sees the bill," I muttered.

Instead of going for pizza, we went to some new pancake parlour Amber liked the sound of. By this time I'd figured out the perfect way to punish Mum for preferring Amber to me. I probably told you, Mum is really diet-conscious? So I ordered this TOTAL calorie-fest. Pancakes, waffles, doughnuts with hot fudge sauce.

Guess what that scheming little Goldilocks did then?

"My, those waffles look so-o good," she cried, like some kid in *The Waltons*. And she ordered EXACTLY the same things!

Our mothers didn't have a clue what was going on. Only Amber and I knew she had just declared war.

The trouble is, I don't like sweet stodgy food that much. And after stuffing my face for fifteen minutes or so, I was already slowing down. But Jilly's daughter kept right on going – dipping, chewing and swallowing.

I've got to admit, all Amber's acting classes had totally paid off. She had this unbelievably innocent expression, like she truly had no idea that she was subjecting me to Death by Doughnut!

Not only that, but my revenge ploy didn't even *work*. Mum actually thought it was funny. She and Jilly got all misty-eyed about the night they stayed at a friend's house, and Jilly got this sudden chocolate craze, and Miggsy (or maybe Buzz) baked them this amazingly gooey cake.

"The trouble was, it wasn't ready until after midnight," Mum giggled. "We were dying to go to bed, but she refused to let us go to sleep until we'd eaten every last crumb!"

Mum always gives everyone the impression she was a real Nikky No-Mates when she was growing up. Now it seemed she'd been sharing midnight cake with crowds of kids, all with cool and groovy nicknames. It made me feel like I didn't really know her.

Quite suddenly I pushed my plate away.

"I think Fliss has had enough," said Amber sweetly. "Don't worry, it won't go to waste."

And she actually took my last doughnut off my plate and popped it into her mouth!!

If I wasn't feeling so miserable (also REALLY sick), I'd have shoved her smiling face right into my plate, saying, "Then DO have the rest of my sauce, Amber, while you're at it!"

But we both knew she'd won, so I just stared straight ahead, waiting for my ordeal to end.

Only it didn't.

That night Mum came to find me in the kitchen, where I was gulping down water, trying to dilute the ill-effects of my fudge-fest.

"Sweetheart," she said. "I've got something to tell you."

I had my second psychic flash of the day. You're not going to like this, Fliss, I thought.

"The thing is, Jilly isn't just my best friend. She's a real soul mate," Mum blurted out.

I stared at her.

"And that makes Amber really special too," she said awkwardly. "Which is why I want her to be one of my bridesmaids."

"You're kidding," I whispered.

"I realise this is a bit sudden," said Mum. "But I just know it would make Jilly really happy."

I didn't plan to sit down – it was more like my legs gave way underneath me, so that I kind of fell into a kitchen chair. My head was spinning with all this urgent stuff I needed to say. But in the end, I just croaked, "But there's only five dresses."

"I know," said Mum sadly. "It's a shame, but there it is."

I couldn't speak. It had been touch and go for some time, but the happy sparkling wedding of my dreams had finally morphed

241

into a total nightmare.

Because in order for Awful Amber to be a bridesmaid, one of my friends would have to stand down.

CHAPTER SEVEN

You know those agony aunts they have in women's magazines? We just *lurve* reading out those letters, don't you? Kenny swears they're made up. She says no-one in their right MINDS would parade their bizarre personal problems for complete strangers to snigger over.

There's two reasons Kenny believes this.

1) She never watches those totally riveting American chat shows.

And:

2) Unlike me, she is not a girl who easily gets her knickers in a twist.

It's like that shopping trip mix-up. My other friends fibbed themselves blue in the face, trying not to hurt my feelings. But Kenny just came clean, like it was no biggie. I'd LOVE to be more like Kenny. I really would. (I just wouldn't want to DRESS like her! *Miaow!*)

But that night when I'd closed my diary (my deadly secret one) and finally switched off my torch, I lay in the dark, composing a letter to some wise agony aunt in the sky.

Dear Auntie Whoever,

Due to circumstances beyond my control, I must inform my friends that one of them can no longer be a bridesmaid at my mother's wedding. I have absolutely no idea how to do this without hurting someone's feelings, and maybe even losing a friend. Can you help? Also, could you please reply by tomorrow, which is when I have to break this disappointing news?

Yours sincerely

Felicity Sidebotham

But by the time I'd finished, I realised that it wasn't an agony aunt I needed after all. What I needed was a miracle.

I could hear gentle breathing from the other side of the room, final proof that Amber totally didn't have a heart. After what she'd done to me, it just didn't seem fair that she was sleeping like a baby. *I* was the innocent person here. So how come it was *me* tossing and turning all night long?

I don't know about you, but when I have a bad night, with the flu or something, I'm usually longing for the first signs of morning. But that night, I was dreading the moment when the sky changed colour over Cuddington and all the little birds began to tweet.

Because I knew that no matter how miserable I felt tonight, it was nothing LIKE as bad as I was going to feel tomorrow.

Don't worry, I promise to spare you the rest of the depressing details.

I'm going to fast forward to the part where I was getting dressed for school – in the bathroom, actually, because not only was

245

Amber using up my oxygen without permission, she'd also totally invaded my privacy.

And as I finished brushing my hair and putting it up in a tidy school ponytail (Mum says a girl should never let herself go, no matter HOW bad she feels), I looked my reflection in the eye.

"Fliss," I said bravely. "Here's your chance to become a stronger, better person, just like Kenny. These are your friends. Just tell them the truth, OK? They'll understand."

My bathroom resolution lasted all the way to school. Right up till the moment I joined my friends in the playground.

The minute she saw me coming, Frankie started humming. The others all joined in, grinning. You won't need me to tell you that this was not the ideal moment for my mates to break into *Here Comes the Bride*.

They looked so incredibly happy that I almost burst into tears. How could Mum make me hurt my friends like this?

"Oh, hi," I said, trying to force a smile.

Rosie giggled. "We've all been getting

totally over-excited, Flissy! We just realised there's only THREE days to go before You Know What!"

"I SO hope I don't get hiccups at the vital moment!" Lyndz bubbled.

Kenny rolled her eyes. "Don't we all," she agreed.

But I'd stopped listening. Suddenly, in a flash of inspiration, I knew where my miracle was coming from. It wasn't like she WANTED to be a bridesmaid, I told myself. I'd practically had to beg her. She'd only agreed in the first place because I went on and on about how much it mattered to me.

As I turned to Kenny, I could already feel a big smile spreading over my face. Miracles happened. They did. You heard about them all the time.

"What about you, Kenz?" I said casually. "Don't tell me you're dying to climb into that meringue, because I won't believe you."

Kenny grinned. "Then you're wrong, Miss Smarty Pants. I know I wasn't keen to begin with. But now I wouldn't miss it for the world."

"Oh," I said. "That's so, erm – sweet." I heard myself sounding like a total fake.

Can you believe it took me until lunchtime to pluck up the courage to tell them the truth? By then I'd worked myself into such a state, I was in extreme danger of going into orbit.

I waited until everyone had finished eating. Everyone except me, that is. I was so nervous, I couldn't eat a thing.

"I think someone's got wedding jitters," grinned Frankie.

I'll do it fast, I thought. Then maybe it won't hurt so much. So in the end, I took a big breath, and blurted out the whole sorry story.

It's weird. I was prepared for just about every reaction, except the one I got. They didn't believe me. Everyone fell about laughing.

"Nice one, Fliss," Kenny chortled. "You really had us going there."

Rosie clutched her chest. "You bad girl!" she giggled. "You gave me a total heart attack!"

"Flissy, sometimes you have the weirdest sense of humour!" said Lyndz in a wondering tone.

Then Frankie's face changed. "She isn't joking," she said. "Look at her!"

Everyone stared at me, and I saw all the laughter go out of their eyes. Tears prickled behind my lids.

"Your mum actually told you to like, SACK one of us to make room for Awful Amber?" gasped Lyndz.

I nodded, and two hot little tears trickled down my cheeks. I kept seeing their happy faces as they sang *Here Comes the Bride*. Now all my friends looked like I'd slapped them.

"Did your mum say which bridesmaid is getting the sack?" Rosie asked finally.

"No," I choked. "She said we've got to figure it out amongst ourselves."

"But HOW?" said Lyndz.

"I don't know," I wept. "I can't believe this is even happening."

I was longing for my friends to comfort me. But they just went scarily quiet. And for a few seconds no-one looked at anyone else.

Then, still carefully not looking at anyone, Rosie said, "Well, I suppose it's got to be Kenny. I mean, we all remember what a terrible time Fliss had getting her to put on a bridesmaid's dress in the first place, right?"

Kenny looked hurt. "How come you're talking about me as if I'm not here?" she demanded in a huffy voice. "But then I suppose you wish I wasn't."

"Don't be stupid, Kenz," said Frankie at once.

Rosie scowled. "I was only saying that it's not fair for one of US to miss out, when everyone knows Kenny hates dressing up and being girly."

Kenny stared at her. "One of US?" she blazed. "What does that mean, exactly? I mean, one of US can't play Let's Dress Up, so suddenly I'm like this ALIEN creature who isn't US?"

"I don't think that's – that's what Rosie meant," I stuttered miserably.

Kenny scraped back her chair.

"I wondered what that was all about this morning," she said in a shaky voice. "All that rhubarb about me and my meringue. It was because you didn't have the guts to tell me the truth!"

"Sssh, Kenny," said Rosie uncomfortably. "Everyone's looking."

But Kenny didn't stop for breath. "Why didn't you just say, 'Laura McKenzie, you'll make a rubbish bridesmaid, so you're FIRED!'" she screamed. Then she ran out of the hall, sobbing as if her heart would break.

The M&Ms must have thought Christmas had come early. It was obvious they were lapping up every moment of our misery.

Then I saw Frankie and Lyndz both glaring at me.

"This is your fault, Felicity Sidebotham," Frankie choked. "I'll never *forgive* you for hurting Kenny's feelings like that."

"Me neither," said Lyndz.

"Hey!" said Rosie. "It's not Flissy's fault if her mum got a bee in her bonnet about Amber being a bridesmaid."

But Frankie and Lyndz just pushed back their chairs and stalked out of the hall.

Have you ever been so upset that you

can't even cry? I sat there at that table with my elbows in everyone's crumbs, the whole school staring at me, and I really wished I could die.

Yet it was like I couldn't even find the energy to get up and leave.

It had all happened so FAST! Like Andy's precious mirror, the Sleepover Club had just shattered into pieces, and I didn't understand *why*. I didn't even know whose fault it was. Was it Amber's, or Mum's, or was it really all down to me, like Frankie said?

As we left the hall, Rosie tucked her arm through mine. "I'm your friend, Fliss," she said fiercely. "I don't care what they say."

All the rest of the day, Kenny sat by herself at the back of the class. I wanted to go up to her and explain that she'd totally got it wrong. But she looked so blank and cold, I didn't dare. It was like she'd put up an invisible force-field which totally stopped the rest of us going near her.

Lyndz and Frankie sat together. When Mrs Weaver wasn't looking, they whispered to each other, darting poisonous looks at me and Rosie.

Without any warning, tears started splashing down my face. Some of them fell on my rough book, smudging the sum I'd been working out in pencil. I scrubbed my hand across my face.

"Don't cry," Rosie whispered. "It'll be OK. I know it will."

I truly couldn't see how. I still believed in miracles and everything. I just didn't think one could happen to me.

That evening I shut myself in the kitchen. I'd told Mum I'd got this work I absolutely had to finish, and that Mrs Weaver would skin me alive if I didn't hand it in by tomorrow. But it was actually because I couldn't stand the thought of spending another evening with Amber and Patsy.

Anyway, there I was, miserably doodling felt-tip hearts on the inside of my work book, when suddenly the phone rang.

It was for Mum. I wasn't in the mood for eavesdropping, to be honest, but I got the vague impression someone had given her some upsetting news. A few minutes after she'd replaced the receiver, the phone rang again. And after Mum had heard what this caller had to say, she sounded totally distraught.

She burst into the kitchen, looking as white as a sheet.

"Did you know about this?" she demanded. "I've just had Frankie and Lyndz's mothers on the phone. Apparently their daughters can no longer perform their bridesmaids' duties on Saturday."

I know it sounds heartless, but I almost burst out laughing. I couldn't help it. Sometimes my friends take my breath away. That's the Sleepover Club all over, I thought. One out, ALL out!

Luckily Mum was too busy ranting to notice my reaction. "What's going on, Fliss?" she blazed. "Have you had some kind of stupid quarrel or something?"

I jumped to my feet. "Stupid *quarrel*!" I screamed. "It's not *us* who's stupid. *You're* the one who forced me to choose between my friends, remember?"

"I didn't do anything of the kind—" Mum began.

"Yes, you did!" I yelled. "You FORCED me. And you know what? I'm proud of my friends for taking a stand. That's what I should have done in the first place. But it's OK, because I'm doing it now!"

I glared at her, breathing hard.

Mum looked alarmed. "What do you mean?" she gasped.

All at once I knew exactly what I was going to say. "It's up to you," I said. "You can have ALL of the Sleepover Club for your bridesmaids, or none of them."

I wasn't shouting now. I was as quiet and reasonable as can be.

"You've got to make up your mind, Mum," I told her calmly. "Is it Amber you want at your wedding? Or is it me?"

CHAPTER EIGHT

It was true what I said to Mum. I should have stood up for my mates at the start. But now that I'd finally done it, I felt like a new person. All my mixed-up feelings melted away like a bad dream, and I knew exactly what I had to do next. But I didn't have much time to do it.

I quickly abandoned my pretend homework, and went to hunt out this fancy writing set which my Auntie Paula gave me last Christmas.

It was the first time I'd used it, actually.

I don't mean to sound ungrateful, but I wasn't too thrilled when I first got it, so I didn't look at it that closely. But as I stripped off the cellophane, I suddenly noticed an eerie coincidence.

My notepaper and envelopes were decorated with cute little cartoons of baby angels. There was also a motto which said, "*Angels fly because they take themselves lightly.*" Isn't that SWEET! Don't tell anyone, but I truly felt like those angels had just popped up to show me I was on the right track.

I was incredibly sleepy after my bad night, but I forced my eyes to stay open until I'd written four letters, one for each of my friends, explaining what I'd just told my mum.

Then I slipped the sealed envelopes into my school bag and zipped it shut. I didn't think it was wise to leave them lying around. If Amber thought it was OK to muscle in on my mates' bridesmaids' dresses, she *might* figure it was OK to read people's letters too.

I went to bed, convinced I'd found the perfect way to put things right. But so far, it was just a theory.

* * *

When I actually went into our classroom next day, I almost lost my nerve. It was like walking into this like, icy wall of HATE. When Lyndz and Frankie saw me coming, they immediately pulled faces, as if I was this really bad smell. But I think you'd have been really proud of me, because I didn't go to pieces. I just reminded myself that the angels were rooting for us all to get back together, then I quickly handed my mates their pink envelopes.

Frankie looked as if I'd dropped a dead mouse in her lap. "What's *this*?" she said in disgust. But she told me afterwards that she was wild with curiosity to know what I was up to, because I'd had such a weird expression on my face!

The four girls read their letters under their desks, while I tried not to look. And I got this sinking feeling. What if it didn't work?

My friends must all read at the same speed or something, because suddenly I heard these soft little sighs as they all reached the last line together.

Then to Mrs Weaver's astonishment, Lyndz, Frankie and Kenny jumped out of their seats and rushed over to gave me a hug. (Rosie was sitting next to me already, if you remember!)

We had to wait till break before we could have our proper reunion, but it was well worth waiting for. Everyone was SO emotional, it wasn't true!! For ten solid minutes, we all cried and hugged and mushily forgave each other. You should have seen us!

"I can't believe you stood up to her like that!" sniffled Frankie. "That was SO brave, Flissy."

I blew my nose hard. "It didn't feel brave," I said. Which was true. "I just couldn't bear the thought of everyone breaking friends, because of me."

And we all had another round of hugs.

But Kenny looked thoughtful. "Fliss, it's so brilliant, what you did. But I really don't think you should back out of your own mum's wedding."

"Nor do I," said Lyndz.

Rosie shook her head. "Me neither."

"I've got an idea," said Frankie suddenly. "We'll put our names in a hat, and whoever Fliss picks out has to stand down."

"Cool," Kenny grinned. "Except we haven't actually *got* a hat."

"Couldn't we use something else?" asked Lyndz.

"I suppose," said Frankie doubtfully. "It just seems more official with an actual hat, somehow."

"We could borrow one from the dressing-up box?" suggested Lyndz.

We all went dashing off to ask Mrs Dwyer – she's one of the infant teachers.

She looked dead suspicious at first. I could see her thinking, "What ARE these weird girls up to now?"

But then Frankie went on about how it was like, the ONLY possible way for us to reach the most important democratic decision in the history of the Sleepover Club, and Mrs Dwyer eventually gave in.

We had four hats to choose from. A straw hat with little daisies and violets on, a beefeater's furry busby, a Red Baron-type pilot's cap with fleecy ear-flaps, and an ancient Roman helmet.

We went for the helmet in the end. As Frankie said, despite being plastic, it was by far the most dignified.

Mrs Dwyer tactfully left us alone in the Year One classroom, while everyone wrote their names on pieces of scrap paper, folded them into squares, and popped them into the Roman helmet.

I shut my eyes, felt around, and drew out one of the squares.

"It's Frankie," I said. "Sorry, Frankie," I added, guiltily.

"Yeah, sorry Frankie," mumbled everyone, though you could see they were all really thrilled that I hadn't picked them!

But to my surprise Frankie took the news really well. "Hey, cheer up," she grinned bravely. "I mean, I'm still coming to the wedding, right?"

Honestly, Frankie's like a different person since her little sister, Izzy, was born. I'm not being mean, but the old Frankie was a typical only child, always expecting to have everything her way. These days she's so mellow, it's unbelievable.

"Does everyone want to come back to my place after school, to tell Mum the good news?" I asked.

I hadn't really spoken to Mum since last night, I realised.

"I bet she was seriously stressed when you told her," said Rosie.

"I'll say," I said. "But everything's been stressing her out lately, I don't know why."

"Weddings are most peculiar things," said Lyndz, putting on a doddery old lady's voice.

"TELL me about it," I grinned.

Miss Dwyer put her head round the door. "Reached that world-shattering democratic decision yet, girls?"

"Yes, thanks!" we yelled.

"Well, praise the Lord and give me my classroom back!" she sighed. She stood aside and a horde of over-excited infants came thundering into the class, all yelling "YAY!" at the tops of their voices.

"Infants are so much smaller than you

think, aren't they?" said Lyndz, as we went back into the playground.

"And they have so much fun," sighed Rosie.

Then we had one of our amazing telepathic moments. We all grinned at each other, and we did something really babyish.

All five of us linked arms and ran across the playground, yelling "YAY!" too!

Further down the playground, the M&Ms were talking to Alana Palmer. As we drew level, all three girls narrowed their eyes at us. It's one of their favourite expressions, and it makes them look exactly like those spiteful Siamese cats in *The Lady and the Tramp.*

"See ya!" Lyndz yelled merrily, as we zoomed past.

"But we wouldn't wanna BE ya!" I added.

And we all cracked up laughing.

I was so happy to be back with my friends, I can't tell you. In a funny way, it seemed as if our quarrel had brought us closer together than ever.

We walked home after school, chatting

and teasing each other, just like always. Plus, we kept telling Frankie what a star she was for the way she'd taken not being a bridesmaid. By the time we reached my house, she was practically walking on air!

But that's NOTHING to how Mum looked when we told her the good news! She was totally *ecstatic*. She insisted on hugging everyone, but I don't think they minded too much.

"I promise you'll still get your special bridesmaid present, Frankie," Mum said.

"Oh, goody," said Frankie greedily, and we all burst out laughing.

After everyone had gone, I gave Mum a specially huge hug to make up for our fight. "Everything's going to be all right from now on," I told her.

A flicker of worry crossed her face. "I hope you're right," she whispered.

"I KNOW I'm right," I said. "Actually, I think I'm getting psychic powers."

Mum gave a tired grin. "Good," she said. "I could really use them."

My mother meant it to come out as a joke,

but I could hear the same scared little wobble in her voice that I'd noticed before.

I watched her anxiously as she rinsed and chopped vegetables for a salad, hoping for clues to her odd behaviour.

Whatever could it be that was making her act so sad and faraway? And why oh *why* wouldn't she tell me? Mum and I always used to share everything. What could be so terrible, I wondered, that she had to keep it such a dark and deadly secret?

After tea, Mum made Amber try on Frankie's bridesmaid's dress.

She revolved slowly, like a cake on a cake-stand, as Mum fiddled around, twitching at seams and yanking down the hem.

Amber's the kind of girl who couldn't look bad if she was covered in slime. Even so, I couldn't help feeling just a tiny bit smug. That dress didn't look anything LIKE as good on Amber as it had done on Frankie!

I don't know why, but all at once, Amber didn't seem nearly such a pain. She didn't mention her fabulous boyfriend once, all night. She also helped me wash up. Though

I'm not sure if these things actually triggered my new tolerant attitude, or whether hating Amber was just getting too much like hard work.

Plus, it had dawned on me that after the wedding, Jilly's daughter would be out of my life forever, but my great friends and my family would all still be here. Anyway, that night, for the first time, Amber and I actually AGREED on something.

We both desperately wanted to watch this funny film on TV, but no-one else was keen, so we watched it on the set in my room. To start with, we were both a bit on our dignity. It was like neither of us wanted to be the first person to laugh out loud. We'd snigger, then instantly straighten our faces. But the film was so silly that soon we were both howling with laughter.

When it was over, Amber went off to use the bathroom, and I trotted downstairs to say goodnight to Mum and Andy.

To my dismay, Andy's mum followed me out into the hall. "I want a private word, Felicity," she whispered.

Oh-oh, I thought. I should have guessed it was all too good to be true. What have I done wrong *now*?

Whatever it was, Patsy didn't want anyone else to hear about my crimes, because she put her finger to her lips and kind of shunted me mysteriously into the kitchen. Then she shut the door.

Did I say before that Patsy always looks and sounds slightly offended?

"I just wanted to tell you," she said in her stiff way, "that I'm really proud of you, dear."

I was so expecting an earbashing that I actually glanced behind me, to see who Patsy was really talking to! "Proud?" I said bewildered. "Of me?"

"You've got strong principles," she said. "I like that. And you're a true friend."

"Oh," I croaked. "Thanks, erm, Patsy."

"I'd like you to bring Francesca back here after school tomorrow. If everything goes according to plan, I may have a surprise for her." And Patsy had this real glint in her eye, like she was actually enjoying our little conspiracy. It was the exact same look Andy gets sometimes, when he's winding Mum up!

"OK," I said, surprised. "I'll ask her."

I couldn't think *what* Patsy was being so cloak-and-dagger about. But I really REALLY hoped her plan wouldn't involve cabbage soup.

I was so tired by the time I switched out my light that I almost fell asleep as soon as I hit the pillow.

Only almost.

Because just as I drifted happily away to dreamland, it hit me!

I'd only got two days until the wedding! And not only had I failed to come up with any of my four somethings, but I still had no IDEA what I was going to get Mum and Andy for a present.

I thumped my pillow angrily.

Felicity Sidebotham, you total fluff-brain! I fumed to myself. How COULD you have forgotten something so important!!

CHAPTER NINE

Bet you thought I was telling serious porkies, didn't you, when I said this story was going to be like a rollercoaster ride! Bet you've changed your mind now though, eh? And guess what! The thrills and spills aren't nearly over yet.

But as this story is being told by that well-known butterfly-brain Felicity Sidebotham, I thought you might be feeling a bit confused by this time. So I thought I'd remind you EXACTLY where we've got up to now, in the wedding countdown. Can you believe it's now actually the day before the wedding?

Me neither!

Have you ever been so incredibly excited, that nothing actually feels quite real? Isn't it the weirdest sensation in the world?

That Friday, I got up and kind of floated through the motions of my usual routine, but it was like I was watching myself in a movie, do you know what I mean? Fliss gets ready for school. Fliss leaves the house. Fliss walks down the street with a soppy grin on her face, dreaming of peach satin dresses, wedding cake and confetti!

"My mother is getting married tomorrow," I whispered, as I walked down the same village street I walked down every day. But I'd been waiting so long, it was like I couldn't really believe my dream was finally turning into reality.

Then I remembered that I still had my little mystery to solve. At break, I took Frankie aside and gave her Patsy's message.

She looked amazed. "Why me?"

"I have no idea," I said truthfully.

"Didn't she even give you like, a tiny CLUE what it's about?"

270

"She said she might have a surprise for you. So can you come?" I asked anxiously.

Frankie grinned. "Do I *look* like a girl who'd pass up the opportunity for a mystery surprise?"

The great thing about this particular Friday was that as well as being Mum's wedding day minus one, it also happened to be the last day of term. This meant we had no actual lessons, YIPPEE! Which, as Kenny said, was really just as well, seeing as by this time all five of us were in like, dizzy nonstop orbit around Planet Wedding!

Frankie and I walked home together, trying to guess what on earth Patsy's surprise could be. Some of our guesses got pretty wild!

"It's her secret recipe for cabbage soup," Frankie suggested. "It's so hush-hush, she's going to write it down in code and make me learn it off by heart. After that she'll make me swallow it. And if I don't, I needn't think I'm going to get ANY pudding!"

"No, I know what it is," I giggled. "You've won an entire five minutes at the Patsy

Proudlove Charm School!"

But the joke was on us, as it turned out.

Andy's mum called out to us as we were coming in through the front door. "We're in the living room, dears," she said. And if it had been anyone else but Andy's mum, I'd have sworn she sounded excited.

Frankie followed me in. "Hi, everyone," she beamed. Then her face kind of crumpled. "Oh, hi Amber," she said bravely. "Wow, that dress really suits you."

No WONDER poor old Frankie didn't know where to look.

Amber was striking this really haughty pose beside the window. But that's not all. She was only wearing her bridesmaid's dress, would you believe! Talk about rubbing Frankie's nose in it. Amber couldn't have been more tactless if she'd tried. Though in passing, I DID notice that the dress looked heaps better on her than it had last night. I hated to admit it, but she looked completely amazing.

OK, now I'm going to let you in on the big secret, right?

In case you hadn't guessed, Mum, Patsy, Jilly and Amber had cooked up a wicked little plot between them. Unknown to Frankie and me, Amber was totally acting her socks off. To be honest, she was the only plotter who managed to keep a straight face (I put it down to all those acting lessons!).

Mum, Jilly and Patsy did TRY to look innocent, bless them. But their twinkly eyes just wouldn't co-operate. So it soon became obvious, even to us, that something very fishy was going on.

Suddenly Frankie couldn't stand the suspense another second. "So is anyone going to tell me about this surprise or what?" she blurted.

"Da-DA," sang Mum, and she whipped a second bridesmaid's dress from behind her back.

Frankie and I stared at it, hopelessly confused.

"Patsy and Amber have been working so hard while you were at school. They really ought to get medals," said Mum.

"It was Patsy's idea," Amber chipped in.

"I still don't get it," I said. "What idea?"

"To make a new dress for Amber, of course," beamed Mum. "Patsy and Amber just didn't think it was right for Frankie to miss out."

And my mum presented the dress to a totally stunned Frankie.

"You mean I can still be your bridesmaid after all?" she gasped.

Mum nodded, beaming.

"Wow!" Frankie breathed. Then she rushed at my mum and hugged her madly around the middle. "Thank you SO much," she said in a muffled voice. "This is a very very happy moment and I think I'm going to cry."

That's one way in which Frankie hasn't changed at all. She's still a TOTAL drama queen!

Amber stepped forward. For the first time since I'd met her she looked really unsure of herself. "Can I hug Frankie too?" she said. "I mean, since we're both going to be bridesmaids now."

All this time, Patsy had been busily inspecting her nails, but suddenly she went zooming towards the door. "I think I'll just go and make everyone a nice pot of tea," she called over her shoulder.

But I got the definite feeling she just wanted to get WAY out of hugging range! And for the first time, it occurred to me that Patsy's prickly hedgehog routine was actually terminal shyness.

"But how did they manage to do it so fast?" I said. "No offence, Mum, but it's taken you AGES to make those other dresses."

"Aha," grinned Jilly. "You obviously haven't heard about Patsy's secret past!"

"Apparently Patsy used to be some kind of dressmaker in London," Amber explained.

Mum acted shocked. "Dressmaker! Patsy used to work for a major French fashion house, darling!"

"So making one itty bitty bridesmaid's dress was not exactly a major problem for her," Jilly explained.

"I don't know what we'd have done without her," sighed Mum. "Patsy's worked absolute miracles today."

I started to giggle. I couldn't help it.

"What?" said everyone.

But it wasn't a thought I could exactly share with them, seeing as Patsy herself had just sailed back in with the tea-things. I DID tell it to my Wedding Diary though, before I went to sleep. Want to see what I wrote?

I kept saying I needed a miracle. It just NEVER occurred to me that a miracle could ever come through someone as scary as Patsy! Maybe that's what our vicar means when he says, "God works in mysterious ways"!!

After Frankie went home, Amber and I figured that the grown-ups in the house were all far too busy with wedding preparations to do anything about food. So we sneaked a tub of Ben and Jerry's Rainforest Crunch out of the freezer, grabbed a spoon each, and went up to my room.

But there wasn't really much on TV and gradually we got talking. Actually it turned into a real heart-to-heart.

"You must have thought I was a real pill," Amber said suddenly.

"Oh, er, not really," I said politely.

She laughed. "Sure you did. The fact is, I was incredibly jealous."

"Yeah, right," I said. "You live in LA, next door to Mickey Mouse and – and lots of other famous people whose names I can't remember just now, and you're jealous of *me*. That makes sense. NOT!"

"Sorry to disappoint you, Fliss, but me and Mickey don't actually hang out on a regular basis," Amber teased. Then she sighed. "I do have a great life though, and I wouldn't change it. Except for one thing."

I stared at her.

"I wish I had great friends, like you guys," she said. "The first time I heard you going on about them, it made me feel kind of lonely." I could tell Amber meant it too. Her voice had this husky little catch in it.

"Don't you have loads of friends in LA?" I said.

Amber grinned. "Don't look so worried. I'm not like, a total hermit or anything. But none of my friends really *know* me. Not the way you guys know each other."

"We have these huge fights sometimes," I said.

"Yeah, but you make up, right?" Amber helped herself to a mega spoonful of Rainforest Crunch. "I did have this really cool friend, once," she said. "Her name was Lauren McGravy."

"You're kidding."

"No, I swear. That's her real name." Amber went into a fit of giggles. "Poor Lauren," she said. "She's allergic to everything, so she's like, sneezing constantly. But this is totally not a human sneeze, right? It sounds like it's made by some cute little Disney cartoon." And she did a wicked imitation of a Lauren McGravy-type sneeze.

"What happened to her?"

She sighed. "The usual thing. Lauren's parents split and her mother took her off to New York."

"You can still phone," I suggested.

"Yeah, yeah," said Amber. "I call her up sometimes. I just hate how after you put down the receiver, you feel like twenty times more lonely than you did before."

There was quite a long silence after she said this. It wasn't a seriously squirm-making silence, but I got the feeling that Amber felt a bit down in the dumps. So it was probably best not to ask her any more about Lauren McGravy just yet.

"Hey," I said suddenly. "There's a really mushy film on later. Want to watch it with me?"

Amber's eyes lit up. "How mushy?" she demanded. "You know, on a scale of one to ten?"

"Twelve at *least*," I giggled.

She wriggled her toes. "I can't WAIT," she said gleefully.

Just then Andy yelled upstairs. Luckily for all our rumbly tummies, my thoughtful step-dad had brought back a carload of pizza for everyone.

"I know it's not very healthy," Mum kept saying merrily, as she handed round massive slices dripping with melted mozzarella cheese. "I'm so disorganised today. But it can't be helped."

She caught me staring at her.

"What?" she said. "I've got tomato sauce on my nose again, haven't I?"

"No," I said. "It's nothing, honestly."

But a wave of wonderful relief washed over me.

Mum was totally her old self again. The scared little wobble in her voice had disappeared. All those stress crinkles in her forehead had been smoothed out. And though she was only wearing the teeniest touch of make-up, my mother looked exactly like brides are supposed to look.

For the first time in over a week, she was really and truly radiant.

And with one of my psychic flashes, I knew I totally didn't need to worry about her scary secret any more. I could tell that it was now well and truly over, and that's all that mattered.

By the way, Amber and I never did get to watch that mushy film.

You see, while we were stuffing ourselves with pizza, I had a private word with Patsy, who immediately set us to work on a secret late-night project. And you're just going to have to wait till the end of the story before I tell you what the project was!

"Mind if I keep the light on?" I asked Amber, when we finally got to bed some time after midnight. "I want to write in my diary for a while."

"I don't know how you can keep your eyes open," she yawned. "I'm exhausted. That Patsy is *such* a slave-driver."

She settled down to sleep, and I started scribbling in my Wedding Diary. I showed you some of this stuff earlier. Plus I also wrote this:

This has been the most amazing week of my life. And now it's almost over, I feel much older and a (tiny) bit wiser. It's like I had this fairy tale going on in my head, where Amber was the beautiful princess who totally didn't have a heart. And I definitely had Patsy pegged as the mean old witch with her evil potions and scary ways!

Well, it turns out I was wrong. (Though Andy's mum does have very useful magic powers. Heh heh heh!)

And here's the icing on the cake. I successfully completed my mission, yippee! Thanks to Patsy's powers, those four somethings are totally sorted. Not only has the wicked ladder spell finally been broken, but I've also got a completely fab and groovy wedding present for Andy and Mum – it's

Oops, I only just shut my diary in time or I'd have ruined the big surprise! I'm not being funny, but I truly can't let you read any more, just yet. These are like, official wedding secrets, OK? Which means they can only be unveiled at the actual wedding!

Are you KIDDING? Of course you're invited. I'm just working up to the most exciting bit of the whole story, you nutcase!

So jump back on the wedding rollercoaster, and get ready to go "ooh!" and "aah!" and "wow!" because that great big water splash is coming up, any minute NOW!

CHAPTER TEN

This is SO embarrassing.

I've been building up to this like, HUGE moment in my story, and now I've come over all wobbly.

It's not just stage fright. You see, in the middle of the celebrations, I got some news which completely blew me away. I took it really calmly at the time. But now I'm in this total DAZE.

I mean, I've been talking all along like this was just about Mum's wedding. But it turns out that the whole time, there was this other mega dramatic stuff going on behind the scenes. So now I'm feeling like, "Fliss, how could you be so DIM!"

OK, OK, I'm probably being about as clear as mud! But my head is just spinning. If you could see my thought bubbles, like in those cartoon strips, I just know they'd be totally haywire.

Bubble 1 is panicking: "Eek, NOW where do I start?"

Bubble 2 is signalling frantically: "Major headache, major headache! A fluff-brain like you shouldn't be attempting to describe the sheer wonderfulness of Mum's Big Day, let alone explaining this like, WILD new strand of the plot!"

But inside Bubble 3 is just a humungous exclamation mark!

In case you were wondering, that's the part of my brain which is still trying to digest my stunning news. You see, it *seemed* to come out of the blue. But, now I look back, I realise there were all these clues staring me in the face, which I totally failed to pick up on.

Phew! Thanks for letting me get that off my

chest. Actually, I think I've calmed down very slightly. So I'll tell you what we're going to do. We'll put my big news on the back burner for now, and just carry on like I originally planned.

So now we're going to zoom straight to that hopelessly mushy scene we've all been waiting for.

The one where we FINALLY get to see (SIGH!!) Mum's dress!

The night before the wedding, Mum had firmly packed Andy off to stay with Dave, Andy's best man. So apart from Callum (who doesn't exactly rate as a real bloke), this was like, an *exclusively* girly moment.

Patsy had been shut in with Mum practically since DAWN, helping her get ready. So there was just Jilly and all six of us bridesmaids, waiting nervously for Mum to come downstairs.

But when she eventually appeared at the top of the stairs, I almost cried. I'm not lying. We all just stared and stared at her, until she came over all shy.

"Do I look all right?" she asked anxiously.

But I think she knew the answer really.

"You look like a fairy-tale princess," sighed Frankie.

Mum had chosen a dress which was utterly perfect for a summer wedding. It was in shimmery ivory satin, with slightly puffy sleeves which came to just below her elbows. The skirt was completely plain, but the sleeves and bodice had all these tiny embroidered hearts and roses done in silver thread, plus silver beads so tiny, you'd hardly know they were there at all.

Oh, and you should have seen Mum's veil! It was the dreamiest thing. It was really long, and edged with more teeny roses and scattered with little seed pearls. To keep it in place, she'd got this gorgeous silver tiara with a cluster of larger pearls in the centre.

Her flowers were really simple – just this absolute *cascade* of creamy blossoms. They smelled so lovely, it seemed like the dress itself was giving off some unique wedding-day scent.

And if Frankie and the others think that sounds soppy, well, that's just too bad. My mum was getting married. I'm *supposed* to feel like that!

Oops, I almost forgot to tell you about her amazing train!

Actually, none of us realised exactly *how* amazing until Mum reached the bottom of the stairs, and suddenly there was absolutely NO room in our hall!

In case you didn't know, most people have at *least* one rehearsal before their actual wedding day, so everyone knows what they've got to do. But for very special reasons I'll go into later, Mum and Andy's schedule was so hectic that they totally couldn't fit one in.

Anyway, you've got to picture like, MILES of satin, all billowing around the hall of our little semi!

Well, naturally we all went into a major panic! I mean, Mum's special wedding car was arriving in five minutes. In other words, the Peaches and Cream Squad (Jilly's nickname for Mum's bridesmaids!) had precisely five minutes to acquire some serious train-management skills!

Poor Mum looked like she might pass out cold at this point.

But Patsy quickly calmed everyone down, explaining that it was really just a question of common sense.

"But you *must* stop walking the instant Nikky stands still," she told us sternly. "And don't lag too far behind, or else you'll all get dragged along behind her like a bunch of bad water-skiers."

This was such a wild picture that my mother and all six bridesmaids, me included, burst into mad fits of giggles. Jilly immediately whipped out her Polaroid camera and took a snap of us all, falling about hysterically, in our long dresses and flowery crowns.

There was only just enough time left for Mum to give us all our special bridesmaids' lockets. They were on these incredibly fine gold chains with the SWEETEST tiny gold hearts on.

"Aaah," said Jilly when we'd put them on. "That is the perfect finishing touch, Nikky. Don't they all look cute!"

I was so proud of Kenny. I mean, imagine Laura MaKenzie allowing herself to be seen in public *looking cute*. That is TRUE friendship!!

But there she was, wearing her peach meringue, a flowery crown and a golden heart locket, with this dreamy little Mona Lisa smile on her face. (Later we found out that the smile was because she'd just thought up this wicked bridesmaid-survival strategy, which I'll tell you later! But who cares – it worked!)

Suddenly I peeped out of the window and almost screamed my head off.

There was a *real Rolls Royce* parked outside our house! A genuine cream-coloured Rolls Royce, decorated with white ribbons. Mum's wedding was really happening at last!!

"Remember, girls," said Patsy fiercely. "Stay calm."

"Peaches and Cream Squad – go go go!" commanded Jilly.

Amber rolled her eyes. "Mum, perleaze!"

"Please God, don't let us trip up, and

please, please don't let me get hiccups," I heard Lyndz pray under her breath.

"Amen," said Frankie fervently.

Then Patsy opened the door and all this lovely summer sunlight flooded in. This is too perfect, I thought tearfully. Even the weather is just TOO perfect.

We followed my mother down the garden path, solemnly keeping all her precious satin out of the dirt. (Now I understand why they call them trains. Mum's practically went on for EVER.) But it wasn't until we got outside that we saw just *how* special her train actually was.

A few metres above the hem, there was this big embroidered A.

Do you get it? Sure you do, you nutcase!

The A was for Andy!! Is that romantic or WHAT!!!

Oh, you did remember the ceremony wasn't going to be in an actual church, didn't you? We all had to drive out to this fabulous old Tudor house out in the country. Belvoir Manor, it's called.

I got this absolute STORM of butterflies in

my tummy when we drove up and I saw all the crowds of people waiting for us. I didn't recognise my step-dad at first in his morning coat. Honestly, it was so sweet! When Andy saw Mum in her wedding dress, he was totally lost for words!

He'd somehow found time to get a really smart haircut since we'd last seen him, and he really did look incredibly handsome. Plus I just *loved* his waistcoat. It was embroidered in exactly the same roses and hearts as Mum's dress. Dave, the best man, was cracking these stupid jokes about how it was so Andy didn't go home with the wrong bride by mistake. But Amber and I agreed that it made Mum and Andy look like they totally belonged together.

I'd have liked to give my step-dad a hug actually, but my official train-management duties made this impossible. So Andy made do with giving me a huge wink, and I gave him a very dignified bridesmaid's smile!

The ceremony passed in a flash. I know you'll be relieved to hear that absolutely no-one tripped over, and Lyndz *didn't* have an attack of her famous hiccups, thank goodness!

But the star of the show was definitely my little brother. I don't think I mentioned what a terrible time we'd had getting Callum into his page-boy clothes earlier? I was probably trying to forget it!

Mum's idea was for Callum to walk along with the wedding rings carefully balanced on a small velvet cushion. I had serious doubts about this. He's not the most co-ordinated boy in the world, and his shoes had seriously slippy soles. He wasn't walking really, so much as *skating* over the carpet.

But somehow, even with total strangers watching him, Callum managed to walk down that long strip of red carpet in his strange new page-boy outfit, plus he hung on to those rings like grim death!

I don't think anyone minded that the tip of his tongue was sticking out the whole time. It was only because he was concentrating so hard. And even our vicar laughed when Callum puffed out his cheeks with relief and said, "So now can we have that cake, Mum?"

And suddenly it was over. Mum and Andy were married. *For real!*

The wedding lunch was held in this big marquee. The food was just amazing. We'd all been loads too nervous to eat a bite of breakfast, so everyone was starving.

Mum and Andy had arranged for us bridesmaids to have a special table of our own. But for the first few minutes we all just stuffed our faces, and now and then one of us would go, "Wow, we actually did it."

But eventually, we were all chatting away at once, like we always do.

"It's so great of you guys to invite me to your big wedding sleepover tonight," Amber said suddenly.

"Well, as we're all going to be staying in Fliss's house," grinned Kenny, "it would be pretty rude to have it without you!"

Rosie looked shocked. "You didn't have to say it like that," she said. "Amber might think you mean it."

But Amber just burst out laughing. In a funny way, I think Kenny teasing her made her feel like she was really one of us.

By this time, all the speeches had started. I don't know why grown-ups insist on having them, do you? Next to school assembly, speeches have to be the most boring invention on this planet.

While they were all going on (and on), everyone at our table carried on talking in whispers. Which is when Kenny shared her secret survival strategy to being a bridesmaid.

"I pretended I was invisible," she said calmly. "You guys didn't realise, but the sixth bridesmaid was totally invisible the whole time."

Well, *honestly* – we all fell about. Can you seriously imagine an INVISIBLE bridesmaid helping to hold up a train? Spooky or what!

But by this time, all those angels who'd been busily protecting Lyndz all morning must have gone off duty. And you know what happens when Lyndz gets the giggles? That's right. That girl just EXPLODED into big-time hiccups.

She'd only just gone back to her normal

colour (i.e. not purple) when everyone in the marquee suddenly went completely wild, all clapping and cheering and laughing.

I looked up in amazement, just in time to see Andy return to his seat beside Mum. For some reason they were both grinning like idiots.

"Wow," breathed Amber. "I don't know what your dad just said, Fliss, but everyone really, REALLY loved him."

And all at once Mum was beside me, hugging all the breath out of me.

"Sorry you had to hear it like that, sweetheart," she babbled. "We'd planned to tell you before we went away on our honeymoon. I don't know what got into Andy, blurting it out in front of everyone like that!"

I struggled up for air. Mum was glowing with excitement.

"So what do you think?" she demanded. "I can't believe I've been worrying myself to death all week, thinking something was wrong. And all the time everything was perfectly normal."

I stared at her. "Mum, I haven't a *clue* what you're on about. What do you mean, *normal*?"

"Normal for twins, of course," she cried. "Isn't it amazing! I had the scan yesterday."

I bet you've never seen six bridesmaids in flowery crowns with their mouths hanging open, have you!

"You're having a BABY!" I breathed.

"Two," Kenny corrected me quickly. "She said twins, dummy!"

Mum's eyes were bright with tears. "I wanted to tell you, Flissy," she said. "But the doctor was worried something was wrong. And you had so much on your plate with the wedding and everything, I couldn't bear you to have any extra worries."

Andy appeared beside her. "So what's the verdict?" he said shyly. "I know we must have acted really weird sometimes this week. Are we forgiven, princess?"

But I just jumped into Andy's arms and buried my head in his shoulder.

"Yes," I said in a muffled voice. "You are both totally *totally* forgiven, but don't you

DARE keep me in the dark like that again, OK."

After that, as you can imagine, all of us partied away like mad. And then it was time for Mum and Andy to go off on their honeymoon.

Sometimes I feel deeply depressed at the end of a party, don't you? But by this time, Mum and Andy's news was sinking in just enough for me to realise this party wasn't like an ENDING. It was the beginning of an amazing new life. And that made me feel incredibly safe and happy somehow. You know what I mean?

All the guests turned out to wave and throw confetti as Andy and Mum made a mad dash for their car. At last they got away and everyone started gradually drifting back to the marquee.

Everyone except me. I stood there by myself, with my long dress fluttering in the breeze, and watched the car disappear down the drive. And I stayed there, watching and watching, until it was a teeny weeny dot in the distance.

The Sleepover Club

And then I went back to the marquee, to do some SERIOUS bopping with the others!

CHAPTER ELEVEN

Phew! That's the big water splash out of the way. Now you can really relax and enjoy the rest of the ride. We're almost home and dry!

There's just a few (very tiny) surprises to go...

Hope you've forgiven me for having that tiny freak-out back there? I mean, how many girls have to cope with getting an official new dad AND find out they're getting two new babies in the family, all on the same day? Not many, is my guess!

It's funny – my mates and I generally think of sleepovers as like, the MAJOR exciting event of our school week or whatever. But after all the excitement of the wedding (AND some!) our actual wedding sleepover felt almost, well – RESTFUL.

Like Lyndz said, you'd think that after stuffing ourselves with all that gorgeous wedding food, we'd be totally full to bursting, wouldn't you? But luckily, by the time everyone had stopped watching videos, we were all feeling nicely peckish again! Which was just as well, because when we finally went up to bed, it turned out everyone had brought LOADS of goodies.

In honour of our special guest, we'd decided to give the sleepover feast an American theme! After Jilly and Patsy had been in to say goodnight, we waited till they'd gone back downstairs, then we turned on our torches and shared out our American loot.

Want to know what we had?

We had real American jelly beans – both kinds. The sweet kind and the really sour ones which make your eyes water. They actually make Lyndz shudder all over, but she says they're so delicious that it's worth it!

We also had some real melt-in-your-mouth chocolate brownies. Good old Frankie brought them. She said she just *had* to make it up to me for my horrendous cabbage soup experience! Plus, we had a HUGE family pack of marshmallows. I truly don't understand how something that is basically just a mouthful of fluff can have so many wicked calories, do you? Oh, yes, and we had Oreo cookies. Everyone else raved about them. Personally I didn't think they were that special.

But the Sleepover Club's unanimous favourite were these totally HEAVENLY sweets that Amber provided. They're called Hershey's Chocolate Kisses, would you believe? Kenny joked that it was the first time in her whole life that she'd seen the point of anyone giving you kisses!

Then it was time for everyone to write in their sleepover diaries. Amber didn't own one, obviously, so I said she could write a few lines in mine. This is what she wrote.

When I get back home, I'm going to invite all my friends to a sleepover at my house, first chance I get! I have had the most fabulous time here. Plus I haven't laughed so much since Lauren McGravy slid down our stairs on a tea tray, sneezing nonstop!!

"Tell us what you put!" everyone pleaded.

So Amber read it out to us in her laid-back Hollywood voice (which sounded even better by torchlight, for some reason). And this time I don't think the others even *noticed* her using the word 'fabulous'!

Of course, then Amber had to explain to the others all about her ex-best buddy Lauren, with the famous Disney sneeze. But she didn't seem quite so sad when she told it this time. Then Amber gave my diary back to me, and I wrote this:

This has definitely been the most amazing twenty-four hours of my life.

Not only have I been a bridesmaid, got a new dad, AND found out I'm getting two new baby sisters or brothers (or maybe one of each!), but I also finally found out what I want to do when I grow up. I have decided to be a fashion designer. Andy's mum promised that when I'm older, she'll teach me how to make really stylish clothes, just like she used to do at that posh French fashion house in London.

I read this out to everyone. Then the others read out all these sweet things they'd written, about what a great time they'd had, being bridesmaids. Then we all totally ran out of steam. The wedding sleepover was over!

You'd think I'd have gone to sleep really quickly, wouldn't you, after the day I'd had? But it's like Mum says. Sometimes it's possible to get TOO tired.

I did almost drift off, but then suddenly I spun off into a serious doom spiral.

For the first time, it really hit me that in a few months my lovely quiet life was going to be disrupted by – shock, horror (*durn durn DURN!*) –

TWIN BABIES!!!

Aaaargh!! What if Mum and Andy's twins

turn out to be rude little boys, I panicked – the kind who go on about bottoms all the time and mess up their big sister's things, and track mud across her nice pink carpet?

Honestly, I lay there worrying for HOURS. Until finally I fell asleep, completely worn out.

And guess what? The sleepover angels must have come back on duty or something, because I had the sweetest, funniest dream. (Don't tell the others though, because it's private.)

In my dream, I walked out into our garden. Suddenly I heard all these soft little cooing sounds drifting over our neighbours the Watson-Wades's hedge, so I peered over to see what was going on.

And there, where grumpy old Mr Watson-Wade always plants his garden peas, were two gorgeous newborn babies, nestling inside a giant pea pod. (For some reason this didn't seem at all weird at the time!)

"You can SO totally tell they're twins," I said to myself in the dream. "They're as alike as two peas in a pod."

Then I realised what I'd said, and woke myself up laughing!

And I felt so ridiculously happy that I tried to stay awake a few minutes longer, to enjoy the joke...

Have you noticed how everything's slowing down now? That's because we've almost reached the end of the sleepover wedding rollercoaster trip. But there's one last thing I've got to tell you.

I expect you noticed that those lucky somethings kind of dropped out of the story? Also that wedding present?

You thought I'd forgotten about them! Well, thanks a BUNCH!!

You didn't seriously imagine that a superstitious girl like me could let her parents drive off into the sunset with all those clouds of bad luck hanging over them? No WAY!

So don't go just yet, OK, because it's time to unveil Patsy's mysterious late-night project at last.

Can you believe that Andy's mum actually came up with a way to combine my four lucky somethings in a totally unique wedding present?

Here's how we did it. With help from Patsy and Amber, I stitched Mum a beautiful little evening bag. And by the time it was finished, my mind was totally at rest. This bag didn't just LOOK good, I knew it had good luck built into every stitch.

We made it from a piece of gorgeous blue satin (something blue *and* something new). Then Patsy kindly donated one of her lovely lace handkerchiefs, so we could edge it in antique lace (something old).

OK, OK, so you can't imagine Andy getting too excited about an evening bag. Plus I've got to admit the "something borrowed" gave me a real headache. But then Amber said she'd lend me her smart new pen so I could write a special message for both my parents, to put inside the bag.

But I had a better idea.

I did borrow the pen, but I didn't use it to write a message, so much as a rather unusual gift voucher.

This is what it said:

The Sleepover Club Bridesmaids

This entitles Nikky and Andy Proudlove to one whole year of good behaviour from their children.

With love from
   Fliss and Callum
***

Sleepover Girls on the Ball

by Narinder Dhami

An imprint of HarperCollinsPublishers

CHAPTER ONE

"Well, I think we should do something *really* cool and totally exciting," said Kenny. "Something we've never done before, like hang-gliding. Or parachute jumps. Or mountain-climbing."

We all fell about laughing. That's Kenny for you. She's totally mad. But you know that, don't you? Or maybe you don't! And if you don't, where have you been all this time? Haven't you *heard* of the Sleepover Club?

"There aren't any mountains in Cuddington," I pointed out. Cuddington's the village where we all live. (What do you mean – who are we? Keep reading, and you'll find out!)

"I wouldn't jump out of an aeroplane," Rosie

said with a shudder. She took a drink of Coke, and put the can down on the grass. Kenny winked at me, and quickly dropped something into the open triangle on the top of the can. Rosie and Lyndz didn't notice. "What if your parachute didn't open?"

"*Ker-splatttt*!" Kenny said. "That's what!"

"I don't like heights," Lyndz said. She opened a bag of prawn cocktail crisps and offered it round. "Anyway, I'd rather go riding."

"Oh, you lot are so *boring*!" Kenny moaned. "Look, we've got six whole weeks of holidays, and we've got to decide what we're going to do. Any ideas?"

We all thought for a bit. It was the last day of term, and we were sitting in the playground after lunch. In a few hours, we'd be free for the whole summer.

"We can have lots of sleepovers," Lyndz suggested.

OK, so now you know why we're called the Sleepover Club. Frankie, Kenny, Lyndz, Rosie and Fliss – that's us.

"Yeah, we can talk about the holidays at the sleepover at Fliss's place tonight," I said.

"Where *is* Fliss, anyway?" Kenny asked.

"She said she had some books to return to the school library," I replied. "She should be here in a minute."

"Oh, well, she'll only want to do *girly* things," Kenny said, pulling a gruesome face.

"There's loads of stuff on the school noticeboard," Lyndz said, "all about summer camps and courses. There's things going on at the local library too."

"Maybe we should take a look," Rosie said, having another drink. She tipped up the can to finish it, then frowned. "Hey, there's something in here!"

"What?" Lyndz asked.

Rosie spat it out into her hand. "Urgh!" she yelled in disgust. "It's a fingernail!"

"Is it one of yours?" Kenny asked, keeping a perfectly straight face. Meanwhile, Lyndz and I were in hysterics.

"No, why would I put a fingernail in my can of Coke?" Rosie screeched. Then she took a closer look. "Hang on, this is plastic!"

"Oh, sorry," Kenny said innocently. "Did you want a real one?"

Rosie burst out laughing. "I'm going to kill you, Laura McKenzie!" she said between giggles.

313

"Let's all help," I said. "Get her!"

Kenny gave a yell as Rosie, Lyndz and I piled on top of her.

"No more jokes for the whole summer, Kenny!" I ordered her. "Is that a deal?"

"No way!" Kenny groaned. "If the summer's going to be dead boring, I'm definitely going to carry on playing jokes."

"There must be *something* we can do," I said, as we all rolled off her. "What kind of things were on the noticeboard, Lyndz?"

"There's a Book Week at the library," Lyndz replied. "And a nature trail walk, and a visit to the local museum."

"Cool," Kenny said sarcastically. "I think I'm going to pass out with all the excitement!"

"Anything else?" Rosie asked.

"There's a week's tennis coaching at the local college," Lyndz added.

"Tennis!" Kenny said in disgust. "I hate tennis. It's so *boring*."

We were a bit surprised. There's not many sports Kenny *doesn't* like.

"It's so dull," Kenny moaned. "All they do is hit a ball over a net."

"Well, all footballers do is try to *kick* a ball

into a net!" I pointed out. Kenny's football-mad. But I knew what she meant. I wasn't that keen on tennis either.

"And then it starts to rain, and everyone rushes inside like a bunch of wimps," Kenny went on. "Footballers don't do that."

"Yeah, and what's with those scores?" Rosie said. "I mean, fifteen, thirty, forty. It doesn't make sense."

"Then there's all that love-this and love-that, too," Lyndz chimed in. "And what's that juice bit all about?"

"You mean deuce," Kenny, Rosie and I said together.

"Oh." Lyndz turned pink. "I thought it meant they were thirsty!"

We got the giggles then.

"You know what I hate," Rosie said, when we'd calmed down a bit. "The way all the other TV programmes are taken off when Wimbledon's on."

"Oh, yeah," I agreed. "We don't get to see *Neighbours* for two whole weeks. How mean is that?"

"My mum's mad on tennis," Lyndz said. "She watches it all day, when it's on."

"Mine too," I agreed.

"So does our Tiff," Rosie added.

"So does Molly the Monster," Kenny said gloomily. That's her sister, by the way.

"OK, so none of us like tennis," I said. "Let's forget about it, and decide what we *want* to do."

"I can't wait for next week," said a snooty voice just behind us. "I'm really looking forward to the tennis coaching. Aren't you, Emily?"

We knew who it was, of course. There's only one person in the whole world who's that snotty. Our arch-enemy, Emma Hughes, and her weedy little sidekick, Emily Berryman, also known as the M&Ms – or the Queen and the Goblin.

"And we'll be able to practise at the Green Lawns club," Emily said in her gruff, goblin-like voice. "I'm really glad we've joined."

"Yes, it's one of the best tennis clubs in England, you know," the Queen said. She is *such* a big fat snob. "And don't forget they're having that special gala afternoon next week to celebrate the club being open for fifty years. That'll be fun."

OK, so we were listening. We couldn't help it. It was *so* typical of the M&Ms to go around boasting at the top of their voices.

Emma Hughes spotted us earwigging. She put this face on like she'd just swallowed a whole lemon.

"Haven't you lot got anything better to do than listen to other people's conversations?" she snapped.

"No," Kenny said.

That floored the Queen.

"Well, just mind your own business," she said feebly.

Kenny shrugged. "I might've known those two wimps would be into tennis," she said, loud enough for Emma and Emily to hear.

Emma glared at us. "And I might've known you idiots *wouldn't* be," she retorted.

"What's that supposed to mean?" I asked.

The Queen and the Goblin smirked. "You lot wouldn't be allowed into Green Lawns," Emma Hughes sniffed snootily. "Tennis is a game for *nice* people who've got lots of money."

"Are you saying we're not posh enough for your stupid club?" Kenny was getting quite annoyed now. I glanced at Lyndz and Rosie.

We might just have to sit on her again to stop her jumping on Emma!

"That's right," Emily said gruffly.

The Queen and the Goblin looked very pleased with themselves, because they thought they'd got one over on us. They soon stopped though, when Kenny took a step towards them.

"I wouldn't want to be in any club that you two were members of, anyway!" Kenny snorted. "And tennis is a load of rubbish. You wouldn't catch me playing a daft game like that."

"Yeah, tennis is for wimps like you who are too scared to play proper games," I joined in.

"So don't worry," Rosie added, "we wouldn't be seen dead at your stupid tennis club."

"Now push off and stop bothering us," Lyndz finished up.

"Take no notice of them, Emma," the Goblin muttered as they walked off with their noses in the air. "They're just jealous."

"I know," the Queen agreed. "Wait till you see my two-handed backhand, Emily. It's my best shot." She swung out with an imaginary tennis racket, and hit the Goblin smack on the shoulder.

"Ow!" Emily yowled. Which had us all in fits, of course.

"Those two have got a nerve," Kenny grumbled. She grabbed Lyndz's empty crisp packet, blew it up and then burst it with a loud bang. "Fancy telling us we're not posh enough to join their tennis club."

"Yeah, fancy that!" I grinned.

"Well, now that we're *definitely* not going to play tennis over the summer, what are we going to do?" Rosie asked.

"Here's Fliss," Lyndz said.

Fliss came hurrying across the playground towards us. She was looking pretty pleased with herself.

"Hiya, Flissy." Kenny waved at her. "We're just talking about what we're going to do over the holidays."

"Yeah, have you got any suggestions?" I asked.

"But not too girly," Kenny added.

"We can't think of anything much," Lyndz said.

Fliss grinned at us.

"It's all sorted," she said. "Well, the first week of the holidays is, anyway. It's going to be really excellent!"

We all sat up, looking interested.

"So what are we going to be doing?" Rosie asked eagerly.

Fliss beamed at us. "I've signed us all up for a week's tennis coaching at the local college!"

CHAPTER TWO

We were all too stunned to say anything for a moment. Then Kenny jumped to her feet.

"You've done *what*?" she roared.

"I knew you'd be pleased," Fliss said chirpily. "We get a whole week of coaching, and..." Her voice tailed off as she looked round at us. "What's the matter?"

"We all hate tennis, that's what's the matter!" I pointed out. "Fliss, why didn't you ask us first?"

Fliss turned pink. "I thought you'd be pleased," she mumbled.

"We've just told the M&Ms that we wouldn't be seen dead playing tennis!" Kenny groaned.

"They're going to laugh their heads off if we turn up for those coaching sessions now."

"Fliss, you're going to have to cross our names off that list," Rosie said.

"But I *like* tennis," Fliss said stubbornly. "Come on, it'll be a laugh. And the guy who's doing the coaching is really nice."

"How do you know?" Lyndz asked.

"I – er – just heard that he was," Fliss replied, blushing madly.

I glanced at Rosie, Lyndz and Kenny. They looked about as impressed as I was. None of us wanted to spend one whole week of our precious holiday doing something we didn't like and just weren't interested in. Then, all of a sudden, I remembered something.

"Hold on a minute, Fliss," I said slowly. "Has this got something to do with your Auntie Jill?"

"No," Fliss said, trying not to look guilty. "Why?"

"Because I remember you saying that your Auntie Jill was going out with a tennis coach." I stared hard at Fliss, and she began to fidget. She was always *hopeless* at telling fibs!

"Oh, all right." Fliss gave in. "Auntie Jill's boyfriend, Mark, is the one who's running the course. And she asked me to get as many people signed up as I could."

"Oh, great," Kenny grumbled. "Why does it have to be *us*?"

"Look, it's only for a week," Fliss pleaded. "And you like my Auntie Jill, don't you? She'd be really grateful."

That kind of made it difficult for us. We *did* like Fliss's Auntie Jill. She was our Snowy Owl at Brownies, and she was a great laugh.

"If you all come, I'll do whatever you want for the rest of the summer," Fliss promised.

"What, anything?" Kenny said with an evil grin.

"Anything," Fliss said bravely.

"OK, I'm in," Kenny sighed, rolling her eyes. "I must be crazy."

Rosie and Lyndz nodded. So did I.

"Oh, great!" Fliss gasped. She was really pleased, but the rest of us looked like we'd agreed to spend a week at the dentist having our teeth pulled out one by one.

Still, it was only for a week. It couldn't be that bad.

Could it?

*   *   *

"Tennis?"

My mum stared at me as if I'd said we planned to spend a week of the summer holidays learning Chinese. "You girls are going to play *tennis*?"

I nodded. "What's so strange about that?"

"Well, for one thing, you moan like mad every time I watch Wimbledon," my mum pointed out, bouncing my baby sister Izzy on her hip. "You said you hated tennis."

"Long story, Mum." I picked up my sleepover bag. School had finished – at last! – and I was in my bedroom, packing for the sleepover at Fliss's. "Anyway, that's what we're doing."

"Oh, well, I suppose it'll keep you out of trouble," my mum said. Then she shook her head. "Why on earth did I say that? *Nothing* keeps you girls out of trouble."

"Thanks a lot, Mum," I grumbled, stuffing my purple pyjamas into my bag. "We're only going to be messing around with rackets and tennis balls, you know. What could *possibly* go wrong?"

"Quite a lot, with Kenny around," my mum replied.

The doorbell rang.

"That'll be Rosie," I said, grabbing my bag. Rosie's mum had arranged to pick us all up and take us round to Fliss's. "'Bye, Mum, 'bye, Izzy."

Rosie was waiting for me on the doorstep, and Kenny and Lyndz were in the car with Mrs Cartwright. I squeezed into the back seat next to them.

"So you're all going to be playing tennis next week," Mrs Cartwright remarked, as she drove off. Like my mum, she seemed to think that this was somehow really funny. Parents! You wouldn't have them if they were being given away, would you? "I hope you're going to behave yourselves."

"Mum!" Rosie muttered, looking embarrassed.

"'Course we will, Mrs Cartwright," Kenny said in that voice which meant she was up to something. I glanced sideways at her. She winked at me.

"Tell you later," she hissed.

Mrs Cartwright dropped us off at Fliss's house, and we all trooped up to the front door.

"Flissy really owes us one for this," Kenny grumbled, ringing the doorbell and keeping her finger on it. "I can't believe what she's got us into."

"It might be OK," Lyndz said hopefully.

"Maybe we could all pretend to injure ourselves on the first day," Rosie suggested. "Fliss couldn't expect us to play if we were in agony."

"Want to bet?" Kenny muttered. "Anyway, don't you think it might look a bit obvious if we *all* sprain our ankles? Oh come on, Fliss!" she added, leaning extra hard on the doorbell.

Fliss opened the door with her hands over her ears.

"Kenny, what're you doing!" she said crossly.

We stared at her. Fliss was wearing a short white dress, and I mean *short*. Fliss loves miniskirts, but this was ridiculous. It was right up round the tops of her legs.

"Aren't you a bit cold?" Kenny asked, as we all went inside.

"This is my new tennis dress." Fliss did a twirl in the hallway. "Do you like it?"

"It's a bit short," Lyndz said.

"Yeah, we can see your knickers," Kenny added.

"You're supposed to see them," Fliss snapped.

"Why?" Rosie asked.

"Well, because tennis dresses are always short," Fliss said feebly.

"Why?" Lyndz wanted to know.

Fliss looked blank.

"So you can run around in them easily, I suppose," I suggested.

"Yeah, that's right," Fliss agreed quickly. "Come on, I've got some really great ideas for the sleepover tonight."

We all looked interested.

"I thought we'd have a tennis sleepover," Fliss said eagerly. "We can play tennis in the garden, and Mum's got some strawberries and cream for tea just like they have at Wimbledon. Oh, and I've got some tennis videos we can watch afterwards."

"You're kidding!" Kenny began indignantly, "That sounds like a load of— OW!"

I took my foot off her big toe.

"That sounds great, Fliss," I said.

"Yeah, great," said Rosie and Lyndz glumly.

Fliss looked pleased. "Come on, let's go into the back garden," she said.

We followed her into the kitchen. Fliss's mum and her mum's sister, Auntie Jill, were sitting at the breakfast bar, having coffee.

"Oh, hello, girls." Auntie Jill grinned at us. "I hear you're going to Mark's coaching sessions next week."

We nodded.

"I didn't know you girls were interested in tennis," Mrs Proudlove said, taking a sip of coffee.

We all started shuffling our feet and looking a bit sheepish.

"Come on," Fliss said hastily. "Let's go outside."

"Jill and I had a game today," Mrs Proudlove went on. "It was pretty close, wasn't it, Jill? I won, though!"

"That was a great overhead lob you pulled off at match point," Auntie Jill said. "It had a lot of topspin on it."

"And what about that forehand drive you won the second game with?" Fliss's mum added. "The way you smashed that down the line was brilliant."

I glanced at Kenny, who rolled her eyes at me. Mrs Proudlove and Auntie Jill might as well have been talking Greek for all we could understand! Were we the only people in the world who weren't tennis-mad?

"Oh, Mum, have you heard anything from the Green Lawns Tennis Club yet?" Fliss asked, as she opened the back door.

Kenny nudged me. That was the same club the M&Ms belonged to.

Mrs Proudlove shook her head. "Not yet," she said. "Your auntie and I played on the tennis courts in the park today. We're still waiting to hear if we can join the club."

"Well, Mark's put in a good word for us," Auntie Jill said. She turned to us and added, "Mark works at Green Lawns. It's one of the best tennis clubs in the country, you know."

"You didn't tell us your mum and Auntie Jill wanted to join that snooty club," Kenny accused Fliss, as we went outside.

"It's not snooty," Fliss said indignantly.

"Well, the M&Ms go there, so it must be," I pointed out.

Fliss pouted. "I don't care," she said. "If Mum and Auntie Jill get in, they can take guests, so I'll be able to play there too."

"Do you reckon Fliss is really keen on tennis?" Kenny whispered in my ear.

"I reckon she just likes the short skirts!" I whispered back.

Fliss was bustling about giving out rackets and tennis balls.

"I've got my own racket," she said importantly, waving it in the air. "You can have this one, Rosie."

Rosie stared at the racket she'd just been given. It was about a hundred years old, and half the strings were broken.

"Sorry," Fliss said. "It's my mum's old one."

"Can't I borrow her new one?" Rosie asked.

Fliss shook her head. "It cost loads of money. She said I could only borrow it over her dead body."

"What about the rest of us?" Kenny asked.

"I've only got two rackets," Fliss said apologetically. "We'll have to take it in turns."

Kenny didn't look very impressed.

"Can't we play something else?" she grumbled.

"We're playing *tennis*." Fliss glared at Kenny. "Now go and sit down. You lot can watch while me and Rosie go first."

"Big deal," Kenny moaned under her breath, as we all sat down on the grass. "This is so boring!"

"Ssh!" I nudged her. "It's Fliss's sleepover, and you know what she's like."

Kenny yawned. "If I die from boredom, you can have my pet rat!"

"Thanks a lot," I said, as Fliss threw the ball into the air, and hit it towards Rosie.

Rosie stepped forward, looking a bit nervous. I thought she'd miss the ball, but she didn't. She gave it a THWACK. At least, she tried to. When the ball hit her racket, there was a snapping sound as it smashed through the dodgy strings, and out the other side. We all watched open-mouthed as the ball sailed over the fence, and into the Watson-Wades' garden next door. Then there was a SPLASH as it fell into their pond.

We all started to laugh our heads off, except Fliss, who turned pale. The Watson-Wades don't like us, and we don't like them either. We call them the Grumpies.

"Quick, into the house!" she hissed, and we all dashed inside. Kenny could hardly walk, she was laughing so much.

"No more tennis!" she whispered gleefully in my ear. "Maybe we can do something more exciting now instead."

"OK, let's watch some of my tennis videos," Fliss said. She was on her knees in front of the TV, sorting through them.

I thought Kenny was going to kill her, but luckily Mrs Proudlove called to say tea was ready.

Tea was pretty boring, too. The food was OK, but Mrs Proudlove, Auntie Jill and Fliss just went on about tennis for the whole meal. They were talking about forehands and backhands and lobs and volleys until our heads were spinning like tennis balls!

We couldn't escape from tennis after tea, either. Fliss put one of her videos on, and we sat and watched them until we went to bed. Kenny fell asleep and started snoring, which really annoyed Fliss.

"That has to be the most mega-boring sleepover of all time," Kenny moaned under her breath, as we trailed upstairs to Fliss's bedroom at the end of the evening.

"Last one in the bathroom is useless at tennis!" Fliss yelled, grabbing her pink pyjamas. She dashed off down the landing, while the rest of us looked gloomily at each other.

"I don't care about being last," Rosie said.

"Me neither," Kenny added. And she's usually the one who pushes us all out of the way!

Lyndz looked round at us. "Maybe we *could* get to like tennis," she suggested.

Kenny chucked a pillow at her.

"No, really," Lyndz went on. "Anyway, even if we don't like it, we can still have a laugh at the coaching sessions. We've got to go to them now, so there's no point in moaning about it."

Kenny grinned an evil grin. "Yeah, Lyndz is right," she said. "Remember I said I'd got something to tell you, Frankie?"

I nodded.

"Well, the M&Ms are going to the tennis coaching too, aren't they?" Kenny went on. "And they take tennis ever so seriously. That means…"

"A chance to play a whole load of jokes on them," I finished up.

Kenny rubbed her hands together with glee. "Yep! Tennis might be boring, but the Sleepover Club will soon liven it up!"

CHAPTER THREE

"I'm sure you're going to have a great time, girls," Auntie Jill said, as she turned into the college driveway. "Mark's a fantastic coach. He'll soon have you all playing like professionals!"

It was the first day of our week of tennis coaching at the local college. Auntie Jill had borrowed the Proudloves' people carrier, and had arranged to drive us to the college.

"So that none of us can make a break for it and escape!" Kenny had moaned to me. Still, we *had* all decided that we would make the best of things, and it *was* only for a week.

Kenny nudged me as we drove through the

334

college grounds, then drew up outside the tennis courts.

"Hey, everyone," she said with a grin. "Don't look now, or you might bring up your breakfast!"

We all looked out of the window. Not many people had arrived yet, but guess who was there already, swanning round the tennis courts as if they owned them? The Queen and the Goblin, of course. Emma Hughes was wearing a white lacy tennis dress which was shorter than Fliss's, if that was possible! And Emily Berryman was wearing this really tight pair of white shorts that looked truly gruesome.

"They really think they're something, don't they?" Kenny said scornfully, as we climbed out of the people carrier. "I'm looking forward to annoying them!"

The M&Ms were carrying rackets that looked really posh. I don't know anything about tennis rackets, but these were definitely pretty flash. None of us had our own racket except Fliss, and we were all wearing different sorts of clothes. Fliss had her white tennis dress on (of course!), and Rosie, Lyndz and I were wearing trackie bottoms and T-shirts in various colours. Kenny had decided to put her Leicester City football strip on, for some reason.

Just then the M&Ms spotted us walking towards the tennis courts. The Queen's eyes almost fell out of her head, and she and the Goblin started nudging each other. They had these big fat smirks on their faces too.

"I'll go and see if I can find Mark," Auntie Jill said, and headed off towards the changing-rooms.

"Funny," the Queen said in this really loud, incredibly smug voice that we were obviously meant to hear. "I thought tennis was for *wimps*."

"Yeah, for people who are too *scared* to play proper games," the Goblin chimed in gruffly. Then they both laughed their heads off as if they'd just said something really funny.

"It is," Kenny retorted breezily. "We're just here to help Mark out."

The Queen and the Goblin stopped laughing.

"Mark?" Emma Hughes spluttered. "You don't know Mark!"

"We do, though," Berryman added. "He's one of the coaches at Green Lawns."

"Yes, well, he goes out with my Auntie Jill," Fliss said, looking pretty smug herself.

The M&Ms glared at her in disbelief – and right at that moment Auntie Jill came out of the changing-rooms with this hunky guy behind her. He looked a bit like Robbie Williams, and he was *gorgeous*!

"Hi, Fliss," he said with a smile. "And these must be your friends. Nice to see you all." He looked at the M&Ms. "Hi, I'm Mark, the tennis coach. And you are?"

The Queen looked a bit annoyed.

"Emma Hughes and Emily Berryman," she reminded him. "We go to Green Lawns."

"Oh, yes, sorry," Mark said. "I'd forgotten."

We all tried not to snigger.

"I'll see you later," Auntie Jill said, and then she left. Meanwhile, Mark took a list from his pocket and ticked our names off.

"I'll just go and check the others off my list," he said. "And then we'll get started."

More and more people were arriving, including Ryan Scott and Danny McCloud, two real idiots who're in our class. Fliss started blushing, and fluttering her eyelashes, though. She's totally in love with Ryan, but she tries to pretend she isn't!

The Queen and the Goblin trotted after

Mark, being real creeps and asking lots of questions. Kenny pulled a face at them, and flopped down on a nearby bench.

"Those two are going to drive me bananas!" she groaned. "Hello, what's this?"

There were two big *Nike* sports bags, by the side of the bench.

"Those are the Queen's and the Goblin's," Rosie said. "I've seen them at school."

"Oh, really," Kenny said with an evil smile. She bounced off the bench, and bent over one of the bags.

"Kenny, what are you doing?" Fliss hissed, in a total panic. "You can't open their bags. If Mark sees us, we're dead!"

"Relax, Flissy," Kenny said. "I wouldn't dream of opening someone else's bag."

Fliss looked relieved. "Oh, good."

"This one's already open," Kenny went on. "Look, it's the Queen's." She pointed at the name written on the handle, then she put her hand into the bag and pulled out a pair of expensive-looking trainers. "Phew, these really stink!"

"Trust the Queen and the Goblin to have special trainers for tennis," I said.

Fliss turned pink. "Actually," she said, clearing her throat, "so do I!"

"Quick," Kenny said urgently. "Stand a bit closer so that no one can see me for a minute."

We all gathered round Kenny and hid her from view. By the time Mark and the others, including the M&Ms, came over, we were all sitting innocently on the bench, and the trainers were back in the Queen's bag.

"Right, welcome to our summer tennis school," Mark said briskly. "A week isn't really very long, but hopefully I'll be able to give you some good advice to improve your game. And if you're a beginner, well, maybe you'll find out if you're any good or not. And maybe you'll find you like tennis a lot more than you thought you would!"

Kenny rolled her eyes at the rest of us. "No chance!" she whispered.

"Now, if you could just divide yourselves into groups of four," Mark went on, "we'll start off with a bit of a knock-up, and I'll come round and see how you're all getting on."

Everyone moved off in groups, and began to spread out around the courts.

"What about us?" Lyndz asked anxiously. "There's five of us."

"It's OK," I said, doing a quick headcount. "There's seventeen people here, so there'll have to be one group of five."

"Come on, Emily." The Queen pushed rudely past us with her nose in the air. "Let's change into our other trainers."

"Here we go!" Kenny whispered with a big grin.

"Oh no." The Queen's face dropped as she pulled her trainers out of her bag. "They're all knotted up!"

We turned our backs, trying not to laugh. Kenny had tied the laces together with about a million knots!

"It's going to take you ages to undo them," the Goblin grumbled.

We left them to it, grabbed some rackets and balls and ran off to bag a court. We were right next to Ryan Scott and Danny McCloud, who were already belting balls around as if they were playing cricket.

"You're supposed to keep it inside the white lines," Rosie shouted at them, as Ryan whacked yet another ball way over Danny's head. Then we all jumped smartly out of the way as Danny mis-hit the next one, and it came thundering towards us.

"Trust us to be next to those two," Kenny grumbled, as we split up into two teams. Rosie and Fliss were on one side of the net, and Kenny, Lyndz and I were on the other. "They're going to do us an injury at this rate!"

Fliss threw a ball into the air, served and smacked it down to Kenny. I don't think Kenny was expecting Fliss to hit it quite so hard. She stuck out her racket, and the ball bounced off the frame instead of the strings. It flew off to the side at an angle, and almost took Danny McCloud's ear off.

"Hey!" Danny shouted indignantly. "Trust us to get landed next to those mad girls," we heard him say to Ryan.

Fliss changed sides, and served to Lyndz this time. She hit the ball hard again, and Lyndz gave a little yelp and jumped right out of the way. She didn't even try to hit it.

"Lyndz, you do know what tennis is all about, don't you?" I said. "You have to try and return the ball."

"I know," Lyndz said gloomily, "But that was scary! Fliss hit the ball too hard."

"Fliss is just showing off," Kenny said to me and Lyndz in a low voice. "Let us serve this time," she called across the net to the others. "Go on, Frankie."

"OK," I agreed. I'd never done it before, but if Fliss could do it, how hard could it be?

I threw the ball up into the air, and then raised my arm above my head to smash it.

"Hey, was that an ace?" I yelled proudly, as Fliss and Rosie stood staring at me. "The ball moved so fast, I didn't even see it."

"Frankie, I think there's something you should know," Kenny said, pointing at my feet. I looked down. There was the ball.

"You missed it," Lyndz said helpfully.

I blushed. I grabbed the ball, bounced it on the ground and just knocked it over the net. Rosie raced towards it, elbowing Fliss out of the way, and hit the ball with all her might. It soared right over the high fence that surrounded the tennis courts, and bounced into some bushes.

"Hey, you're supposed to keep the ball *inside* the courts!" Ryan Scott shouted, and he and Danny laughed themselves silly.

"Come on," Kenny said impatiently, "I'm getting bored with this. I want to try out my trick shots."

"What trick shots?" Fliss asked suspiciously, as Rosie tapped another ball over the net to Kenny. It was a lot lower and slower this time. Kenny immediately ran round the ball so that she had her back to the net. Then she scooped it up and flipped it over her head. It dropped gently over the net, and then rolled away from Fliss, who was running towards it.

"Kenny, that's not a proper shot!" Fliss said disapprovingly.

"What a load of rubbish," the Queen sniffed. She and the Goblin had come over, and had stopped to watch what we were doing. "Some people will *never* be good at tennis."

"We've got to play with you," Emily Berryman said to Ryan and Danny. "There aren't any more courts left."

We saw Ryan and Danny pull faces at each other.

"OK, but don't try to boss us around," Ryan said shortly.

The Queen and the Goblin started playing against each other, on the side of the court closest to us. Kenny was still messing around and having a go at all sorts of tricks, like trying to catch the ball on her racket instead of hitting it back, and trying to hit the ball between her legs. It was driving Fliss crazy.

Anyway, I couldn't help watching the M&Ms. To my surprise, they were pretty good. They aren't exactly sporty types, but they looked all right at tennis. The other thing that surprised me was that Fliss was good too. Whenever she managed to get the ball, she always did something I was *sure* I wouldn't be able to do myself.

While Rosie and Fliss were collecting up the balls we'd hit all over the place, I nudged Kenny. "Have you seen the M&Ms? They're not bad at this."

"What?" Kenny's eyes almost popped out of her head. She watched the Queen and the Goblin for a few moments, and then nodded reluctantly. "Yeah, I suppose they're OK. Sick-making, isn't it?"

"Fliss is good too, isn't she?" Lyndz added.

"Hmm." Kenny was frowning. I knew exactly what was going through her mind. "Come on, let's start practising. We don't want the M&Ms getting one over on us."

"But I thought we were here to have a laugh?" Lyndz said.

"Never mind that," Kenny ordered us. "We'd better start taking this a bit more seriously."

Just then Mark came over to us. He'd been walking round the courts, watching everyone and talking to them, and now it was our turn.

"Over here, girls," he said, beckoning us over to the net. "How are you getting on?"

"Fine," Fliss mumbled, glaring at Kenny. I felt a bit sorry for her. She was way better than the rest of us, and she was fed up with Kenny and the rest of us messing around when she wanted to have a proper game.

"Good." Mark nodded. "Now, I've been watching you for the last few minutes, and I think you've got the makings of a very good forehand drive there, Kenny."

Kenny looked amazed. "R-really?" she stuttered.

Mark grinned. "Yes, but I don't think the trick shots are helping, so cut them out, OK? And Frankie – we'll be working on our serves later, so don't worry about that."

345

I turned red.

"Carry on knocking up for another few minutes," Mark said, glancing at his watch. "And then we'll all get together for some practice shots."

"Come on, you lot," Kenny shouted, herding us back on to the court. "And *concentrate* this time!"

Fliss looked smug. "See?" she said. "I told you you'd enjoy it!"

And we *were* starting to enjoy it. Once we stopped messing about, and began trying harder, we got better. Fliss showed us some of her shots, and we tried to copy her. We weren't very good, but at least we were better than before. She also showed us how to serve, and this time I actually managed to hit the ball!

Then Mark called us all together, and began talking to us about different types of shots.

"We're going to start with a simple forehand," he said, and then he told us how important it was to hold the racket properly, and have the right grip. We all had to practise holding our rackets, and swinging them at an imaginary ball. There was so much to remember, I couldn't take it all in. It wasn't just about how you hit the ball

– you also had to follow through properly, and end up with the racket in a certain place *after* you'd hit the ball. Confused? I was!

"Right, line up behind the net," Mark called. "I want you to step forward one by one, and hit the ball back to me with your forehand. Remember what we've just been talking about, and try to follow through correctly. Fliss, you first."

Mark hit the ball over the net to Fliss, and she hit it back. It looked pretty good to me. Then Kenny stepped up.

"Just watch her make a mess of this!" we heard the Queen whisper to the Goblin.

Kenny didn't say anything. She whacked the ball, and it whizzed neatly just over the net and bounced into one corner of the court.

"Excellent, Kenny!" Mark called, and the Queen and the Goblin turned red with rage.

Lyndz, Rosie and I didn't do too badly either. Lyndz's effort was a bit feeble and only just made it over the net, but Rosie and I hit ours pretty hard, even though Rosie's was a bit high. We had another couple of goes, and then Mark came over to speak to us again.

"Right, I want you to go back on to the courts and practise those forehands," he said. "Oh, and before you go, I want to tell you all about the tournament we'll be having at the end of the week."

Tournament? We looked at each other. That sounded interesting.

"We'll be finishing the summer school with a doubles tennis tournament," Mark went on. "So you'll need to get into pairs, and let me know who you'll be playing with. Now off you go."

The Queen and the Goblin were looking smugly at each other.

"I reckon we've got a great chance of winning that, Emily," the Queen said gleefully. "There's no one here who's as good as we are."

"We'll walk it!" the Goblin chortled. "Especially as we'll be able to practise at Green Lawns every afternoon."

Kenny turned to the rest of us, as the M&Ms went off, grinning from ear to ear. "Did you hear that?" she said urgently. "We can't let them win!"

"We'd better start practising then," Rosie said. "Because at the moment, Fliss is the only one of us who's any good."

"Hang on a minute," I cut in. "We've got another problem to sort out first."

"What's that?" Fliss asked.

"It's a *doubles* tournament, and we need to get into pairs," I pointed out. "Do the maths. There's *five* of us…"

CHAPTER FOUR

Everyone's faces dropped.

"Maybe one of us could play with someone else," Lyndz said hopefully.

I shook my head. "No, remember I said that there were seventeen of us? That means one person's always going to be left over."

"And it looks like that's going to be one of us," Kenny said gloomily, "because everyone else is already in twos."

"What are we going to do?" Fliss asked.

"I'll drop out," Lyndz offered bravely. "I'm rubbish anyway."

"You're no worse than me," Rosie argued.

"Or me," I said.

"We could spin for it," Fliss suggested, twirling her tennis racket on the ground to show us what she meant. "That's the fairest way to choose the lucky four."

We all nodded. So we gathered round in a circle, and Fliss spun her racket. It came to a stop, pointing at Lyndz.

"OK, Lyndz, you're in," said Kenny. "And now for your partner."

The next spin left the racket pointing at Rosie.

"You two are a team then," said Fliss. She looked really envious. I was pretty jealous too because I really wanted to play. Once we'd stopped messing about and started playing properly, I was surprised by how much I'd enjoyed myself.

"Lyndz, you spin it now," Kenny said. "And then it'll be fair."

Lyndz spun the racket, and it ended up pointing at Fliss. Fliss tried not to look too pleased.

"So it's between me and Frankie," Kenny said.

My heart was pounding as Lyndz spun the racket again. It stopped really slowly, and pointed straight at...

Kenny.

"Sorry, Frankie," said Fliss and Rosie together.

"Poor old Frankie," said Lyndz sympathetically.

"Yeah, bad luck, Frankie." Kenny thumped me on the back.

"It's cool," I said, trying not to sound like I minded too much. "You're a better player than me, anyway."

"Come on, girls." Mark was calling and waving at us from another court. "You should be practising your forehands."

We spread out across our court, and began knocking the ball to each other. I didn't feel much like playing any more, but I didn't want to let the others down. After all, they had to practise if they were going to beat the M&Ms.

Fliss hit a forehand drive towards Kenny, who ran forward to return it. At just that moment, Emily Berryman came charging on to our court, chasing a stray ball. Kenny bashed straight into her, and knocked the Goblin flying.

"Help!" Emily shrieked, as she fell backwards on to her bottom. "You did that on purpose, Laura McKenzie!"

"No, I didn't," Kenny retorted. "*You* got in *my* way."

The Queen came stomping over to stick her nose in, as usual.

"You're just trying to make sure we don't win the tournament," she snapped, hauling the Goblin to her feet. "You tried to injure Emily by pushing her over!"

"Oh, go stuff a tennis ball in your mouth!" Kenny replied. "On second thoughts, try two tennis balls – your mouth's big enough."

"You won't be laughing when we win that tournament," the Queen said threateningly, and she stalked off, dragging the Goblin behind her.

"The trouble is, they *could* win it," Kenny muttered. "They're good."

"And did you hear Emily say that they were going to practise every afternoon at that posh tennis club?" Rosie said gloomily.

"Well, we can practise too," I pointed out. "We don't need a posh club. We've all got gardens. Or we could go to the park."

The others cheered up a bit. Although I wasn't going to be playing in the tournament, I reckoned it was going to be a full-time job keeping the others from getting too depressed!

353

We went back to practising our forehands, and then Mark called us all together again. This time he showed us how to serve properly. And guess what? Surprise, surprise (and nobody was more surprised than ME), I turned out to be quite good at it. I banged down quite a few good serves, and everyone (except the M&Ms) looked pretty impressed.

"Frankie, maybe you *should* be playing in the tournament," Lyndz said, when we'd been sent off to practise on our own again. "I don't mind dropping out."

I shook my head. "Nope, you were all chosen fair and square."

"I don't think me and Lyndz have got much of a hope," Rosie said. "I'm rubbish."

"No, I'm worse than you," Lyndz argued.

"No, *I'm* the worst player."

"No, I am."

"Shut up, you two," Kenny said, giving them both a shove.

"Kenny and Fliss are in with a good chance," I said. "Fliss is brilliant."

Fliss turned pink with pleasure.

"What about me?" Kenny demanded.

"You'll be all right, as long as you don't fool around," Fliss said sternly.

"Me? Fool around?" Kenny snorted. "Do I ever?"

"Yes!" we all shouted, and pelted her with tennis balls.

About ten minutes later, Mark announced that it was the end of the coaching session for today. None of us wanted to go home though – we could have stayed there and played all day long!

"There's my mum and Auntie Jill," Fliss said, as we put the tennis balls in the boxes.

"Hurry up, Emily," called the Queen in a loud voice which just about everyone could hear. "My mum will be here soon to take us over to Green Lawns."

"They're really getting on my nerves, going on about that tennis club," Kenny muttered. She did a double-take in the direction of Mrs Proudlove. "Hey, what's the matter with your mum and Auntie Jill, Fliss? They look like they've won the lottery!"

Mrs Proudlove and Auntie Jill were hurrying towards the tennis courts, looking really excited. We went to meet them. So did Mark.

"We're in!" Mrs Proudlove announced. She was waving a small piece of card in the air. "We just heard this morning."

"In what?" Kenny asked, looking puzzled.

"The Green Lawns Tennis Club," Auntie Jill said triumphantly, showing us her membership card. She flung her arms around Mark and gave him a hug. "Thanks for putting in a good word for us."

"That's great," Mark said.

"Excellent!" Fliss beamed. "I'll be able to practise there too, for the tournament."

"Are you ready, girls?" Mrs Proudlove called. "Jill and I want to go to the tennis club this afternoon, and I have to take you all home first."

Kenny nudged me. "What do you reckon?" she whispered in my ear.

I blinked at her. "What're you talking about?"

Kenny grinned at the rest of us. "How annoyed do you think the M&Ms would be if the whole of the Sleepover Club turned up at their posh tennis club this afternoon?"

"They'd go totally mad," I said. "But it's not very likely to happen, is it?"

"We're not members," Rosie pointed out, looking puzzled. "They only let members in."

"*We're* not members." Kenny winked at us. "But Fliss's mum and Auntie Jill are – and you heard what Fliss said before. They can take guests!"

Fliss turned a sickly shade of white, while Rosie, Lyndz and I burst out laughing.

"Do you really think my mum is going to let us all go to the club with her this afternoon?" Fliss spluttered. "Dream on, Kenny!"

Kenny grinned. "Why not? We can ask her, can't we?"

"You can ask her, but she won't say yes!" I replied. "Not in a million years."

The M&Ms were sitting on the bench near us, changing their shoes. Now they got up, and picked up their bags.

"Come on, Emily," said the Queen, shooting us a poisonous sideways glare. "Let's go. At least we'll be able to have a *proper* game at Green Lawns without stupid people mucking about."

Kenny gave them a cheery wave. "We'll see you there!" she called.

The Queen's mouth fell open as she goggled at us.

"*What* did you say?" she roared.

"We're coming to the tennis club this afternoon," Kenny retorted coolly. "We're going to be there regularly from now on."

Emma Hughes couldn't think of a single thing to say. She turned bright red with rage and stomped off, with Emily scurrying along behind her.

"Oh, Kenny, what've you done?" Fliss moaned, looking terrified. "I am *not* asking my mum if she'll take us to the tennis club!"

"Calm down, Flissy," Kenny said breezily. "I'll ask her myself."

CHAPTER FIVE

"Oh, no," said Fliss's mum, folding her arms. "I don't think that's a good idea at all."

"Why not?" Kenny said, trying to look all innocent. "We wouldn't be any trouble."

Mrs Proudlove looked even more doubtful. "Yes, well…" she said. "I've heard *that* before."

"Oh, go on," Kenny nagged her. "We'd only sit and watch. We wouldn't *do* anything."

"And maybe we could learn something by watching you and Auntie Jill," I added. "Then we could get better at tennis ourselves." OK, so I was doing some serious sucking-up here. But if we didn't turn up at the club now, after

359

everything Kenny had said to the M&Ms, we'd look like prize prats.

"Oh, that would be great," Rosie said, joining in to help me out. "I'm so rubbish at tennis. I bet I'd be loads better if I could watch someone *really* good."

"Me too," Lyndz added.

"And you and Auntie Jill are brilliant at tennis," Fliss finished up.

"Well, I don't know about that." But Fliss's mum looked pleased. She turned to Auntie Jill. "What do you think?"

"Oh, let them come," said Auntie Jill with a smile. "There's two of us to keep an eye on them, after all. And they can't get up to much, if they're just sitting watching us play."

"Well, all right then," Mrs Proudlove said, and we all cheered. "But I'm warning you," she went on sternly, "I don't want *any* messing around." She stared hard at us. "We've waited a long time to get into this club, and we don't want anything going wrong. Is that clear?"

We all nodded.

"I'll see you there later," Mark said, kissing Auntie Jill on the cheek. "'Bye, girls."

"Yes!" Kenny said triumphantly, as we hurried over to the Proudloves' people carrier. "I knew we could swing it!"

"You heard what Mum said, Kenny," Fliss reminded her. "If we get into any trouble, I'm dead – and so are the rest of you."

"We'll all be really good," I said. "Won't we, Kenny?"

"Yep, cross my heart and hope to die," Kenny said loudly. "Unless the M&Ms annoy me, of course," she added under her breath.

Mrs Proudlove drove us all home, and dropped us off one by one, after she'd arranged to pick us up in an hour or two.

"Mum!" I dashed into the house, yelling my head off. "Mum, is lunch ready? And is it OK if I go out this afternoon? Fliss's mum is taking us to her tennis club."

My mum was working in the study, with Izzy in the playpen next to her. She looked up from the computer and stared at me.

"A tennis club? I thought you hated tennis, and you were only going to the coaching sessions because Fliss forced you into it?"

"Oh, Mum, you're *so* out of date!" I groaned. "Tennis is *cool*."

361

Fliss's mum turned up again bang on two o'clock to pick me up. She'd already collected the others, so I dived into the back of the people carrier to join them.

"I was just saying," Mrs Proudlove remarked, as she pulled away from the kerb, "that I expect you all to be on your best behaviour, and not to show me up."

"This is worse than going on a school trip!" Kenny whispered in my ear. "We've been getting the big lecture for the last five minutes."

Auntie Jill, who was in the front seat, turned round and winked at us. "I'm sure they'll be fine," she said.

The Green Lawns Tennis Club was just outside Cuddington, in the countryside. I'd been past it and seen the big iron gates loads of times, but I'd never been in before. There was a large car park at the front, and large, brightly-coloured flowerbeds.

"Right, you can get out," said Mrs Proudlove, switching off the engine. "But stay together where I can keep an eye on you."

"Does she want us to hold hands like five-year-olds?" Kenny grumbled.

We went over to the entrance. Fliss's mum insisted on walking in front, and she kept looking round at us nervously, as if she thought we were already up to something. There was a turnstile next to a little green-roofed hut, and a man with a big moustache and grey hair was sitting inside the hut, reading a newspaper. He glared suspiciously at us.

"Members only," he snapped. "Membership cards?"

"Oh, yes, of course," said Mrs Proudlove. She and Auntie Jill held theirs out, and the man took them. "And these girls are our guests," she added.

The man looked down his nose at us as if we were a bad smell.

"Nobody's allowed to play on our courts unless they're wearing white," he said, giving Kenny's football strip a disgusted glance.

"They're not playing," Fliss's mum said quickly. "Just watching."

The man didn't want to let us into the club at all. He handed the membership cards back really slowly, after he'd spent ages looking at them, and then he operated the turnstile, grumbling all the time to himself.

363

"He's a real misery-guts, isn't he?" Kenny said, as we went through. "I've seen more cheerful people at funerals!"

"Hey, this is pretty cool," I said, looking around.

The tennis club was really big. There were lots of courts, and quite a few people were playing on them. There were landscaped gardens around the courts, filled with flowers, and there was a fountain too, of a boy riding on a dolphin. In the middle of it all was a big clubhouse, next to a posh-looking restaurant with tables set outside on a patio. We were all pretty impressed.

Rosie pointed at a poster pinned to the clubhouse door. "Look at that. That's what the M&Ms were going on about last week."

**COME AND CELEBRATE 50 YEARS OF
THE GREEN LAWNS TENNIS CLUB!**

A SPECIAL GALA AFTERNOON ON JULY 29th

**EXHIBITION MATCHES
REFRESHMENTS PROVIDED
ALL MEMBERS WELCOME!**

"That's in two days' time," Fliss said eagerly. "Maybe Mum will bring us to that."

"That would really get up the M&Ms' noses!" Kenny grinned.

"I have to pop into the clubhouse, and find out which court we're playing on," Fliss's mum said. She fixed us all with a laser-beam stare. "Don't move, or touch anything while I'm gone."

We stood outside the clubhouse with Auntie Jill, staring at everything going on around us.

"I wonder if the M&Ms are here yet," Rosie said.

"Maybe we can have a wander round the courts, and find out," Kenny began, but she shut up when Auntie Jill gave her a look. "Oh, I forgot. We're not allowed to move!"

Fliss's mum came back. "Court Seven," she said to Auntie Jill. "Let's go and get changed."

We went over to Court 7. We looked at all the other courts we passed on the way, but there was no sign of the M&Ms.

"Maybe they haven't arrived yet," Lyndz suggested, as we reached the changing-rooms.

"You girls had better come with us while we get changed, so that we can keep an eye on you," Mrs Proudlove began, but then she stopped as Auntie Jill pointed at a sign on the door.

ONLY PLAYERS ARE ALLOWED IN THE CHANGING-ROOMS

"Oh." Fliss's mum looked worried. "You'll have to stay outside then. But—"

"We know," said Kenny. "Don't move!"

"Can't we go on to Court Seven, and wait for you there, Mum?" Fliss asked.

Mrs Proudlove glared at her. "No, Felicity, you stay right here," she snapped, and she and Auntie Jill went into the changing-rooms.

We all stood there, shuffling our feet for a few moments and getting really bored. Then Kenny started walking towards the tennis courts, which were right ahead of us.

"Kenny!" Fliss began to panic. "Come back!"

"Don't get your knickers in a twist, Fliss," Kenny said impatiently. She leaned against the fence and peered into the nearest court. "Is this ours? Because it looks like someone's playing on here already. There's some rackets and tennis balls lying on the ground."

I went over to her. "No, that's Court Eight," I said, squinting at the number on the fence. "Ours must be the next one."

"Frankie, come back," Fliss wailed, but I didn't take any notice. After all, we were only about two metres away from her!

"Hey, what about a knock-up?" Kenny nudged me, and nodded at Court 8.

"Not a good idea, Kenny." I shook my head. "Fliss's mum would go mad."

Kenny shrugged. "Oh, she'll be ages yet. And anyway, why would someone leave tennis rackets and balls lying around, if they didn't want people to use them?"

"Kenny," I said warningly as she pushed open the door of the court, but that didn't stop her. She walked in, and picked up one of the rackets.

"Kenny, what're you doing?" Lyndz said. She and Rosie hurried over to join us, with Fliss trailing after them looking terrified. "Put that down!"

"It's OK," Kenny grinned. She brought the racket over to the fence and showed it to us.

"This racket is *really* gross. I'm sure no one would mind if we had a game with it."

Kenny was right, the racket was really awful. The strings weren't broken, but it was made of wood, not like Mrs Proudlove's posh metal one, and nearly all the paint had flaked off.

"Come on, who's going to play against me?" Kenny asked, waving the racket around as she tried out her shots.

The rest of us looked at each other. We weren't quite as brave as Kenny. None of us wanted to annoy Fliss's mum.

"You lot are so boring!" Kenny announced. "Hey, have you seen what some of the players do when they win a match at Wimbledon? They throw their rackets right up into the air."

"How do you know?" I asked. "I thought you hated tennis until this morning!"

"Well, I've seen the *end* of some of the matches, haven't I?" Kenny retorted. "You know, while I was waiting for *EastEnders* to come on."

"What happens when the rackets fall down again?" Rosie asked. "Do they catch them or what?"

"What if they don't get out of the way in time, and it hits them on the head?" Lyndz wanted to know.

Kenny considered that. "I dunno," she said. "Let's give it a go!"

"Kenny, no!" Fliss yelled, but it was too late. Kenny had flung the racket into the air as hard as she could.

"Don't worry, Fliss," Kenny called, "I'll catch it on the way down."

The racket started hurtling downwards.

"Kenny, you're not going to catch it!" I shouted. "Get out of the way!"

Kenny looked alarmed at the speed with which the racket was falling. She leapt out of the way, and the racket hit the hard surface of the court.

CR-R-R-ACK!

We all stared in horror. The wooden frame of the racket had split.

"What's going on here?" said a loud voice behind us.

Luckily, it wasn't Mrs Proudlove. Instead, a tall, plump woman with grey hair, wearing tennis whites, was marching towards us, followed by a much weedier woman of about the same age, who looked really scared. Not as scared as we were, though!

Before any of us had a chance to say anything, the tall woman spotted her broken racket lying on the ground.

"My racket!" she roared furiously, hurrying on to the tennis court. She snatched it up, inspected the damage and glared at Kenny, red-faced. "My lucky racket, the one my Aunt Fiona played with at Wimbledon in 1951!"

"Oh," Kenny said politely. "I'm really sorry, but maybe it was time you got a new one anyway, then."

She was trying to be helpful, but the woman almost had a fit.

"How dare you!" she shouted, waving the racket at Kenny. "This is part of my family's history!"

"Steady on, Dorothy," said the other woman in a wobbly voice. I think she was as frightened of her friend as we were!

"We're really, really sorry," Fliss stammered, looking as if she was about to faint with fright.

"Do you know who I am?" The woman glared round at us. "I'm Mrs Morgan, the club secretary. And I'm going to make sure you never set foot in Green Lawns again!"

CHAPTER SIX

"Well, how was I supposed to know that the racket belonged to the club secretary?" Kenny moaned in a low voice. "I mean, it was really tatty. I didn't think anyone would mind if I played with it."

"Ssh, Fliss's mum is looking at us," Rosie hissed.

Mrs Proudlove was glaring at us in the driver's mirror, so we all shut up. The atmosphere in the car was colder and frostier than the North Pole. While Mrs Morgan had been telling us off, Fliss's mum and Auntie Jill had come out of the changing-rooms just in time to find out what had happened. Mrs

Morgan gave *them* an earful too. Fliss's mum had been so furious and embarrassed, she'd hauled us off home straight away without even bothering to change. Now we were pretty much in doom forever.

"It's a wonder Mrs Morgan didn't throw us out of the club there and then," Fliss's mum said through her teeth.

"I think she only let us off because she knows I'm Mark's girlfriend," Auntie Jill muttered.

"I don't know if I'll ever be able to show my face there again," Mrs Proudlove groaned, changing gear with a lot of crunching and banging. "I certainly won't be going there for the next few days."

"Me neither," said Auntie Jill.

"Sorry," Kenny said again, for about the millionth time. "But that racket was just *lying* there. She shouldn't have left it lying around if it was that important."

Auntie Jill turned round, and directed an icy stare at Kenny. "Everyone at Green Lawns knows about Mrs Morgan's special racket," she said. "And nobody would *dare* to touch it. The reason why it was lying on the court was that

Mrs Morgan and her friend were about to have a game."

"Sorry," Kenny muttered again.

"I knew this would happen," Fliss's mum grumbled. "Well, that's it." She shot us another glare in the mirror. "None of you will be coming to Green Lawns with me ever again. Is that clear?"

"But, Mum—" Fliss began.

"Is that *clear*?" Mrs Proudlove said again in a louder voice.

We nodded. We didn't dare to speak, not even to each other, but I knew what everyone else was thinking. We'd been boasting to the M&Ms about how we were going to be practising at the tennis club from now on. If they didn't see us there, we'd never hear the end of it…

"Look, there are the M&Ms waiting for us," Fliss said gloomily, as we drove through the college grounds.

"Are those girls friends of yours?" asked my dad, who was dropping us off. Mrs Proudlove had refused to give us a lift after what had happened the day before.

We all made being-sick noises.

"Dad, we ARE not friends with those two losers," I told him.

"So why are they waiting for you then?" Dad said.

I rolled my eyes. "Don't ask."

"I don't think I want to know," my dad said with a grin. "See you at lunchtime."

We all climbed slowly out of the car. The M&Ms were watching us gleefully, just waiting to find out why we hadn't been playing at the club yesterday after all Kenny's boasting.

"Look, we'll just say we were there, and they didn't see us," Kenny hissed.

"Well, we *were* there – for about ten minutes!" Lyndz pointed out. "So it's not really a fib."

"You don't think the Queen and the Goblin heard about what happened to Mrs Morgan's racket, do you?" Fliss squeaked, looking really worried.

Kenny groaned. "I hope not – they'll laugh their heads off if they know it was us."

"If they know it was *you*, you mean," Fliss said grumpily. She was in a bit of a bad mood this morning. Her mum must have had a right go at her.

"Not wearing your magic cloaks today, then," the Queen called as we walked on to the court.

We all stared at her. None of us had a clue what she was going on about.

"Your magic cloaks," the Queen repeated. The Goblin was sniggering away beside her. "You know, the ones that make you *invisible*."

"Yeah, because if you were at the club yesterday afternoon, you *must* have been invisible," Emily Berryman explained sarcastically. "Because *we* didn't see you!"

"We were there," Kenny said shortly. "We had a quick game, and then we left."

"Oh, yeah, right," the Goblin chortled. "You must think we're stupid!"

"We do, actually," I chimed in.

"You didn't go to the club!" Emma Hughes said. "I knew you were making it all up."

"We're not," Kenny snapped. "Actually we're going to be there this afternoon as well!"

"What?" I muttered. "Kenny, what're you talking about?"

"We're going to the club this afternoon, right?" Kenny turned round and eyeballed the rest of us really hard.

"Er – yeah…" we all muttered. Fliss was looking nervous, and I didn't blame her. Kenny and her big mouth had gone and dropped us right in it *again*!

"Are you totally and completely bonkers, Kenny?" I demanded, when the M&Ms had stomped off, looking a bit less smug. "There's no way we can get into that club again!"

"My mum won't take us," Fliss said anxiously. "She'll kill me if I ask her."

"And we're not members, so how can we get in?" Rosie added.

"Kenny, what have you done!" Lyndz groaned.

"Leave it with me." Kenny grabbed a racket, as Mark came over to join us. "I'll have a think about it, and I'll come up with one of my super-duper, fantastically cool ideas."

"You mean, you'll think of a way to get us into even more trouble," Fliss said gloomily.

Mark gave us all a talk to start with, reminding us of what we'd learned yesterday. We lined up and did some more forehand practice shots, then he sent us off to practise against each other.

Things went a bit better than yesterday. Even Rosie managed not to hit the ball right over the fence this time. The most difficult thing was trying to hit the ball hard and still keep it within the white lines. Kenny could whack the ball really hard, but she kept knocking it out of the court.

Mark came over to give us some advice.

"Remember what I said yesterday," he told us. "The forehand can be a really easy shot, but if you want to be a good player, there are some things you need to remember. You have to think about your grip, and the position of your racket when you hit the ball." He took Rosie's racket from her to show us what he meant. "Move the racket back as fast as you can, to get ready for the shot, and keep it vertical. And try to finish up with your racket pointing towards the place you want the ball to go."

"There's so much to remember," Kenny groaned, as Mark went off again.

"And you thought tennis was just about hitting a ball over a net!" I reminded her.

The morning went by really quickly. We were getting so into the game that we didn't take any notice of the M&Ms, who were playing on the same court as Ryan and Danny again. But when the session was over, they started hanging around as we packed up the rackets and balls, smirking all over their faces.

"So we'll see you this afternoon," the Queen said loudly. "At the club."

Kenny glared at her. "That's right."

"Don't bring your magic cloaks this time then," the Goblin chortled, "or we won't be able to see you!"

And off they went, laughing like drains.

I looked at Kenny. "So what's your big idea then?" I asked. "If you've got one at all!"

"'Course I've got an idea." Kenny was looking well pleased with herself, which usually means trouble. "We're going to get into that club, no problem."

"How?" Lyndz asked, looking puzzled.

"I'm not climbing over the fence!" Fliss said firmly.

"Don't be daft, Fliss," Kenny said. "We're not going to do *that*."

"So what *are* we going to do?" Rosie asked.

Kenny grinned. "Fliss is going to borrow her mum's membership card, pretend to be her mum and sign us all in as guests!"

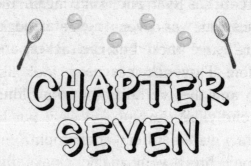

CHAPTER SEVEN

"Kenny!" Fliss howled. "That's the most stupid idea I've ever heard!"

"Why?" Kenny asked crossly. "I thought it was brilliant, even though I say so myself."

"You've really gone bananas this time, Kenny," I told her. "It'll never work."

"How can I pretend to be my mum?" Fliss demanded. "She's twenty-eight!"

"So?" Kenny shrugged her shoulders. "Her age isn't on the membership card, is it? Just her name. You can easily call yourself Nicola Proudlove."

"Hang on," Rosie said. "I got a quick look at the card when we went to the club yesterday, and there's a photo of Fliss's mum on it."

"Oh, rats!" said Kenny. She thought for a minute, and then beamed at us. "OK, no problem. Fliss and her mum look like each other, and they've both got long blonde hair. Fliss can wear shades, and we'll put loads of make-up on her to make her look a bit older, and more like the photo."

"Yeah?" Fliss brightened up a bit, and stopped looking so nervous. She loves doing girly stuff with make-up. "Do you really think it'll work?"

"Of course it won't work!" I said, and Rosie and Lyndz nodded in agreement.

"Have you got a better idea, Francesca?" Kenny asked me.

I shook my head. "Nope."

"OK, then, so this is what we'll do," Kenny went on. "After lunch, we'll meet at Fliss's house, and get her all made up. Then we'll cycle to the club, so bring your bikes."

Fliss was looking nervous again. "I don't think my mum will be very pleased if you all come round to my place. She's still really annoyed about yesterday."

"Just tell her we're doing homework

together," Kenny said. "The oldies always like that."

"All right," Fliss agreed.

"See you all there then," Kenny grinned, as my dad drew up outside the tennis courts.

"Quick, get inside before my mum comes down to see who it is," Fliss whispered, hustling me through the door of the Proudloves' house. I'd left my bike outside in the front garden, along with the others which were already parked there. "She keeps checking up on us, so we have to pretend to be doing homework."

"Where *is* your mum?" I asked, stepping into the hall.

"She's with a client," Fliss replied, pushing me towards the stairs. Her mum is a beautician, and she has a sort of beauty salon in one of the spare bedrooms where she does all sorts of treatments. "Come on, we're in my room."

We tiptoed up the stairs, and Fliss opened her bedroom door.

"Yikes!" Kenny gasped, jumping a mile into the air. She was in the middle of tipping a make-up bag full of lipsticks and nail varnishes on to the floor. "I thought you were Fliss's mum."

"Come on, let's get on with it," Fliss said, looking nervous.

"One of us had better be on guard," Rosie suggested.

"Good idea," I said. "I'll do it."

I went over to the door and opened it, so that I could see right down the landing.

"Now, which one do you think I should wear?" Fliss held up two lipsticks. She's got loads of make-up that her mum lets her wear when we're playing dressing-up or having fashion shows. "Peachy Kiss or Purple Pout?"

"Oh, Fliss!" Kenny groaned. "It doesn't matter. Just slap some lipstick on, and then we can go."

"Don't be silly, Kenny," Fliss retorted. "I've got to do it properly. My mum's taught me all about make-up."

"Peachy Kiss is nice," Lyndz said, twisting the lipstick up out of its tube.

"OK," Fliss agreed. "But I've got to do my blusher and mascara first."

We all sat around waiting as Fliss did her face. Kenny was so impatient, she couldn't sit still. She kept hopping around from foot to foot, like she wanted to go to the loo or something.

"OK, I'm all done." Fliss fluttered her eyelashes at us. "What do you think?"

"You *do* look a few years older," Rosie said.

"Fourteen, maybe." I added, "But not twenty-eight!"

"Yes, but Fliss's mum looks really young for her age, anyway," Kenny pointed out. "We'll get away with it."

"What if the man on the gate asks me how old I am?" Fliss said, looking panicky.

"Say you're fourteen," Kenny instructed her. "And if he says you look older in the photo, just tell him you were having a bad hair day when it was taken."

"I hope it's not the same man who was on the gate yesterday," Lyndz said suddenly. "He might remember us."

"We'll just have to risk it," Kenny said in a determined voice.

A door opened further down the landing. And I nearly died when I saw Fliss's mum come out and head in our direction.

"Mrs Proudlove's coming!" I hissed.

"Help!" Fliss gasped. "What about my make-up?"

"Lie down on the bed with your back to the door, and stick your head in a book," Kenny told her. Between the four of us, we bundled her on to the bed, and thrust a book into her hand. "And whatever you do, don't look up!"

By the time Fliss's mum opened the door, we were all sitting quietly and reading.

"Everything all right in here?" Mrs Proudlove asked suspiciously.

"Fine, thank you," we replied politely.

"Mum, we've finished our homework," Fliss mumbled without looking up. "Is it OK if we go out on our bikes now?"

Mrs Proudlove frowned. "I suppose so," she sighed. "But just *try* to stay out of trouble, please."

She went out again. We all heaved a sigh of relief.

"Come on, let's get going," Kenny said. "Fliss, have you got some sunglasses?"

Fliss nodded, and picked up a really funky pink, heart-shaped pair of shades. Then she grabbed her sports bag.

"How're we going to have a game, if we do get in?" I asked. "Fliss is the only one of us who's got a racket."

"Oh, we can always borrow one from somebody," Kenny replied.

"As long as it's not Mrs Morgan!" Rosie giggled nervously.

"We'd better make sure we stay out of her way," I said. "And Mark's too, just in case he tells Auntie Jill that he saw us there."

We went out of the bedroom.

"Don't forget the membership card," Kenny reminded Fliss.

"That'll be downstairs by the phone," Fliss said confidently. "My mum always keeps stuff like that there."

We all went down the stairs really quietly, just in case Mrs Proudlove came out to check on us again. Luckily, she didn't. Fliss stopped by the phone table in the hall, and quickly went through the letters and bits of paper which were lying there.

"It's not here!" she gasped.

"Oh no!" Kenny groaned. "Well, where else would it be?"

"It might be in my mum's sports bag," Fliss

said doubtfully. "Hang on, no, it isn't. I remember her saying that she'd emptied everything out."

"It could be *anywhere*!" Rosie said, looking around.

"I've seen it this morning." Fliss frowned, trying to remember. "I *know* I've seen it."

"Think, Fliss, think!" Kenny urged her.

We all stood around, while Fliss racked her brains.

"The kitchen!" Fliss said triumphantly, at last. "I saw it lying on the worktop."

We were just about to dash into the kitchen, when we all froze. A door had opened overhead, and there was the sound of footsteps.

"My mum must have finished with her client!" Fliss wailed. "If she sees me with all this make-up on, she'll guess we're up to something."

"Quick, we've got to get that card!" Kenny hissed.

Fliss ran into the kitchen. As we heard Mrs Proudlove and her client at the top of the stairs, Fliss dashed out again, waving the card in the air.

"I've got it!"

"Let's get out of here," I said, and we all raced out of the front door.

We collected our bikes from the Proudloves' front garden, and cycled off to the tennis club. It was a really warm and sunny day, and we were all sweating a bit by the time we got there. Or maybe it was just nerves!

"I'm scared," Fliss moaned, as we locked our bikes up in the club car park.

"You'll be fine," Kenny said. "Just think about the M&Ms' faces when they see us inside the club."

"I hope they're there," I said. "Or this will all be a big waste of time."

"They'll be there," Kenny said.

We didn't go straight up to the entrance. Instead, we hung around on the edge of the car park, trying to see if the same man from yesterday was on duty.

"It's OK," Kenny said in a low voice. "It's a different guy."

We all marched up to the entrance. Fliss's knees were knocking together so much, though, we practically had to carry her.

"Membership cards, please." The man at the turnstile was a bit younger than the one from yesterday, and not quite so snooty.

"Er – yes." Fliss fumbled in her pocket. Her voice was a bit high and squeaky because she was nervous. "I'm a member, and these are my guests."

The man took the card and looked at it for what seemed like ages.

"You're Nicola Proudlove?" he said at last.

"Um – yes," Fliss muttered.

The man eyeballed Fliss sternly. "How old are you?" he asked.

"I'm fourteen," Fliss said in a wobbly voice.

"Oh, really." The man turned the membership card round, and held it out so that we could see it. "And how long have you been married, *Mrs* Proudlove?"

We all squinted at the card. There, next to the photo, it said *Mrs Nicola Proudlove.*

"Goodbye, Mrs Proudlove," said the man sarcastically. "And just make sure you give that card back to its rightful owner."

We all trailed gloomily back to the car park.

"Why didn't anyone notice the card said *Mrs* Proudlove?" I asked, glaring at Fliss.

"I didn't have time to look at it properly," Fliss snapped. "I was in too much of a rush."

"So the M&Ms win again," Rosie said.

"Maybe we should just give up," Lyndz suggested.

"Give up!" Kenny spluttered. "What do you mean, give up? I've just thought of another *brilliant* idea!"

CHAPTER EIGHT

We all groaned.

"Kenny, you're not serious!" I said.

"You haven't heard my idea yet," Kenny said indignantly. She took the membership card from Fliss, and waved it at us. "See this? How about if we make our *own* membership cards?"

"What, fake them, you mean?" Lyndz gasped.

Kenny nodded. "Look at this card," she said. "For a posh club, it's pretty ropey. I reckon we could copy it, no problem."

"That sounds a bit dodgy," I remarked.

"It's got to be against the law!" Fliss wailed.

"Don't be a bunch of wimps," Kenny retorted. "We're not doing anything wrong. Not really."

"How do you work that one out?" I asked.

"Because all we're going to do is hang around inside the club until the M&Ms have seen us," Kenny replied. "It's not like we're going to nick anything or cause trouble."

"How about if someone spots us and realises we're not members?" Rosie asked. "Like that Mrs Morgan, for instance."

"Or Mark," I added.

Kenny grinned. "That's why my plan's so cool." She pointed at a poster for the gala afternoon, which was stuck on the fence. "Look, this is on tomorrow. There's going to be loads of members there, and I bet there'll be a lot of people who've come as guests too. So we aren't going to stand out in such a big crowd."

"I suppose not," Fliss said doubtfully.

"We won't be able to bag a court to have a game, though," I said. "No way. If there's going to be loads of people there, I bet all the courts will be booked, anyway."

"Yeah, we'd better not draw any attention to ourselves," Lyndz said, and the others nodded.

"OK, we'll just hang around until the M&Ms have seen us, and then we'll leg it," Kenny said.

"We'll need some photos if we're going to copy those membership cards," Rosie pointed out.

"There's a photo booth in the Post Office in the High Street," Kenny replied, jumping on her bike. "Come on!"

We all pedalled after her. We cycled back into Cuddington, and left our bikes in the car park behind the supermarket. The Post Office was right next door.

"Look, it's £3.50 for five photos," Kenny said, nodding at the photo booth. "How much money have we got?"

We all turned out our pockets. We had exactly £3.50 between us.

"See? This is our lucky day!" Kenny grinned. "Who's going first?"

"Wait a minute," I said. "How are we going to get in and out of the booth quick enough?"

"Just don't hang about," Kenny ordered us. "As soon as the flash goes off, get out of there as fast as you can. Frankie, you go first."

I went in and pulled the curtain. Then I sat down and adjusted the stool so that my face was in the middle of the little square in front of me.

"Don't have the stool too low." Kenny stuck her face round the curtain all of a sudden, nearly giving me a heart attack. "We won't have time to adjust it, and we're not all beanpoles like you!"

I put the stool up a bit higher, and started to put the money into the slot.

"Ready?" I called.

"Ready!" the others called back.

I dropped the last coin into the slot, and put on this really cheesy grin. I thought the flash was never going to come, but when it did, I jumped straight up. At the same moment, Kenny came hurtling through the curtain like Superman, and we banged heads.

"Aaargh!" Kenny groaned. "Get out of my way, you idiot!"

I fought my way past the curtain, and got out just in time before the second flash went off.

"You're next, Fliss," Rosie said, giving her a shove.

Looking flustered, Fliss hurried into the booth. We heard Kenny shout "*OW*!", and then she hopped out of the booth, clutching her foot. "Fliss trod on my toe," she moaned.

"Go on, Rosie," Lyndz said, as the flash went off again.

Rosie pulled the curtain aside. Fliss was down on her knees, hunting around on the floor.

"I dropped my sunglasses," she gasped.

"Stay down, Fliss!" I told her. Rosie crammed on to the stool, trying not to tread on Fliss, who was crouched in a ball. The flash went off, and both of them hurried out. Lyndz dashed in, and just about got there in time to have her picture taken.

"What did you say about this being our lucky day?" I remarked to Kenny, who was clutching her head and rubbing her foot.

"Here are the photos," Fliss announced.

We all crowded round to take a look as the photos popped out of the machine. They were really and truly gruesome. I'd put the stool a bit too high, and the top of my head had been cut off. Kenny was pulling a face like she was in agony, which she probably was after we'd banged into each other. Fliss looked totally panicked, and Rosie was all hunched up because she was trying not to step on Fliss. Only Lyndz looked in any way normal.

"If they let us in with these, they must be mad," Rosie said. "We look awful!"

"We've got to make the cards now," Kenny said. "Whose place shall we go to?"

"Somewhere the oldies won't interfere and want to know what we're up to," I suggested. "So my place is out. My mum's got eyes in the back of her head."

"Not mine either," Fliss said quickly. "My mum keeps checking up on us."

"We could go to my house," Rosie said. "Tiff's got a holiday job, so she won't be there, and Adam's gone to summer camp." Adam and Tiffany are Rosie's brother and sister. "My mum'll be there, but she'll be studying."

"OK, let's go then." Kenny glanced at her watch. "We'll have to get a move on. Mum told me I had to be home by four."

We grabbed our bikes and pedalled like the wind to Rosie's house, which luckily was quite close by. Mrs Cartwright was working on the computer, and she just popped out to say hello, then left us to it. We scooted out into the garden, while Rosie went to get us some drinks and something to eat. We really needed it, after the afternoon we'd had!

"Right, we need card, black felt pens, scissors and glue," Kenny said, ticking the items off on her fingers.

"Look, Fliss's mum's card is covered in this kind of clear plastic to protect it," I said. "How are we going to do that?"

"We've got some clear sticky-back plastic," Rosie said, coming out with a tray of orange squash and a family-sized bag of cheese and onion crisps. "My mum uses it to cover her college books."

"Excellent," Kenny said. We were sitting round the garden table, and she put Mrs Proudlove's card in the centre, so that we could all see it. "Now remember, it has to be exactly the same size and everything."

Rosie fetched the stuff we needed, and we got to work. Like Kenny had said, the cards weren't that posh-looking. They were just plain white with Green Lawns Tennis Club in black letters at the top, and they had the member's photo, name and signature on the front. I'd thought that Kenny's idea was really daft, but I was surprised by how good the cards looked as we worked on them.

"Rats," Kenny said, looking at her watch. "I've got to go. I'll have to finish mine at home."

"Me too," I said, slipping the card into my pocket.

Fliss and Lyndz decided it was about time they went home as well. Rosie cut us some squares of sticky-back plastic so that we could finish the cards off that evening, and then we went to get our bikes.

"What happens if we don't get into the club tomorrow?" Lyndz asked.

"I'll think of another plan!" Kenny said firmly. "I'm not letting the M&Ms think they've got one over on us…"

"You can play a backhand with one or two hands," Mark said, and held up his tennis racket, showing us the different ways to hold it. It was the following morning, and we were at our coaching session. Lyndz's mum had taken us, and she was a bit late picking us up, so we'd got there just as Mark had started the session off. At least that meant that we didn't have to put up with the M&Ms going on at us. They'd just sniggered and nudged each other when we'd arrived.

"There are a few important things to try and remember, whether you play a one-handed or two-handed shot," Mark went on. "Hold the racket head straight. If you tilt it slightly, you can get backspin on the ball, but for the moment just practise keeping it straight."

Someone poked me in the back. I glanced round, and Emma Hughes and Emily Berryman grinned unpleasantly at me.

"I thought you were going to the club yesterday afternoon," the Queen said.

"We did," I replied. No need to say we hadn't actually gone in!

"You didn't," Emily said accusingly. "We were there for most of the afternoon, and we didn't see you."

"Well, you must need glasses then," I retorted, and turned away.

"You lot are big fat liars!" the Queen said. "You're not members, and you've never been there at all!"

"Yes, we have." Kenny joined in. "And we're going to be at the gala afternoon today, too."

"Huh! I'll believe that when I see it," Emma Hughes snorted.

"Emma, could you be quiet please?" Mark said sharply, and the Queen turned bright red.

We spent the session practising our backhands, and then Mark let us actually have a proper game for the last hour, with scoring and everything. He gave us each a sheet of paper, which explained exactly how to do it. Some of the others played doubles, but we decided to play singles and take it in turns to play each other, although we had to limit each match to just three games.

Of course, Fliss was easily the best, and she beat the pants off all of us, but Kenny was good too (when she wasn't belting the ball right out of the court and giving points away), and I wasn't too bad either. My serve was quite good, but I couldn't hit the ball as hard as Kenny. Rosie and Lyndz were OK too, although they weren't as good as Fliss and Kenny.

"I think you and Kenny might have a chance of winning the tournament on Friday," I said, as we packed away when the coaching session was over.

"Yeah, if I can stop losing points by whacking the ball out of play," Kenny grumbled.

"You just need a bit more practice," Fliss said.

"Well, we've only got today and tomorrow, and then the tournament's on Friday," Kenny pointed out.

"The M&Ms aren't as good as they think they are, though," Rosie chimed in. "I was watching them today, and Emily's really weedy."

"Yeah, she didn't return half the shots, and Emma was telling her off," Lyndz added.

Kenny waved at the M&Ms as they went past. "See you at the gala afternoon," she called.

"Oh, shut up," the Queen snapped. "If you think you can wind us up by always pretending you're there when you're not, it won't work!"

"Yeah, we *know* you're making it up," the Goblin added.

The Queen turned to her. "Tell you what, Em," she said. "If we don't see them there this afternoon, we'll ask Mrs Morgan, the club secretary, if she knows them."

"Ooh, that's a good idea," the Goblin said, and they walked off.

"Did you hear that?" I hissed. "If the M&Ms speak to Mrs Morgan, she might tell them that we're the ones who broke her racket."

"The M&Ms would love that," Kenny groaned. "So we've got to make sure we get into that club this afternoon!"

We arranged to meet up at my place, ready to cycle to the tennis club later. Then we hung around, waiting for Lyndz's mum. Mrs Cartwright was late again picking us up, so when I got home, lunch was ready. I quickly got changed, and I'd just sat down and picked up my cheese and pickle sandwich when the phone rang. My mum went to answer it, and came back, looking suspicious.

"It's Fliss for you," she said, "and she sounds in a right old flap. Are you girls up to something?"

"'Course not, Mum," I said airily. "You know what Fliss is like. She panics about *everything*."

I waited till my mum had gone back into the kitchen, and then I dashed into the hall.

"Frankie?" Fliss squealed, nearly deafening me. "You'll never guess what's happened!"

"What?" I asked.

"My mum and Auntie Jill have decided to go to the tennis club this afternoon!" Fliss wailed.

CHAPTER NINE

"Oh, you're joking!" I groaned. "I thought they were too embarrassed to go after what happened?"

"Yeah, that's what they *said*," Fliss replied. "But then Mum said there'd be loads of people there for the gala thing, so maybe it wouldn't be so embarrassing. And Mark's talked Auntie Jill into going."

"What about you?" I asked. "Are you going with them?"

"No, that's the other thing," Fliss said gloomily. "Me and Callum are supposed to go to Dad's for the afternoon."

"Ask your mum if you can come round here

instead," I said, thinking fast. "The others'll be here soon, and we can decide what to do."

"OK," Fliss said glumly, and put the phone down.

"Problems?" said my mum. She was standing right behind me.

"No," I said innocently. "We're all going on a bike ride this afternoon, like I told you before."

"That's all right then," said my mum. "Because I know you wouldn't lie to me, Frankie."

"No," I said. Well, it wasn't lying, was it? We *were* going on a bike ride – to the tennis club!

I finished my sandwich and toffee yoghurt in double-quick time, and then went out into the front garden to wait for the others. A few minutes later, Rosie came cycling down the street, followed closely by Kenny.

"We've got a problem, guys," I said, as they wheeled their bikes into the garden. "Fliss's mum and her Auntie Jill have decided to go to the gala afternoon."

Kenny's face fell. "Oh, rats!" she exclaimed.

"Well, we can't go then, can we?" Rosie asked. "If they spot us, we'll be deader than dead!"

"Hey, we can't give up now," Kenny said. "There's going to be loads of people there. I bet we can keep out of their way."

Fliss and Lyndz came pedalling like mad things down the road.

"What're we going to do?" Fliss gasped, jumping off her bike and nearly tripping herself up.

"We'll have to go," Kenny said. "Otherwise the M&Ms are going to start talking to Mrs Morgan, and then they'll find out everything that happened."

"But what about my mum?" Fliss looked as if she was about to faint with fright.

"Look, like I said before, we'll just find the M&Ms, prove that we're there and then leg it," Kenny said. "Come on, let's go."

"Has everyone got their membership cards?" I asked, as we climbed on to our bikes. Everyone nodded, and we cycled off.

When we got to the tennis club we had to hide behind the trees at the side of the road, while we checked the car park to make sure Fliss's mum wasn't parking the car. Then we had to dash out, lock up our bikes and rush over to the entrance, hoping that Mrs Proudlove and

Auntie Jill didn't turn up while we were trying to get in. There was quite a long queue at the turnstile, and we joined the end of it.

We were so worried about Fliss's mum, we'd forgotten to check which man was on the gate. Luckily, it wasn't the man from yesterday – it was the same elderly man who'd been there the first time we came. I hoped he wouldn't remember that two days ago, we'd all been guests and not members!

The man was looking a bit stressed out, probably because there were so many people around.

"Membership cards, please," he snapped.

Kenny went first, and handed her card over, looking pretty confident. The guy hardly looked at it this time. He gave it back to Kenny, then flicked his eyes over mine, Fliss's, Lyndz's and Rosie's without even taking them from us.

"Go through," he said shortly.

I could hardly believe it – we were in! Kenny's plan had worked.

Kenny gave us a big grin, and pushed hard against the turnstile.

"Hey!" she gasped, as it didn't move. "It's not working."

The man was staring suspiciously at Rosie. "Give me your card, please," he said, frowning at her.

Rosie looked pretty scared as she handed it over. The man looked at it, and then glared at us.

"We spell *tennis* with two 'n's here," he said angrily, holding the card up so that we could see it.

Green Lawns Tenis Club was printed in black across the top of Rosie's card.

"You idiot, Rosie," Kenny said crossly under her breath.

"I didn't notice I'd spelt it wrong!" Rosie muttered, turning bright red in the face.

"I'll have the rest of those fake cards, please," the man said sternly, holding out his hand. He collected them all up while the people in the queue behind us watched, goggle-eyed. It was totally embarrassing.

"Now be off with you," the man shouted, "or I'll call Security!"

We slunk off back towards the car park, with everyone in the queue turning round to watch us go.

"Rosie, don't you know how to spell *tennis*?" Fliss groaned.

"Of course I do," Rosie said miserably. "Sorry, guys."

"We'd better get our bikes and go," Lyndz suggested, "before Fliss's mum turns up."

We hurried across the car park, but we had to wait as a white van turned in from the road and drove in front of us. It had *Archers Catering Company* written on the side in blue letters.

"It'll be just my luck to meet my mum while we're cycling back to Cuddington," Fliss grumbled, bending down to unlock her bike. "If she ever knew what we'd been up to, I'd be—"

"Don't unlock your bikes yet," Kenny cut in. "Wait a minute."

"Why?" I asked, surprised.

Kenny didn't answer. She was watching the white van very intently. The driver had got out and gone across to speak to the man operating the turnstile. Now he got back in the van again. Slowly, the big iron gates began to open. They must have been controlled automatically by the man in the hut.

"Come on," Kenny whispered.

We hurried over to the gates. The van drove through, and we dashed into the club after it, just before the gates started to close again.

"Hey! Come back!"

We could hear the man at the turnstile shouting behind us, but we didn't stop.

"No chance, mate," Kenny grinned, punching the air.

CHAPTER TEN

"What do we do now?" Fliss asked, panicking as usual.

"Lose ourselves in the crowd, just in case that guy comes after us," Kenny instructed.

There were loads of people around, and once we'd moved away from the entrance, we felt reasonably safe. The place was packed. By the look of it, there were matches going on on all the courts, and there were lots of people sitting watching them. The restaurant and the clubhouse were full of people eating and drinking and having a good time. There were also a couple of big, white marquees set up on the grass, and people were standing around in

411

the sunshine eating bowls of strawberries and cream. There was bunting in the trees, and stalls selling tennis stuff.

"Right, let's find the M&Ms," Kenny said, looking around.

"It's not going to be easy with all these people," Fliss said. Then she gave a shriek, and grabbed my arm.

"I thought we weren't going to draw attention to ourselves," I reminded her.

"Over there – it's Mark!" Fliss stammered, "He mustn't see us, or he'll tell Auntie Jill."

Mark was standing chatting to another man by the fountain.

"Let's get out of here," Kenny said urgently. She spun round, and knocked a bowl of strawberries and cream right out of the hand of the woman standing behind her.

"Well, really!" said the woman, who was another snooty type in a straw hat and a posh flowery frock.

"Sorry." Kenny scooped the strawberries up, dropped them into the bowl and handed them back to the disgusted woman. "Come on, let's hide!""

We ran off round the side of the clubhouse,

412

out of sight. Then we peered round the building to see if Mark had noticed us. He hadn't. He was still chatting to the same guy.

"That was close," Rosie whispered.

"Quick, let's find the M&Ms and get out of here," Fliss pleaded.

Cautiously we came out from behind the clubhouse. But we hadn't gone more than a few steps when we suddenly saw Mrs Proudlove and Auntie Jill, making their way towards us.

"It's my mum," Fliss gasped. As if we didn't know that already!

"Look, follow me," Kenny said quickly, leading us towards one of the marquees. We crept round the side of it, and stood there, our hearts pounding. Well, mine was, and I'm sure everyone else's was too!

"It's OK," said Kenny, who was keeping watch. "They've joined Mark, and now they're all going into the restaurant."

"That'll keep them out of the way for a bit," Fliss said, relieved.

"Let's go to the courts," Rosie suggested. "The M&Ms could be watching one of the matches."

"Good idea, Rosie-Posie," I said. "Come on, then."

Fliss was staring at the flowerbed nearest the marquee. "Hang on," she said, pointing at a plant with big scarlet flowers. "What's that?"

"Fliss, this is no time for gardening questions!" Kenny hissed crossly. "We need to find the M&Ms and get out of here."

"Not the plant, you idiot," Fliss retorted. "That little blue box lying underneath it."

She bent down and picked the box up. It was made of dark blue leather, and had *Masterson's* printed in gold on the top.

"It looks like a jewellery box," Fliss said eagerly. "I wonder if there's anything inside it?"

She was just about to open it, when we heard two angry voices in front of the tent, only a metre or so from where we were standing.

"And first of all they tried to fool me with fake cards, and then they ran inside when the catering van came in!"

We all looked at each other in horror. It was the man from the gate.

"Yes, Mr Harper, you've already told me, several times." I glanced at the others. I

414

recognised that voice. Last time we'd heard it, she'd been telling us off for breaking her precious racket. Mrs Morgan! "And from your description, it sounds like those terrible girls who were responsible for ruining my Aunt Fiona's racket."

Kenny pulled a face. "She's on to us!" she whispered.

"Shall I make an announcement over the tannoy, Mrs Morgan?" Mr Harper went on. "I could put out a description, and ask people to keep an eye open for them."

I rolled my eyes at the others. Honestly, this guy was acting like something out of *The Bill*! It wasn't like we were criminals or anything.

"No, I don't think that's a good idea," Mrs Morgan said. "But, as we both know what they look like, we'd better search for them ourselves."

We didn't dare look to see which direction they were going in. If one of them came round the side of the marquee, we were as good as dead!

"Quick!" Kenny gasped. "Under here!"

She lifted up the canvas, and we all crawled underneath it and into the marquee as fast as we could. Fliss was trying to shove the little blue box in her pocket, and kept dropping it, which held us up a bit.

The marquee was the place where they were serving the strawberries and cream, and what looked like champagne in crystal glasses. It was packed with people, and it could have been a bit embarrassing if we'd been spotted. But luckily, there were lots of long tables, covered with white cloths dotted about, and one of these happened to be positioned right where we'd crept under the canvas. So we were able to slide under the table without anyone seeing us. The tablecloth hung almost right down to the ground, so we were pretty well hidden. We could just see people's shoes moving about.

"What now?" Fliss whispered.

"We'll stay here for a bit, and wait until Mrs Morgan and Mr Harper have gone off somewhere else," Kenny said.

"I'm getting cramp in my legs," I grumbled. The tables were pretty low, and I was so hunched up, I was starting to ache all over. It was all right for the others, they weren't as tall as me.

"Stop moving around, Frankie," Rosie said in a panicky voice. "You're rocking the table."

I groaned, trying to stretch my aching arms and legs a bit. "I'm never going to be able to stand up straight again!"

"Hey, what's that?" Kenny jumped as something fell on to the grass, right next to her foot. She peered at it, then grinned at us. "It's OK, guys," she whispered. "Someone's just dropped a spoon."

It took us about two seconds to realise that if somebody had *dropped* a spoon, they'd probably be bending down to pick it up. But it was too late. Someone had already pulled the tablecloth aside, searching for the spoon...

We all looked into the startled face of a woman in a straw hat and a flowery frock. The same woman whose strawberries Kenny had sent flying a little while ago!

"Aargh!" the woman shrieked, jumping backwards. I didn't think we were *that* scary-looking, but I don't suppose she was expecting to see anyone under the table, let alone five of us.

"Quick, let's get out of here!" I gasped. We yanked up the edge of the marquee, and wriggled our way out. Then we jumped to our feet, and dashed off. A few minutes later, we were in the middle of a large crowd, and feeling a lot safer.

"Where are we?" Kenny asked, looking around.

"Near the changing-rooms." I pointed them out. "And there are the courts."

"If we walk along the fence, we can check out the people watching, and see if the M&Ms are there," Lyndz suggested.

"Good idea," I began. But then I nearly *died* as a hand grabbed my shoulder from behind.

"What do you girls think you're doing?" said a stern voice.

We all turned as white as ghosts. But when we looked round, it wasn't Mrs Morgan standing there. It was a shorter, thinner woman wearing glasses and carrying a clipboard.

"N-nothing," I stammered. "We're not doing anything."

"Exactly!" the woman said crossly, rolling her eyes. "What are you hanging around here for? Haven't you been told what to do?"

I glanced at the others. We didn't have a clue what this woman was going on about, but at least she didn't seem to know that we were being hunted by Mrs Morgan.

"Er – no," I said, trying to look as if I knew what she meant. "Not exactly."

The woman tutted loudly. "Come with me," she snapped. "We don't have much time."

She bustled over to the changing-rooms, taking us with her.

"Go and get changed," she said impatiently. "And hurry up about it. I'll wait for you here."

"What?" I stared at her. Get changed? Into what?

"Your uniforms are in the junior changing-rooms," the woman said. "Now get a move on. We haven't got all day."

Feeling a bit dazed, we all trailed into the changing-rooms.

"We need to get away from that mad woman!" Kenny said urgently. "Is there another way out of here?"

I stopped by a door labelled:

JUNIOR CHANGING-ROOM – GIRLS

"Let's look in here. There might be a window we can climb out of or something."

419

We went in.

"Look." Fliss pointed at five pairs of dark green shorts and five green sports shirts, hanging on pegs near the door.

"Are those our uniforms?" Lyndz asked, puzzled. "What are we supposed to be?"

"She thinks we're ballgirls," Fliss gasped.

"Pardon?" Rosie said.

"Ballgirls," Fliss repeated. "You know, ballboys and ballgirls run around the courts and collect the spare tennis balls during a match."

"What!" Lyndz squeaked anxiously. "I wouldn't have a clue what to do!"

"We've got to get out of here," Kenny said urgently. She went over to the window, climbed on to the bench and tried to open it. "Oh, rats, it's locked."

"What are we going to *do*?" Rosie wailed. "She's waiting for us outside."

"We'll just have to go and tell her we're *not* the ballgirls," I said.

"I'll do it," Kenny offered. She went over to the door, walked out and then leapt back in again. "She's talking to Mrs Morgan!" she hissed.

We all nearly *died*.

"Mrs Morgan's probably telling her all about us," Fliss whispered.

"It's OK," Rosie pointed out. "She thinks we're the ballgirls."

"We'll have to go along with it for the moment, until we can leg it," Kenny said. "Come on, get changed."

We all started taking our clothes off, and putting the ballgirls' uniforms on. We had to do a bit of swapping around to make them fit, and even then mine was too tight, and Rosie's shorts were too long.

"It's OK, Mrs Morgan's gone," Kenny said, peering round the door. "Come on."

"Are we *really* going to have to be ballgirls?" Lyndz asked.

"'Course not," Kenny replied. "We'll try and get away as soon as we can."

But it wasn't as easy as that. The woman was still waiting for us outside, and she herded us over to the courts. One of them, Court 3, was absolutely packed with people waiting for a match to start, and as we got closer, we heard the umpire talking to the audience.

"Ladies and gentlemen, thank you for coming to our gala afternoon. Today we have a very special match for you. The winner of the women's club championship last year, Barbara Browne, will be playing the winner from the previous year, Marina Warner."

There was loud applause.

The woman with the clipboard stopped right by Court 3. "Go on, then," she said, pushing the door open. "They're ready to start."

"What, *here*?" Kenny gasped, shooting the rest of us a panicky look. "But there's about ten million people watching!"

"So?" The woman looked at us suspiciously. "You know what to do, don't you? You *are* ballgirls. Aren't you?"

CHAPTER ELEVEN

We were all too nervous to say anything, except Fliss. For once, she didn't panic.

"Of course we are," she said coolly.

"Good." The woman glanced at her clipboard. "Don't forget that one of you has to be in charge of the scoreboard."

Fliss nodded. "Come on, girls," she said confidently, pushing the door open.

We trailed on to the court behind her, trying to make ourselves look as small as possible. The umpire was introducing the players to the audience, so no one was taking much notice of us.

"Look," Fliss said urgently. "You know how to

be ballgirls, don't you?"

We all shook our heads.

"You've seen Wimbledon, haven't you?" Fliss asked, beginning to look desperate.

We shook our heads again.

"OK, listen to me," Fliss went on. "Two of us have to be at the end of the net, one on each side of it, to collect the balls that don't go over."

"Frankie and me can do that," Kenny volunteered.

Fliss nodded. "Then there has to be one person at each end to pass the balls for the players to serve."

"That sounds easy," Rosie said hopefully. "Maybe me and Lyndz can do that."

"All right," Fliss agreed. "But remember, you have to do it like this." She raised one hand high in the air, and pretended to bounce an imaginary ball towards a player. "And I'll do the scoreboard," she went on.

The scoreboard was in the corner, and was just a black board, with white numbers on it, a bit like a cricket scoreboard. It wasn't an automatic one, so the numbers had to be changed by hand. Fliss went over there, and Lyndz and Rosie each went to different ends of the court. They both looked terrified. Meanwhile Kenny and I went over to the net, and hung about. The two players were busy unpacking their sports bags, and having a drink before the match began.

I nudged Kenny. "Fliss is trying to tell us something," I said.

Fliss was pulling faces and pointing at us.

"What's she going on about?" Kenny wanted to know.

Fliss was pointing at her knees, and bending up and down.

"Oh, I get it," I said. Even though I used to hate tennis, I'd seen bits of Wimbledon when my mum was watching it. "She's telling us to remember to crouch down when the match starts."

The players were coming on to the court now, ready to warm up. Marina Warner went down the end where Rosie was standing, and Barbara Brown took the other end. They started knocking the ball around to each other, and practising their serves.

"Hey, Frankie, look," Kenny whispered suddenly. "It's the M&Ms!"

She pointed at the crowd. The M&Ms were

sitting in the middle of a row near the front. They were staring at me and Kenny, their faces absolutely crimson with fury.

"They're really annoyed," Kenny said gleefully. "Wave at them, Frankie."

We flapped our hands at the M&Ms, and they stared back at us, stony-faced. We'd obviously *really* wound them up. I bet they never *dreamt* we'd turn up at the club as ballgirls. Then again, neither did we!

"Do you mind!" Marina Warner came over, glaring at us. "Stop distracting me. And aren't you supposed to be picking these balls up?"

With a bad-tempered look on her face, she pointed her racket at a ball lying by the net. We'd been so busy waving at the M&Ms, we hadn't noticed that there was a ball waiting to be collected.

"OK, don't get your knickers in a twist," Kenny retorted, and she strolled on to the court and picked the ball up.

"I think we're supposed to do it a bit quicker than that!" I told her.

"What do I do now?" Kenny said, staring at the ball in her hand. "Shall I put it in my pocket or what?"

Fliss was jumping up and down by the scoreboard, trying to attract our attention as the umpire announced that the game was about to start. I squinted at her.

"I think she's saying you roll it down the court to Lyndz," I told Kenny.

"OK." Kenny shrugged, and rolled the ball down to one end of the court. Unfortunately, Lyndz wasn't looking.

"Lyndz!" Kenny hissed. "*Lyndz!*"

Lyndz jumped, looked down at her feet and saw the ball lying there. At last she picked it up.

"Miss Browne to serve," said the umpire.

The whole court went quiet. Barbara Browne, who looked a whole lot nicer than grumpy Marina Fleming, turned to Lyndz, waiting for a ball to be passed to her so she could serve. Lyndz just smiled at her.

"Lyndz!" I groaned under my breath. "Give her a ball, or the match can't start."

"Oops!" Lyndz said suddenly, turning pink, as she remembered what she was supposed to do. "Sorry." But instead of bouncing the ball to the player like Fliss had shown her, she dashed over and handed it to Barbara Browne. There was a ripple of laughter round the court.

"Quiet, please," said the umpire sharply.

"We've got to do better than this, or we're going to look like real idiots," Kenny fretted. "And won't the M&Ms just love that."

We started concentrating then. It was actually pretty easy, once we got the hang of it. All Kenny and I had to do was dash on to the court and pick up any balls which hit the net, and then roll them down to Rosie or Lyndz, depending on which player was serving. And once Lyndz realised that she was supposed to *bounce* the ball to the player and not *hand* it to them, things went really well.

The only problem was that Marina Warner was a bit bad-tempered. She wasn't such a good player as Barbara Browne, and she got annoyed every time she lost a point.

"She's a miserable so-and-so, isn't she?" Kenny remarked to me, as Marina Warner stomped back to the baseline after hitting the ball into the net.

"Ssh," I said, as Marina shot us a poisonous glare.

Her next serve was in, and Barbara Browne returned it. Marina hit the ball with a forehand drive, and it fell just over the net, near to where Kenny was crouched, but about a centimetre outside the white line.

"Out," called the umpire.

"That was definitely in," Marina snapped, rushing over to him.

"No, it wasn't," Kenny said helpfully. "It *was* out. I saw it."

Marina Warner turned purple. She was so angry, I thought she was going to grab Kenny and shake her.

"Since when have the ballgirls been umpires?" she snorted scornfully.

"I've got eyes, haven't I?" Kenny retorted. "And it was out!"

"Quiet!" the umpire said with a frown. "Carry on with the game, please."

"She's a right pain in the bottom, isn't she?" Kenny said, pulling a face at Marina's back. "I hope she loses!"

She did. Barbara Browne won by two sets to love, and when she hit the winning point, everyone started cheering. So did we! The umpire didn't look too impressed at us joining in, but we didn't care.

"I'm tired out," Kenny moaned, as we joined up with the others. There was a fifteen-minute interval before the next match, and most of the audience were leaving. "You don't think we've got to do this for the *next* match, do you?"

"How about if we swap over?" Rosie suggested. "You and Frankie can change with me and Lyndz."

"Hang on a minute," said Lyndz. "Shouldn't we be getting out of here? I mean, we've seen the M&Ms and they've seen us."

The M&Ms were just leaving the court. They were whispering to each other, and shooting us furious looks.

"Yeah, we've well and truly rubbed their noses in it," Kenny said with satisfaction. "I suppose we'd better go."

"We've been pushing our luck," I pointed out. "Mrs Morgan could have walked on to that court and spotted us at any moment."

We hurried over to the door, and went out with the last few spectators.

"Let's get changed, and get out of here," I said urgently.

"Wait." Kenny grabbed my arm, and yanked me back. "There's that woman again, the one with the clipboard."

The woman who'd sent us to get changed was standing talking to a group of five girls, a little bit older than us.

"Do you think they're the *real* ballgirls?" Fliss asked nervously.

We crept behind a nearby bush, and listened hard. We could just about hear what they were saying.

"And your mum's car broke down," the woman was saying suspiciously. "That's why you're late."

"That's right," one of the girls replied.

"Hm, that's strange," the woman went on. "Because we've actually got all our ballgirls, and we've got no uniforms left, anyway."

"But we're *supposed* to be ballgirls," the girl said firmly. "Ask my mum, she's a member here."

"There's something funny going on," the woman said, sounding puzzled. "Come with me, and we'll find Mrs Morgan and see what she says."

They all went off. Immediately we dashed out from behind the bush, and into the changing-rooms.

"Hurry up," Kenny urged us.

We didn't need much persuading. We changed out of our clothes in double-quick time, and then ran for the door. We peered outside to check that the coast was clear, and then we hurried outside.

"Keep a look-out for my mum," Fliss told us, as we headed for the exit.

We nearly made it safely out of the tennis club, too. We wouldn't have stopped if we hadn't seen the M&Ms standing by the fountain...

"Oh, there you are!" the Queen said. Funnily enough, she didn't look annoyed any more. She looked like a cat who'd just had a big saucerful of cream. "We were looking for you."

"Where are you going?" the Goblin chimed in.

"Home," Kenny said breezily. "We've finished being ballgirls. You *did* see us, didn't you?"

"Oh, yes." The Queen folded her arms, looking smug. "But are you *sure* that's what you were meant to be doing?"

She couldn't be on to us – could she?

"What are you talking about?" I asked.

"We heard Mrs Morgan talking to somebody, and she said five girls had got into the club, who weren't members," Emma Hughes said gleefully. "It was *you*, wasn't it?"

We all tried not to look guilty.

"Don't be stupid," Kenny retorted. "How could we have been ballgirls if we weren't meant to be here?"

"I don't know." The Queen frowned. "But we're going to tell Mrs Morgan right away, aren't we, Emily?"

"Yeah," Emily agreed eagerly.

"I wouldn't do that if I were you!" Kenny growled, taking a sudden step towards them.

Emma Hughes panicked, and jumped backwards. She knocked into the fountain behind her, sat down in surprise for a moment on the edge of it, and then tipped backwards, her legs and arms waving.

"Help!" she shrieked as she fell into about half a metre of not-very-clean water.

We all burst out laughing, except for the Goblin, of course.

"Serves you right," Kenny grinned, walking up to the edge of the fountain. "*Aaargh!*"

We all gasped as Kenny slipped on a patch of water, and went flying. She landed heavily on the ground, and we rushed over to her.

"Are you OK, Kenny?" Lyndz said anxiously.

Kenny's face was white. "No," she said through gritted teeth. "I think... I think I've sprained my ankle!"

CHAPTER TWELVE

"Serves *you* right, Laura McKenzie!" yelled Emily Berryman. She was trying to help Emma out of the fountain. The Queen was dripping wet from head to toe.

"Everyone's looking," Fliss said nervously. People sitting outside on the restaurant patio were staring at us. "Can you walk, Kenny?"

Kenny was trying to pull herself to her feet, hanging on to the edge of the fountain. "I don't know," she gasped, looking as if she was in a lot of pain. "You'll have to help me."

Lyndz and I put our arms round her, and we began to make our way slowly towards the exit, with Kenny leaning on us and hopping along.

We left the Goblin trying to dry the Queen off with her hanky.

"How is Kenny going to cycle home?" Rosie asked suddenly.

We all looked at each other in dismay.

"She isn't," I said at last.

"I can try," Kenny said bravely, putting her injured foot down on the ground for a second. "Ow!"

"So what're we going to do?" Lyndz asked.

"We could find Fliss's mum and tell her what's happened," Rosie suggested. "Then she could give us a lift."

Fliss turned a sickly green colour. "She'd be so mad, I'd be grounded till I'm eighteen," she muttered.

"There must be a phone here," I said. "We could ring one of our parents, and get them to pick us up."

"Then *they'll* want to know what we're doing here," Rosie said gloomily.

None of us could think of anything to say. We seemed to have got ourselves into the worst mess *ever*. It didn't look like there was anything we could do except own up.

"Hello, girls," said a voice behind us.

We all nearly jumped out of our skins. We turned round to find Mark standing there. He was frowning, and looked pretty upset.

"H-hello," we gulped, waiting for him to start yelling at us.

But Mark didn't seem too worried about us being there. In fact, he just didn't seem interested at all. He wasn't even looking at us. He was glancing all around him, as if he was looking for someone or something.

"Maybe you could help me, girls," he said urgently. "I've lost something, and it's really important that I find it again. You could help me search for it."

"Sorry," Kenny said. "I've sprained my ankle."

"And we were just leaving," Fliss added quickly.

"What have you lost?" I asked. I felt a bit sorry for Mark, he looked so worried.

"A little blue box," Mark told me, "with gold writing on the top."

"Oh!" Fliss dived into her pocket, and pulled out the box she'd picked up in the flowerbed when we were hiding round the side of the marquee. "I'd forgotten about it, what with – er – everything going on. Is this it?"

Mark's face lit up as if someone had just given him a million pounds.

"That's it!" he said, looking hugely relieved. "It must have fallen out of the pocket of my shorts. I can't thank you enough, girls." He took the box from Fliss, then frowned. "How did you girls get in here, anyway? You didn't come with Nikky and Jill, did you?"

We'd been rumbled. Should we own up, or try to think of a way out? Kenny was in too much pain to come up with one of her 'brilliant' plans, and to be honest, I couldn't think of anything myself.

"Felicity! What are *you* doing here?"

Too late. Fliss's mum and Auntie Jill had appeared from nowhere, and were charging towards us. Fliss almost fainted on the spot, and the rest of us weren't far behind her.

"I can't believe it!" Mrs Proudlove said, looking dazed. "What on *earth* are you girls doing here?"

"And how did you get in?" Auntie Jill added.

No one got a chance to say anything more though. Suddenly the M&Ms came out of the clubhouse. Emma Hughes had a towel round her shoulders, and she looked triumphant when she saw us.

"There they are, Mrs Morgan!" she shouted.

We were all horrified. Next moment the club secretary rushed out of the clubhouse behind the M&Ms, and glared at us.

"Aha!" she said loudly. "So there you are. You've led me a merry dance, haven't you?"

She stomped down the clubhouse steps, and rushed over to us. The M&Ms followed her, grinning.

"Oh, dear," Fliss's mum said nervously. "I hope these girls haven't been a nuisance again, Mrs Morgan."

"Worse than that." The club secretary folded her arms grimly. "I have reason to believe that they forced their way into this club without proper membership cards."

We all hung our heads and looked sheepish. We were really in for it now. And didn't the M&Ms just love it. They were both lapping it up.

"Actually that's not true, Mrs Morgan," Mark said suddenly.

What?

"The girls are here as my guests," Mark went on. Mrs Morgan and the M&Ms looked really taken aback, and Fliss's mum and Auntie Jill stared at him.

"*Your* guests?" Mrs Morgan repeated fiercely.

Mark nodded. "You see," he went on, "this is a very special occasion."

Suddenly, for some reason, he got down on one knee. We all goggled at him.

"What's he up to?" Kenny whispered. "Has he gone barmy?"

Mark took Auntie Jill's hand, and then flipped the box open. We saw the sparkle of a diamond inside.

"Jill, please will you marry me?" he said.

CHAPTER THIRTEEN

Everyone was *stunned*. There was silence for a few seconds, and then Auntie Jill burst into tears.

"Just say YES!" Kenny whispered.

"Yes, Mark," Auntie Jill sobbed happily, as he slid the ring on to her finger. "Of course I'll marry you!"

We all began to cheer. Fliss was nearly wetting herself with excitement, Mrs Proudlove was crying too and hugging her sister and Mark, and the people in the restaurant stood up and started clapping. Even Mrs Morgan looked pleased. Only the M&Ms slunk off, still looking grumpy!

"This is great!" Lyndz grinned.

"Yeah, maybe I'll get to be a bridesmaid," Fliss said excitedly.

Mark came over to us. "Thanks, girls," he said, with a wink. "If it hadn't been for you, I might never have got that ring back. And I'd been saving up for it for weeks."

"Thank *you* for saving our necks," Kenny whispered.

Mark smiled at us. "No problem. Especially as Fliss and I are going to be related now."

Fliss turned pink. "Yeah, you'll be my uncle," she said.

Mrs Proudlove and Auntie Jill came over to us, and we all crowded round to look at the engagement ring.

"Mrs Morgan has very kindly offered us glasses of champagne to celebrate," Fliss's mum told Mark.

"Great!" Kenny said.

"It's orange juice for you, girls," Mrs Proudlove said with a smile. "And Kenny, I think we'd better get you to the first-aid tent, so that they can take a look at your ankle."

Half an hour later, we were all sitting out on the patio in the sunshine. We had orange juice, and big bowls of delicious strawberries and cream, and we scoffed the lot! Kenny's ankle had been looked at, and she was resting her leg on a chair. The guy in the first-aid tent had given her an ice-pack, and told her that it was a bad sprain, and not to walk on it if she could help it.

"You know, maybe we should join the tennis club ourselves," Kenny said, finishing off her strawberries. "I reckon we could become members, if Mark put in a good word for us."

"Hm, we'll have to see about that," said Fliss's mum.

"Hang on a minute, Kenny." Fliss suddenly put down her spoon. "Now that you've sprained your ankle, you won't be able to pay in the tennis tournament on Friday."

Kenny's face fell. "Oh, rats!" she said. "And I was looking forward to thrashing the M&Ms. Today's only Wednesday, though," she went on hopefully. "Maybe I'll be OK by Friday."

"No, you won't be," said Mrs Proudlove firmly.

Kenny turned to me. "It's up to you, then, Frankie," she said. "You'll have to take my place."

"But I'm not as good as you," I said, feeling a bit scared, even though I really did want to play.

"Don't put yourself down, Frankie," Mark cut in. "You've got the makings of a killer serve, and your ground shots aren't bad either, for a beginner."

"Thanks," I mumbled, turning red. "OK, I'll play then."

The others cheered. Fliss leaned across the table and clinked glasses with me.

"We're going to beat the pants off the M&Ms," she said. "Just you wait and see."

"And don't forget that there's a sleepover at my place on Friday evening," Lyndz added.

"We'll be celebrating!" Fliss boasted confidently.

"You bet," I said, trying not to sound too nervous…

"I'm really nervous," I said to Fliss, for about the millionth time.

It was the last day of our week of coaching, and the day of the tournament. We were hanging around, waiting for Mark to tell us who we would be playing.

Most of our parents had come along to watch, and they were sitting on folding chairs which had been placed around the courts. Rosie's mum was there, my mum had come with Izzy, and Lyndz's mum had come with her baby brother Spike. Kenny had arrived on crutches her dad had given her (he's a doctor, remember?) with Mrs McKenzie, and Mrs Proudlove and Auntie Jill were there too. They were going to help with the umpiring, and so were some of the other parents.

The M&Ms were all dressed up in their gruesome tennis whites and looking completely smug, which annoyed me. They kept well away from us, though, after what had happened at the club!

Mark came over carrying a clipboard.

"Morning, everyone," he called. "Now, let me explain what's going to happen. We've got eight pairs of players, so there'll be four matches to start off with. We're going to draw names out of a bag to see who plays first."

Mark had a box with folded-up bits of paper in it, and Auntie Jill came over and drew them out one by one. Rosie and Lyndz got Ryan and Danny in the first round, and me and Fliss got Seema and Zoë, who we didn't know very well.

"I don't think they're very good though," Fliss said to me in a low voice.

The M&Ms got Jack and Katie Marshall. They were twins, and they were quite good players, but, of course, the M&Ms were so sure they were going to win, they didn't even look worried.

"Wouldn't it be great if they got knocked out in the first round?" I said to Fliss, as we went over to our court. Rosie and Lyndz were playing Ryan and Danny on the court next to us, so that Kenny could watch both matches at the same time. One of the other parents was umpiring our match, and Fliss's mum was in charge of Rosie and Lyndz's. Each match was only going to be one set long, to save time.

"Come on, Sleepover Club!" Kenny bawled, waving her crutches in the air as we took our places on the court.

"I hope I can remember what to do," I said, feeling worried, as I got ready to serve. Seema and Zoë were already standing on the other side of the net.

"You'll be fine," Fliss said. "I'll remind you if you get things wrong."

Rosie and Lyndz were waiting to start their match, but Ryan and Danny were arguing about which one of them was going to serve first. Fliss's mum went over to sort them out. Meanwhile, we waved at Rosie and Lyndz, and yelled, "Good luck!"

I was really nervous, as I tried to remind myself of all the things Mark had told us. I threw the ball up into the air, and hit it. It bounced on the other side of the net, and zoomed past Seema. It was an ace!

"Fifteen-love," called the umpire.

After that, I started to relax a bit. I wasn't really very good, whatever Mark said (after all, I'd only been playing for a week!) but Seema and Zoë were worse than I was! They gave loads of points away because they kept hitting the ball out of the court. Anyway, Fliss was brilliant, and she won most of our points, although I did manage another couple of aces. By the end of the set, the score was six games to two, to me and Fliss. We'd won!

"Brilliant!" Kenny yelled, hobbling around on her crutches and getting a telling-off from her mum.

About ten minutes before our match ended, Rosie and Lyndz finished thrashing the pants off Ryan and Danny. They'd beaten them 6-0. Not surprising really, considering that Ryan and Danny spent the whole time arguing!

"Great stuff," Kenny said, beaming all over her face when we went to speak to her.

"Looks like the M&Ms won as well though," I said.

We looked at the M&Ms, who were strolling back from their court. They were so cocky, it was sickening.

"Well done, all the winners," Mark called, "and bad luck to the losers. Now, I need the four winning teams over here, and we'll draw the names again for the semi-finals."

Mark asked one of the other parents to do the draw this time. The four winning pairs were me and Fliss, Rosie and Lyndz, the M&Ms and two girls called Tania and Natalie. We'd already worked out that either me and Fliss or Rosie and Lyndz could be playing the M&Ms. If we weren't, we would be playing against each other. I didn't know which was worse.

"Right, our first semi-final is between Natalie and Tania," Mark called out, "and Fliss and Frankie."

"That means Rosie and Lyndz have got the M&Ms," I groaned to Fliss.

Rosie and Lyndz both looked glum. Meanwhile, the Queen and the Goblin could hardly stop themselves laughing.

"We're going to walk it!" I heard Emma Hughes crowing.

Poor old Rosie and Lyndz looked really down as they trailed over to the court behind the M&Ms.

"Good luck," Fliss and I said together.

Rosie and Lyndz were too depressed even to reply. They just nodded miserably.

"Oh no!" Kenny gasped, when Fliss and I went to tell her who we were playing. "Do you think Rosie and Lyndz will beat the M&Ms?"

"I don't know," I said doubtfully. "Emma Hughes is good."

"You and Fliss could be playing the M&Ms in the final," Kenny pointed out.

"We've got to win first," Fliss said. "And Natalie's pretty good too."

The M&Ms were already knocking up on the court next to ours. Instead of hitting the ball straight back to Rosie and Lyndz, so that they could practise their shots too, they were showing off by belting it out of their reach. Rosie and Lyndz were looking gloomier and gloomier.

Meanwhile, me and Fliss started our game against Tania and Natalie. For the first few minutes, I kept squinting at the next courts, trying to see what was going on between Rosie and Lyndz and the M&Ms. But then I had to start concentrating on *our* game. Natalie was nearly as good as Fliss, and me and Tania were about the same, so it was a really close match.

"That's four games all," Mrs Scott, Ryan's mum called, as Fliss did this really excellent, cross-court backhand to win us the fourth game.

"Try to hit the ball towards Tania, if you can, Frankie," Fliss whispered to me, as Natalie got ready to serve. "She's not very good."

"About as hopeless as me, you mean!" I said. Natalie's serves were quite powerful, and I'd hardly managed to return one of them yet. If it wasn't for Fliss, we'd be losing.

I waited for Natalie to serve to me again. This time, for some reason, it wasn't as hard as the others had been. I returned it with a forehand which sent the ball flashing right past Tania, who just stood and looked at it helplessly. It was a fluke, but we'd won the point!

"Love-fifteen," Mrs Scott called.

"Well done, Frankie!" Fliss said, looking thrilled.

Natalie served to Fliss next, and Fliss won the point with a scorching backhand that just skimmed the top of the net. Love-thirty. I lost the next point when Natalie served an ace, which made it fifteen-thirty, but then Fliss won the next. Thirty-forty. We needed one point to win the game, and then one more game to win the set.

"Come on, Frankie," I muttered, as Natalie prepared to serve to me again. "Concentrate."

The ball bounced over the net towards me – and I completely mis-hit it! But it didn't matter. The ball fell gently back over the net, and although Tania made a run forwards, it was too late.

Well, after we'd won that game, there was no stopping me and Fliss. She served for the match, and we won the last game in about two minutes. I think Tania and Natalie had given up by then!

"We're in the final!" Fliss crowed, slapping me on the shoulder.

I suddenly remembered the other match. "Yeah, but who are we playing?" I asked.

We both looked over at the next court. Rosie and Lyndz were walking off, looking depressed, and the M&Ms were laughing and doing high fives.

"It looks like poor old Rosie and Lyndz lost," Fliss said sadly.

"So that means you and me are playing the M&Ms," I groaned.

CHAPTER FOURTEEN

I was so nervous, and it was so quiet, I thought that everyone watching would be able to hear my heart thumping away. I tried to stop my knees wobbling, and looked across the court at Emma Hughes. She was getting ready to serve to me, and she was taking *ages*, bouncing the ball and pulling her skirt down and fiddling with her racket.

"Emma, get on with it, please," called Mark, who was umpiring the match.

Kenny had warned us that the Queen would try to distract us. She'd done the same in the match against Rosie and Lyndz. *And* she'd kept arguing that balls were in or out when they're weren't. Well, Fliss and I were ready for her…

Er – well, maybe we weren't. Emma's serve came zooming towards me, and I hit it weakly into the net. First point to the M&Ms. I heard Kenny groan from the side of the court.

The M&Ms won the first game without me and Fliss winning a single point, which was a bit worrying. As we swapped ends, I was beginning to feel more and more nervous. Fliss would have had a much better chance if she was playing with Kenny, I kept telling myself, and that made me feel even worse.

And now it was my turn to serve. I felt sick.

"Just take it slowly, Frankie," Fliss said. "Remember the things Mark told us."

I nodded. But that was easier said than done. My first serve didn't even get over the net. Neither did my second.

"Love-fifteen," Mark called.

My serving was *hopeless*. I just about managed to get the rest of them in, but they were so slow and pathetic, the M&Ms were banging the ball back all over the place. It was only because Fliss was so brilliant, and Emily

Berryman not very good, that we actually won the game. Now it was 1-1.

I cheered up a bit when Emily Berryman had to serve. She was pretty rubbish. Her first serve was just over the line, and Mark called "Out."

"I thought that was in," the Queen said, glaring at him.

Mark shook his head. "Play on, please," he said. He obviously wasn't going to let the Queen get away with wasting time.

Emma looked furious, but she shut up. Anyway, the M&Ms won that game, and the score was 2-1.

It was Fliss's turn to serve, to the Goblin. It was a really good one too, but Berryman just about managed to hit it back over the net. It came towards me, pretty slowly – I pulled back my racket, whacked it and it sailed right out of the court.

I felt *terrible*. And the M&Ms' nasty grins weren't helping. Luckily, Fliss just about managed to turn the game by serving two aces in a row, and then the Goblin fluffed an easy shot, and hit it into the net. So now it was two games each.

That was how it went on for a bit. 3-2. 3-3. 4-3. 4-4. I was so wrapped up in the game, I even forgot about the audience, although I could hear Kenny, Lyndz and Rosie cheering every time we won a point. But if it wasn't for Fliss, we'd have been losing really badly.

The M&Ms had just won the last game, and the score was 5-4. They only had to win one more game, and they'd won the match. As we swapped ends, the Queen smirked at Fliss and me.

"You losers haven't got a hope," she said gleefully. "It's Frankie's turn to serve, and she's useless!"

"Yeah, bye-bye, losers," the Goblin added.

I clutched my tennis racket angrily. That had *really* wound me up.

"Don't get mad, Frankie," Fliss whispered, as the game began again, "Get even!"

"I will," I promised grimly.

The Queen was faffing around on the other side of the net, trying to put me off. I took no notice. I threw the ball into the air, and hit it. It was so fast, the M&Ms didn't even *see* it.

"Fifteen-love," Mark called.

I served again. This time Emma Hughes hit it back, straight into the net. Love-thirty.

The M&Ms were starting to look rattled, and that cheered me up no end. I fired down another ace! Love-forty.

The last point of the game was quite a long rally, and Fliss won it with a brilliant backhand. The score was now 5-5.

Emma Hughes was beginning to look really worried. It was the Goblin's turn to serve, and we all knew she wasn't very good. I gritted my teeth, telling myself to concentrate. Fliss and I now had a chance to win this match!

The Goblin was so nervous, she began by serving a double fault. Love-fifteen. The Queen started telling her off, and that made Emily even more nervous. She hit this pathetic, weedy serve that just about made it over the net, and I hit it back, a bit too hard. Luckily, it just stayed inside the white lines, and Emma returned it, in Fliss's direction. Fliss sent it whizzing back, straight between the M&Ms, who both stuck their rackets out and missed.

The score was now love-thirty, and Kenny and the others were going mad at the side of the court. Two more points, and we'd won the match!

The Goblin did us a real favour then, by serving another double fault. The Queen was so furious, I thought she was going to bash Emily over the head with her tennis racket!

"One more point, and we've done it, Frankie," Fliss whispered.

Emily was serving to me now, and pulling all these faces to put me off. I ignored her, and kept my eyes on the ball. It came over the net towards me, I stepped forward, I hit it – and what a shot, even though I say so myself! It zoomed across the court in front of the M&Ms, bounced neatly in the corner and rolled out of play. We'd done it!

"Frankie!" Fliss squealed, flinging her arms around me. "We won! We won!"

I just about had time to catch a glimpse of the M&Ms, red in the face and stomping off the court, when Rosie and Lyndz came dashing over to grab me and hug me too. Kenny couldn't run, obviously, but she was waving one of her crutches in the air like a mad thing.

"You were great, Frankie," she shouted.

"Thanks," I yelled back. "Wimbledon, here I come!"

"Show us your winning forehand again, Frankie," Kenny said, with a big grin.

"OK." I got up from the grass, and picked up my new racket. "I kind of stepped forward like *this*, and hit the ball like *this*."

Everyone clapped. It was Friday evening, and we were round at Lyndz's house. We were having our tennis sleepover, and to start with, we'd been having a sort of game in the back garden. It wasn't a proper court, of course, but it was good fun. Kenny had been umpire, and had made up all sorts of stupid rules, like we lost a point if a ball hit a tree, or if it bounced on the path. Or if Buster, Lyndz's mad dog, ran off with the ball!

"I can't believe I've got my own racket," I said proudly. The prize for the winners of the tournament had been a new racket each, and Fliss and I were showing them off. Fliss had brought her old racket, too, for Rosie and Lyndz to share. After playing a game for a while, we'd had some daft competitions, made up by Kenny. One of them was seeing how long you could bounce a tennis ball on your racket for, and another was trying to balance the end of your racket on your finger!

"I'm going to ask for a racket for my birthday," Rosie said.

"Me too," Lyndz added.

"And me," Kenny agreed. "Or maybe I could just use my crutches!"

"Stay where you are," I ordered her, as she started to struggle to her feet. "Your mum said you're not to move around."

"Weren't the M&Ms really sick at losing to us?" Fliss said with satisfaction. "I've never *seen* them so mad!"

"I thought the Queen was going to hit someone with her tennis racket!" Rosie said, and we all giggled.

Just then Lyndz's mum called down the garden. "Tea's ready, girls," she said. "I've laid it all out on the patio."

We were all starving, and we charged down the garden. Well, except for Kenny, of course! We couldn't believe what we saw – Mrs Cartwright had really gone to town. She'd tried to make all the food something to do with tennis. There were racket-shaped sandwiches that must have taken her ages to cut out, and round things like Maltesers and cheesy footballs in bowls. There were strawberries and cream, of course, and right in the middle of the table was a big cake, with a tennis court iced on top of it. There were mini-rackets and tennis balls made of marzipan, and across the court was iced Well Done Frankie and Fliss!

"This is brilliant!" Fliss gasped.

We all stuffed ourselves silly, then we went inside to watch some of Fliss's tennis videos, which she'd brought with her. This time we didn't complain at all – we were glued to the screen. Watching the world-class players made you realise just how difficult it was to play tennis properly. Anyway, I was determined to get better, now that I had my new racket!

"Time for bed, girls," said Lyndz's mum, coming into the living room. "Kenny, you'd better go upstairs and use the bathroom first."

"OK." Kenny pulled herself to her feet, and grinned at us. "We really showed the M&Ms, didn't we?"

"Yeah, we did!" we chorused gleefully.

"Let's carry on playing tennis over the summer," Rosie suggested, as Mrs Cartwright helped Kenny upstairs. "When Kenny's ankle's better, we could go to the courts at the park."

"Maybe my mum will take us back to Green Lawns," Fliss said hopefully. "Or maybe Mark will, now that he's going to be my uncle!"

"When's the wedding?" Lyndz asked.

Fliss shrugged. "I don't know," she replied. "But Auntie Jill's asked me to be a bridesmaid."

"Maybe all the bridesmaids should wear tennis dresses!" I joked.

Fliss gave me a look. "I don't think so," she snorted, as we went upstairs. "I want a *proper* bridesmaid's dress, thank you!"

Kenny was already in bed when we went upstairs. Usually we all lie in our sleeping bags on the floor, but Lyndz's mum thought that Kenny would be better in Lyndz's bed, what with her bad ankle. So Lyndz was on the floor with the rest of us.

"I was thinking," Kenny said, as the rest of us came back from the bathroom. "We ought to carry on playing tennis for the rest of the summer, once my ankle's better."

"That's just what we were saying." I replied, chucking my toothbrush into my sleepover bag.

"We could have our own tournament at the end of the summer," Kenny suggested, as everyone unzipped their sleeping bags, and crawled in.

"EEK!" Rosie shrieked suddenly. She was the first one to snuggle down into her sleeping bag. "There's something hairy at the bottom!"

"There's something in mine too!" Fliss screamed, wriggling out again.

"And mine!" Lyndz yelped.

I could feel something too. I pulled myself out of my sleeping bag, and turned it upside-down. Three tennis balls fell out.

"Very funny, Kenny!" I said, as the others did the same and more balls bounced out. Meanwhile, Kenny was laughing her head off in the corner!

"Fifteen-love to me!" she said gleefully.

"No way," I said. I picked up the balls and began chucking them at her, and so did the others. Kenny gave a yell, and tried to hide under the duvet. "Fifteen-all, I think!"